Anne Rice

Twayne's United States Authors Series

Frank Day, Editor

Clemson University

TUSAS 644

ANNE RICE.
Photo by Karen O'Brien courtesy of Alfred A. Knopf.

Anne Rice

Bette B. Roberts

Westfield State College

Twayne Publishers • New York
Maxwell Macmillan Canada • Toronto
Maxwell Macmillan International • New York Oxford Singapore Sydney

Anne Rice
Bette B. Roberts

Twayne Publishers
Macmillan Publishing Company
866 Third Avenue
New York, New York 10022

Maxwell Macmillan Canada, Inc.
1200 Eglinton Avenue East
Suite 200
Don Mills, Ontario M3C 3N1

Library of Congress Cataloging-in-Publication Data

Roberts, Bette B.
    Anne Rice / Bette B. Roberts
        p. cm.—(Twayne's United States authors series; TUSAS 644)
    Includes bibliographical references and index.
    ISBN 0-8057-3961-0
    1. Rice, Anne, 1941– —Criticism and interpretation. 2. Horror tales, American—
History and criticism. 3. Gothic revival (Literature)—United States. I. Title. II.
Series.
PS3568.I265Z85 1994
813'.54—dc20   93-40509
                                                                              CIP

The paper used in this publication meets the minimum requirements of American
National Standard for Information Sciences—Permanence of Paper for Printed Library
Materials, ANSI Z39.48-1984.™ ⊚

10 9 8 7 6 5 4 3 2 1

Printed in the United States of America.

Contents

Preface

Though Anne Rice has written two historical novels and five erotics, she is best known for her Gothic fiction beginning with *Interview with the Vampire* in 1976. Besides adding three more novels to *The Vampire Chronicles*, she has also explored other areas of the occult with *The Mummy* (1989), *The Witching Hour* (1990), and *Lasher* (1993). The film *Interview with the Vampire*, based on Rice's script, is scheduled for release in 1994.

Many reviewers and gothophiles responded enthusiastically to her fresh, original approach to conventions of the Gothic in *Interview with the Vampire;* since then, however, reception has been more divided. Some critics praise her restoration of Romantic dignity and power to the vampire figure and her use of vampirism as a vehicle for commentary on our current human condition, while others see only a blatant contrast between the erotic, sensational adventures and philosophical debates about values and meaning. Nearly all reviewers respect her talents in telling a gripping story and creating a true sense of place, yet several critics note her tendency toward repetition. Some praise her lush, ornate prose as baroque and connect it with the southern literary tradition, while others regard her writing as stilted and overly dramatic.

Clearly distressed that she has been considered primarily a popular writer, Rice indicated in an interview in the 14 October 1990 issue of the *New York Times Magazine* that she would like to be taken seriously by the academic community. Her request throws down the gauntlet for a researcher of the Gothic, and this study is a response to that request. After exploring the significant happenings of her life that contribute to her novels in the first chapter, I devote chapter 2 to a discussion of Gothic fiction. I believe the answer to the question of whether Rice should be taken seriously rests primarily on our placing her Gothic novels in the history and context of the genre. Each of *The Vampire Chronicles* books—*Interview with the Vampire, The Vampire Lestat, The Queen of the Damned,* and *The Tale of the Body Thief*—receives separate treatment in chapters 3, 4, 5, and 6, with chapter 7 focusing on her Gothic but non-vampiric novels, *The Mummy* and *The Witching Hour*. Finally, I take up her other works that are non-Gothic altogether but still indicative of

important elements she brings to the Gothic: the two historical novels—
The Feast of All Saints and *Cry to Heaven*—and the erotic fantasies.

My interest in Gothic fiction goes back to a University of
Massachusetts dissertation in 1975 (later published by Arno Press in
1980) on the relationship between Gothic conventions and female writers and readers in late eighteenth-century England. This interest has
continued with shorter studies exploring the persistent appeal of the
Gothic with popular audiences of the Victorian period and our own
times. Struck by Rice's modern adaptations of the vampire myth in
Interview with the Vampire, I explored her domestication of Dracula in a
short article in 1979. Unlike most of her female contemporaries writing
Gothic novels according to formulas, Rice continues to create striking,
original, and complex variations of the genre, especially with vampirism,
that justify our comparing her works with those of her famous forerun-
ners. I propose, in fact, that Rice's vampires Louis, Lestat, and Akasha
are metaphors that are just as meaningful to our own fin-de-siècle climate as the infamous Dracula was to late-Victorian decadence.

Acknowledgments

I wish to thank two graduate assistants, Joseph Dragon and Robert Schaaf, for their help with bibliographical work. I have been fortunate to have an excellent editor from Twayne Publishers, India Koopman. Her thoughtful reading and meticulous attention to detail have strengthened the text. I am also grateful to a dear and patient first reader whose suggestions have been invaluable to me, my husband, Jeffrey.

In addition, I wish to thank Alfred A. Knopf, Inc. for permission to quote excerpts from the following novels by Anne Rice: *Interview with the Vampire,* copyright © 1976 by Anne O'Brien Rice; *The Vampire Lestat,* copyright © 1985 by Anne O'Brien Rice; *The Queen of the Damned,* copyright © 1988 by Anne O'Brien Rice; *The Witching Hour,* copyright © 1990 by Anne O'Brien Rice; and *The Tale of the Body Thief,* copyright © 1992 by Anne O'Brien Rice. I also thank Dutton Signet, a division of Penguin Books USA, Inc., for permission to quote excerpts from *Prism of the Night: A Biography of Anne Rice* by Katherine Ramsland, copyright © 1991 by Katherine Ramsland; Afterword copyright © 1992 by Katherine Ramsland.

Chronology

1941   Anne Rice (named Howard Allen) born 4 October in Mercy Hospital, New Orleans, to Howard and Katherine O'Brien.[1]

1956   Death of Anne's mother.

1957   Attends St. Joseph Academy boarding school. Father remarries and moves family to Richardson, Texas. Anne meets Stan Rice in high school.

1959   Graduates from high school and enrolls in Texas Woman's University.

1960   Drops out of college and goes to San Francisco.

1961   Returns to Texas to marry Stan Rice on 14 October.

1962   Lives in Haight-Ashbury with Stan and attends college.

1964   Graduates from San Francisco State with a B.A. in political science.

1966   Moves with Stan to Taraval. Daughter, Michele, born 21 September. Anne attends graduate school.

1969   Family moves to Berkeley.

1970   Anne enrolls in Ph.D. program at the University of California at Berkeley. Leaves to pursue master's in creative writing at San Francisco State University. Daughter is diagnosed with leukemia.

1972   Earns master's degree in creative writing. Daughter dies 5 August.

1976   *Interview with the Vampire* published.

1977   Travels to Europe, Egypt, and Italy.

1978   Son, Christopher, born 11 March.

1979   *The Feast of All Saints* published. Short story, "The Art of the Vampire at Its Peak in the Year 1876," appears in January *Playboy*.

1982   *Cry to Heaven* published.

1983   *The Claiming of Sleeping Beauty* published under pseudo-
       nym A. N. Roquelaure. Essay on David Bowie appears
       in November *Vogue.*

1984   *Beauty's Punishment,* second of the *Beauty* series, pub-
       lished under pseudonym A. N. Roquelaure. Short story,
       "The Master of Rampling Gate," appears in February
       Redbook.

1985   *Exit to Eden* published under pseudonym Anne
       Rampling. *Beauty's Release,* third of the *Beauty* series,
       published under pseudonym A. N. Roquelaure. *The
       Vampire Lestat* published.

1986   *Belinda* published under pseudonym Anne Rampling.

1988   *The Queen of the Damned* published.

1989   Anne and family move to New Orleans. *The Mummy or
       Ramses the Damned* published.

1990   *The Witching Hour* published.

1991   Father, Howard O'Brien, dies on 29 November.

1992   *The Tale of the Body Thief* published. Short story, "The
       Tale of the Body Thief," appears in October *Playboy.*

1993   *Lasher* published.

Chapter One
Rice's Life and Art: Liberation in the Savage Garden

Studying a living novelist is hazardous, since the last word cannot be written and the quality and extent of future literary output cannot be predicted. Yet there is the advantage of being able to witness the writer's evolution and of having the writer around to talk about it. In a 1990 interview Anne Rice told Susan Ferraro that she was annoyed by reviewers' dismissing her as strictly a popular writer.[1] Later, in a November 1992 television interview, she no longer expressed the same frustration. Though still eager for academic attention, she very much appreciated the enthusiastic response of her popular audience and her Dickensian relationship with her readers. Unlike many writers, who prefer to maintain silence on their work, Anne Rice has been quite forthcoming in sharing her views with television commentators, interviewers, reviewers, and her biographer Katherine Ramsland.

Ramsland's *Prism of the Night: A Biography of Anne Rice* views Rice's novels as "a progression from Anne Rice to A. N. Roquelaure to Anne Rampling [pseudonyms she used for her erotic fiction] and back to Anne Rice that traces the journey of an author toward a sense of personal clarity and ever greater experiments with creative expression."[2] Ramsland's thesis on the progression of Rice's fiction is based not on literary assessment but on the psychological and philosophical maturity that she sees Rice achieving as a result of learning from her life while exploring different forms and devices of literary expression. "Anne herself evolved as her characters evolved," writes Ramsland (350). Her fiction reflects the author's journey toward "self-realization"; in it she has found a release from her own fears that has led her to a "faith in a positive future for herself and for humankind": "She had traveled into her own darkness, transforming monsters, forbidden sexuality, restrictive femininity, and the threat of eternal chaos and anonymity into images no longer frightening, more human and acceptable, and even possessing a transcendent power" (351). Rice's fiction may not evidence a steady artistic progression, but it does demonstrate the extent to which the conventions of traditional literary forms, especially the Gothic and the historical romance, can provide a powerful outlet for an author's personal pain, lead to psychological discovery, and reveal philosophical depth while still striking a sympathetic chord in modern readers.

A summary of her life indicates that Rice writes a good deal from experience, as is evident in her repeated preference for the settings of New Orleans and San Francisco, where she has lived, and, less obviously, in her use of nightmarish, mysterious images that represent her own personal and painful preoccupations. Tonio's relationship with his alcoholic mother, Marianna, in *Cry to Heaven* clearly reflects Rice's own childhood with her mother, Katherine; the vampire Louis's mourning the loss of the five-year-old Claudia in *Interview with the Vampire* conveys Rice's grief over the death of her daughter, Michele; and the vampire Lestat's gift of eternal life to David Talbot in *The Tale of the Body Thief* coincides with Rice's wish to keep her own father alive (Ramsland, 361). In addition to the specific connections between her life and her art is the more general and pervasive way that her unconventional upbringing, her formal education in the humanities, her rejection of Catholicism, and her living through the 1960s as a young adult give rise to the pervasive existential sensibility that values individual freedom in her fiction.

The metaphor of the savage garden is consistent in her work, and however tormenting the circumstances, Rice's positive characters mature by confronting life's lack of meaning and establishing their secular morality. They must create their own moral systems and make choices in a world where the only truths are aesthetic ones. Though Louis's absorption in art fails to lift his spirits in *Interview with the Vampire,* Lestat reiterates Keats's "Beauty is truth, truth beauty" philosophy: "A thousand other things can be said about the world, but only aesthetic principles can be verified, and these things alone remain the same."[3] Accepting the violence of his vampiric nature, Lestat informs the reader at the beginning of *The Queen of the Damned* that "[r]ight and wrong we will struggle with forever, striving to create and maintain an ethical balance; but the shimmer of summer rain under the street lamps or the great flashing glare of artillery against a night sky—such brutal beauty is beyond dispute."[4] Marcel Ste. Marie's maturation in *The Feast of All Saints* involves a similar awareness when he tells Christophe why he is afraid: "Because if it's really true that there's no order, then anything can happen to us. Anything at all. There's no real natural law, no right and wrong that's immutable, and the world is suddenly a savage place where any number of things can go wrong."[5] Finally, in *The Witching Hour,* Michael Curry, at a later stage in the maturation process, still maintains his faith in human goodness and free will despite the wrenching loss of his wife, Rowan: "I believe finally that we are the only true moral force in the physical world, the makers of ethics and moral ideas, and that we must be as good as the gods we've created in the past to guide us."[6]

What these characters share with Anne Rice is a pattern of growth and awareness similar to that of Hemingway's heroes and existential protagonists, whom she studied in college. Like Hemingway's characters, they experience a loss or violent confrontation that causes a reevaluation of self in relation to the world and a replacement of traditional values with those of individualism. Unlike Hemingway's heroes, however, Rice's characters learn the truth through the power of the supernatural instead of the impact of stark reality, through vampiric thirst and incineration rather than war or the bull ring. Though Rice's characters seldom triumph as a result of their fictional experiences, they are indeed strengthened and, more important, liberated, as they shed their illusions about life and achieve independence. Whatever truths they face and accept about themselves—the conditions of vampirism, the humiliations of racial prejudice, the inescapable demands of their own sexuality—the outcomes are positive and suggest a new beginning.

Born on 4 October 1941, in New Orleans, Anne Rice was originally named Howard Allen to carry on the name of her Irish parents, Katherine Allen and Howard O'Brien. Uncomfortable with having a boy's name in public school, Rice often changed her name and finally settled on Anne (Ramsland, 18, 28). She was the second of four daughters: Alice, born in 1939; Tamara, in 1947; and Karen, in 1949. Being a member of a large Irish family amidst the rigid social hierarchies of southern society at that time fostered a sense of inferiority outside the home: "segregation laws were strictly enforced, and the poor Irish were regarded as just a step or two above blacks" (Ramsland, 4).

Anne's burning desire to be special and to accomplish something may have been born of a desire to overcome the prejudices of her surroundings; it was also fueled by her mother. Both of her parents were well educated and provided intellectual stimulation for their children, but Rice's mother, Katherine, in particular "strove to raise healthy, perfect children, each of whom would be a genius. To be a good mother, she believed, was to be the operative force behind a brilliant child, and that meant allowing them the freedom to express themselves in whatever way appealed to them, and encouraging their imagination" (Ramsland,

15). Recounting several situations when the children's behavior shocked relatives and neighbors, Rice fondly remembers a "wonderful mother" who was tolerant and permissive, providing a free, undisciplined childhood where the fantasies of the imagination were nurtured and the restrictions of prejudice discounted. At the same time, her mother's strict Catholicism set up boundaries. Encouraging her daughter to read many books, Katherine forbade others. According to Rice, "Art existed for God's sake. Anything that did not conflict with those values was fine" (Ramsland, 19). While not problematical for Katherine, her active devotion to Catholicism and her insistence on its importance in the household later became a major source of tension for Rice. She relished the sensuous rituals of the religious ceremonies and even dreamed of joining the convent during her childhood, yet she recoiled from the oppressive rules.

Ramsland reports that the "mix of freedom and censorship in the home was reinforced when Anne eventually went to school by juxtaposing the discipline of parochial education against a free-spirited household, deepening the tensions of paradox" (20). Rebelling against the regimen of the Catholic school day yet wanting desperately to fit in with the other students, Rice "always felt estranged," since the imaginative, uncontrolled intellectual life at home set her apart. Rice claims that her mother's encouragement made her feel free of the traditional limitations placed on females, but she found the different opportunities and expectations afforded for male and female students at school irritating (Ramsland, 52). It was her "determination to become great that kept her going in the face of social and religious pressures to succumb to submissive female roles" (Ramsland, 53).

Adding to her sense of being different was her mother's increasing dependence on alcohol. Describing a now all-too-familiar process of children's responses to alcoholic parents, Ramsland explains how Anne and her sisters had to deal "with feelings of guilt, secrecy, depression, helplessness, and insecurity over their mother's unpredictable affections. At times she overflowed with emotion; at others, she withdrew. They never knew what to expect" (23). Some children become permanently disabled emotionally by parental alcoholism; others may find an early "independence and strength," a determination to please others and avoid the pitfalls they know so well. As will become apparent later, the significance of these particular family circumstances cannot be overstated in a consideration of Rice's development as a writer: "It was within the alcoholic family system, coupled with the tensions of freedom and restraint, that Anne first developed the ambivalence between self-sufficiency and the need for love that pervaded her life, her secret fantasies, and later, her art" (Ramsland, 23).

Though her more stable father worked away from home much of the time, he still managed to be "a significant literary influence on Anne." He not only read to the children but wrote stories and poems for them, walked with them all over New Orleans, exposed them to classical music, and introduced them to the public library (Ramsland, 22, 24, 27). Throughout her adult life, until her father's death in 1991, Rice enjoyed her father's pride in her accomplishments. She often asked him to read her novels, with the exception of the erotica, and respected his reactions (Ramsland, 214, 160). Responsive to the lush sensuality and historical atmosphere of the city, Rice was especially drawn to ghost stories about the old mansions. She read Gothic fiction and tried her hand at writing it. With encouragement from her parents, she explored the images of mummies and vampires she saw in movies and relied on her writing as a "natural and intimate way of dealing with her world" (Ramsland, 40).

She was also excited by the dark mysteries of the church that stimulated her imagination, particularly the transubstantiation that precedes Holy Communion during the ritual of the Mass (Ramsland, 28). As an adolescent, she "felt sexual stirrings toward the dark and lurid images that confronted her every day in her spiritual exercises" (Ramsland, 30). Her Catholic background not only aroused her enduring interest in the spiritual and the supernatural but also the erotic. Her mother reiterated the "double messages" of the church that sexual feelings were "sinful," though sex was "beautiful and natural." The repression of these feelings during puberty became somewhat "entertaining" for Rice: "As a result of the excitement and dread of participating in the forbidden, and anticipating possible punishment, she had sexual fantasies with a masochistic flavor" (Ramsland, 31). The repression and immersion into things spiritual that Rice experienced through Catholicism find expression in both her Gothic and erotic novels, where she emphasizes liberation from restraint.

Rice's transition to adulthood begins with the loss of her mother, who died at age 48 in 1956, shortly before Rice turned 15. According to Ramsland, the changes after her mother's death affected her profoundly: her enrollment in a Catholic boarding school, her father's remarriage to Dorothy Van Bever in 1957, and the family's move from New Orleans to Richardson, Texas, a suburb of Dallas. Ramsland believes that Rice's grief and anger created "an edge of darkness" that she would eventually attempt to work out in her fiction, a "need to regain her mother's presence and a desire to conquer death" (47). At the time, she became more independent and assumed responsibilities in the household (Ramsland, 48). Later in her life she saw her mother as someone unable to conquer the tests of life, a victim. "Perhaps trying too hard to be a conqueror," her mother, Rice suggests, "succumbed all the more easily to the other extreme of being a victim" (Ramsland, 49). Rice herself would later be tested through a terrible loss, but she would not become a victim.

After finishing her senior year at a Baptist high school in Texas, where she met and dated her future husband, Stan Rice, she enrolled in Texas Woman's University for one year. She transferred to North Texas State University for six months of her sophomore year, and finally moved to San Francisco to continue her college education at the University of San Francisco at night and then at San Francisco State University, where she received a B.A. in political science in 1964 and an M.A. in creative writing in 1972. Having to support herself made college a difficult experience. She describes her exhaustion during that time: "I don't think anyone should have to work as hard as I did. To watch the college world through the cafe window while you're wiping tables fifty hours a week is a bitter experience. I survived it because I was very strong and had a tremendous ambition to succeed, not to be stuck cleaning that cafe table for life" (Ramsland, 65).

Rice's formal education, particularly her studies in literature and philosophy, proved to be as important to her development as the nonconformist atmosphere of San Francisco in the 1960s. Her exposure to existential writers and philosophers fostered her independent thinking, her questioning of social institutions, and her search for personal truths, causing her finally to abandon the religious certainties of her childhood. Within the larger philosophical influence of such writers as Hemingway and Sartre, echoes of literary classics reverberate throughout Rice's fiction. For instance, she acknowledges her favorite Dickens novel, *Great Expectations,* in *The Witching Hour* with many allusions, particularly to Miss Havisham, whose physical surroundings emit decay in the same way the Mayfair mansion exudes the horror and stagnation of the family legacy. Hawthorne's dark view of sin and the fortunate fall imaged in Edenic gardens are also evident in this novel, along with the Jamesian observation that Rowan is a person "upon whom almost nothing is lost" (*Hour,* 914). Nearly an exact paraphrase of James's advice to prospective writers in "The Art of Fiction," this observation calls up themes concerning the nature of human perception and the relativity of reality pertinent to Michael's and Rowan's experiences. Readers familiar with the works of Shakespeare, Dostoevsky, Donne, Keats, Kerouac, and Blake benefit from allusions to these writers in Rice's Gothic and historical novels.

Thrilled with the intellectual stimulation of her independent life in San Francisco, she nonetheless felt "adrift" without her family and longed for a "relationship with someone who would return her intense affection, respect her mind, and encourage her ambitions" (Ramsland, 72). That "someone" turned out to be her first romantic interest, Stan Rice, whom she married in October 1961. The influence of a supportive and loving husband, himself an accomplished poet, has been extremely fortunate. From comments that Rice has made to interviewers (she told Ferraro in 1990 that she fell in love with Stan Rice right away and has never fallen out of love) and her biographer, and from their appreciation of each other's literary efforts in public, it would appear that the marriage has provided the stability, the family closeness and love, and the mutual devotion to artistic endeavor in which Rice's writing could flourish.

Rice's husband, in fact, encouraged her to write to cope with the most devastating event of her life, the death of the couple's daughter, Michele, in August 1972, shortly before her sixth birthday. Rice admits that writing *Interview with the Vampire* was "cathartic." According to Ramsland, "She had dealt with her pain and guilt by projecting them into the first-person point of view of Louis. People close to her believed she had 'saved' herself from her grief" (166). Moving away from the alcoholism and arguments that characterized the Rices' relationship after Michele's death, they each offered up a literary response—Stan, a collection of poetry, *Some Lamb,* and Anne, *Interview with the Vampire.* "The history of a blood disease led into images of the vampire," says Stan, "and in my work . . . the idea of the lamb that is sacrificed, the blood of the lamb. We started out in different places, but a lot of our ideas came together" (Ramsland, 167).

Since the publication of *Interview with the Vampire* in 1976, Rice's life has been marked by increased family stability and literary recognition, despite the typically mixed responses to her fiction. Two years after the book appeared, the Rices had a son, Christopher. His name is significant in Rice's fiction, symbolizing new beginnings (Ramsland, 203). The derivative Christophe provides the education central to Marcel's maturation in *The Feast of All Saints,* enabling him to begin his adult life, while Christina in *Cry to Heaven* teaches Tonio to transcend sexual identity. As the unborn child of Rowan and Michael in *The Witching Hour,* "Little

Chris" is intended to be a new beginning, despite his transformation into Lasher. Christopher was a new beginning for the Rices as well in 1979, when, according to Ramsland, they gave up drinking and avoided the personal ruin of Rice's mother, Katherine.

In 1989 the Rices left California for New Orleans, a move that may reflect Rice's coming to terms with her past, transforming a dark place into one illuminated by her maturity (Ramsland, 351). While Louis and Lestat are fictional vehicles through which she has revisited painful events of her life (especially the deaths of her mother and daughter and the loss of her religious faith) and responded with despair and rebellion, one of her most recent protagonists, Michael Curry of *The Witching Hour,* begins as an older and wiser man who sees it is essential to recapture his past in order to fulfill his role in the present and confirm his faith in the future.

Lestat, too, having come to understand the absence of moral direction in the universe and his own insignificance in the large scheme of things, embarks on a personal adventure in *The Tale of the Body Thief,* rather than a cosmic attempt to make a difference in mortals' lives. The journey from innocence to experience caused by loss or change that forces Rice's characters to confront nothingness, the liberation of self that comes through this awareness, and the construction of an individual morality that affirms a human capacity for goodness are what it means to realize the potential of being human. These are the themes in her life and her art.

In addition to the liberties she has taken with traditional forms (discussed in chapter 2), Rice has also experienced a personal, artistic liberation similar to that of her protagonist Jeremy Walker in *Belinda,* who takes the risk of jeopardizing his success as a writer and illustrator of children's books by exhibiting nude paintings of his teenaged lover. The revelation of Jeremy's secrets turns out happily in the end, freeing him from repression and enabling him to grow and find independence as a painter who pours out his passions onto the canvas. Like Jeremy, Rice has explored her sexual fantasies, writing erotic books under the pseudonyms of Anne Rampling and A. N. Roquelaure and identifying herself later as the author.

Rice's novels have always included a strong element of eroticism, reflecting her belief that acknowledging sexuality and overcoming repression are part of a liberating process for the artist. In particular, she views vampires as affording a gender-free perspective, or images of "lovers as equals" (Ramsland, 148). As many reviewers have noted, the androgynous nature of vampire unions and blood exchanges in the vampire novels has attracted a large following among homosexuals and women, who praise the transcendence of restrictive gender roles. In her historical fiction, too, the mentor voice in *The Feast of All Saints* comes from the bisexual Christophe, who is free of southern prejudices and determined to educate his students. In *Cry to Heaven,* the homosexual intimacies of the castrated Tonio allow him to transcend male sexuality and accept himself in his relationship with the equally liberated Christina. In the novels of sexual fantasy and erotica, Rice focuses entirely on sexuality, especially sadomasochism, as a liberating force.

While overcoming repression through art may be as important to Rice, with her Catholic background and her 1960s exposure to the ideal of unrestricted self-fulfillment, as it is to Jeremy Walker, there is a difference between the fictional artist and the real novelist. Jeremy's erotic paintings receive praise for their passion and power, but Rice's erotic novels, whatever purpose they may have served her, have not been well-received. Despite her efforts to avoid the violence and sexism of erotic books that appeal mainly to male readers and outrage feminists, Rice's exclusive emphasis on erotic awareness as the source of personal liberation in these novels tends to dehumanize the characters. This focus lacks the artistic blending of the physical, philosophical, and spiritual that humanizes her vampires and moves her historical human characters toward complex growth and self-knowledge.

As with Dickens's orphans, the characters who undertake these journeys tend to be outsiders like Rice herself, a southern child of Irish parents and an alcoholic mother. Often their conflicts begin within the family. The alienated and guilty Louis feels responsible for his brother's death; Lestat relies on his mother's love to counteract the estrangement from his father and brothers; Tonio learns that his brother is his father; and Marie Ste. Marie never experiences maternal love because her mother is jealous of her whiteness. Belinda, too, comes to terms with an alcoholic and extremely defensive, self-centered mother, and in the most extremely dysfunctional family, Baby Jenks's emotional confusion results in the grisly murder of her parents.

Though her vampires are the most exaggerated social outcasts, cut off eternally from mortality, Rice's other protagonists also suffer alienation and loneliness: in *Cry to Heaven* castration removes Tonio from the Italian aristocracy; in *The Feast of All Saints* Marcel and Marie are *gens de couleur*—neither black nor white; in *The Witching Hour* Rowan Mayfair, removed from her family, is rootless in California despite her successful career; even Lisa Kelly in *Exit to Eden,* because of her sexual needs, finds herself more comfortable on a remote island away from the mainstream of American values. All of these characters feel the pangs of estrangement and yearn for some kind of close relationship and meaningful role in the community.

In the *Chronicles,* as in the historical novels, family patterns among the vampires are created, dissolved, and reshaped again and again. Vampires can endure a timeless sentence in a godless, seemingly meaningless universe, but they cannot abide the isolation and loneliness of their condition. In addition to seeking out intimate companions, as Lestat first reaches out for Louis, then later to Marius, then Akasha, and finally David Talbot, the vampires live in groups that often resemble a triangular family structure, perhaps reflecting Anne Rice's own recovered family of herself, husband, and son: Louis, Lestat, and Claudia, and then Louis, Madeleine, and Claudia in the *Interview;* Lestat, Gabrielle, and Nicolas in *The Vampire Lestat;* and Maharet, Mekare, and Miriam (replaced by Jesse) in *The Queen of the Damned.* Moreover, in the sequence of the vampire books, small family-like groups grow into an international community of vampires. Historical protagonists also know the importance of "being connected." Tonio Treschi, cast out by his brother at the beginning of *Cry to Heaven,* puts off his revenge in an attempt to preserve the family name by giving his brother time to have children. As he tries to understand his purpose in the unfolding horrors of his family, his worst fear is that he has no role at all, that the dark secrets of his life are *"not* connected."[7] In *The Feast of All Saints,* Marcel takes his place amidst life in New Orleans, as Marie finds hers with Richard Lermontant. Rowan is determined to seek out her place in the family legacy in *The Witching Hour,* and even in the erotic fantasies men and women move from sensual attachments to permanent commitments, as Lisa Kelly agrees to marry Elliott Slater and Jeremy Walker weds the teenaged Belinda.

Obstacles to the characters' journeys toward self-realization are more internal than external, particularly in the Gothics, and are rooted in misconceptions and delusions, which are similar to Rice's experience with Catholicism. Louis's quest as a vampire is to discover his moral nature and to find Satan in order to affirm his own purpose. Lestat determines to use his evil nature "to do good," that is, to show mortals what evil really is, and Marcel believes that he can escape the limitations of color and find freedom by going to Paris. Repeatedly, a confrontation with religious faith is part of the process, as the protagonists face the meaninglessness of traditional values and recognize the accidental nature of their lives. In Rice's fiction, the elements of Catholicism so familiar to her as a child become important resources and metaphors for creating unconventional, sometimes ironic effects, such as the powerful communion between vampire and vampire in the exchange of blood, the intimacy between Jeremy and Belinda in his "Communion" paintings, the new religion that Akasha envisions with herself as God and Lestat as Christ, and Lasher's birth on Christmas Eve that results from a diabolical invasion of spirit into body rather than from immaculate conception.

When the conflicts are more external, they concern battles with the rationalists like Akasha in *The Queen of the Damned* and Lasher in *The Witching Hour,* or with representatives of inhumane social institutions like the oppressive whites in *A Feast of All Saints* and the Italian clergy and aristocracy in *Cry to Heaven,* who come up with ethical systems and strategies to justify acts of violence and oppression that benefit themselves or maintain their power. The voices of their adversaries reflect the antiestablishment 1960s sentiment of Rice in repeatedly rejecting what she sees as the false rules of religions and hypocritical laws of society that prevent people from finding their own values and making their own choices. As Akasha's adversary, Maharet, tells her, "Look on the effect of your religions, those movements that have swept up millions with their fantastical claims. Look at what they have done to human history. Look at the wars fought on account of them; look at the persecutions, the massacres. Look at the pure enslavement of reason; look at the price of faith and zeal" (*Queen,* 408).

As if to belie further the idea of restricting human development and to encourage faith in human potentiality, Rice engages her characters in experiences that exaggerate their independence and their transcendence from conventionality. Often this theme comes from their bold sexuality, whether it is expressed through the passion of vampiric lust or the pleasure of sexual intimacy between men and women or members of the same sex. Focusing more on the larger picture of liberation for both sexes, Rice does not depict women as being more repressed and therefore needing more freedom than men. In the historical novels, both male and female characters demonstrate the same themes, though the focus is more upon the male perspectives of Marcel Ste. Marie and Tonio. Marie and Christina, however, are equally effective illustrations of victories over oppressive social attitudes. In the erotics, Rice is careful to bring in men who enjoy the same masochistic pleasures as women, as well as women who take on the dominant role in sex. Beauty becomes the master of an

intended suitor, while Lisa assumes power over Elliott, and Belinda
seduces Jeremy. In the Gothics, the androgynous sexuality of the vampires, inviting male and female identification, implies that the liberating
life of Lestat is intended for both sexes.

Though a few of Rice's female characters conform to stereotypical
romantic roles (Julie Stratford in *The Mummy* comes immediately to
mind), the majority of them exhibit unusual independence and atypical-
ity, particularly the vampires: Gabrielle, Akasha, Maharet, and Jesse.
They not only demonstrate the same themes as her male characters but
reflect Rice's own sense of individualism as a woman. Two of her human
females are women of courage and talent who choose lives of professional nonconformity. Christina, the artist in *Cry to Heaven,* devotes herself to
art instead of having children and assuming her place in the Italian aristocracy. Rowan Mayfair, who inherits strong genes from dominant
female ancestors in *The Witching Hour,* combines her personal needs as a
woman with those of her professional goals as a scientist in a union with
Lasher. Minor female characters memorable for their fortitude and social
unconventionality in *The Feast of All Saints*—Dolly Rose, Anna Bella,
Aunt Josette, and Juliet Mercier—suffer oppression for being women of
color and assume significant roles in the historical conflicts of the novel.

The importance of even these minor characters is not that they are
female or male but rather that, like the protagonists, they become
metaphors of hard-won personal survival and peace. Refusing to become
victims, they manage to rise above the accidents and realities of life in
the savage garden while retaining their faith in human nature. Having
suffered horrendous loss, Michael Curry can still write at the end of *The
Witching Hour:* "I suppose I do believe in the final analysis that a peace of
mind can be obtained by faith in change and in will and in accident; and
by faith in ourselves, that we will do the right thing, more often than
not, in the face of adversity." Noting the signs of early spring in his New
Orleans garden, Michael affirms his trust in human nature: "We are
capable of visions and ideas which are ultimately stronger and more
enduring than we are" (*Hour,* 964).

As a novelist, Rice chooses enduring forms of fiction, especially the
Gothic and the historical romance, which have provided outlets for the
expression of women's fears and fantasies since the late eighteenth century. As Joseph Grixti explains in defining the continuing appeal of the
Gothic, "stereotypes and literary/cultural archetypes (like 'fantasy') do
not just develop out of thin air; they form part of complex meaning-
making processes which are inspired by identifiable social and psycho-

logical purposes. They also form part of the myths which societies con-
struct in order to help make sense of the world of experience, as well as
derive reassurance about perceived aspects of that experience which
appear to pose a threat to control, comprehension, happiness, and/or survival."[8] Anne Rice approaches the conventions of the genre with the
same independent spirit of her protagonists. The results of her creativity
are Gothic novels that transcend the categories of male and female
Gothic types, provide new images that appeal to the modern reader, and
establish fresh possibilities for the genre. It is no accident that Rice
regards Michael Curry of *The Witching Hour* as her most autobiographi-
cal character (Ferraro, 77); looking out at the Mayfair garden made less
savage by his restorations, he affirms her personal faith in aesthetic
truths and the human spirit.

Chapter Two
Rice and the Gothic Tradition

To present a critical study of Anne Rice's work just 20 years ago would have required a major justification; Ian Watt's influential 1957 *The Rise of the Novel,* with its emphasis on realism, virtually dominated critical assessment of the novel. Analyzing the supernatural was acceptable so long as the research was confined to Romantic poetry, such as Keats's "Lamia" figure, Coleridge's mysterious "Christabel," or Poe's "Ligeia." When these fantasy figures and the medieval ruins they inhabited moved over into the novel, the novels themselves were relegated to the realm of popular fiction and deemed unworthy of critical attention because they failed to conform to the standards of realism. Before the mid-1970s few doctoral candidates wrote dissertations on the novels of the Romantic period, and courses in the British Romantics seldom included writers like Ann Radcliffe or Mary Shelley. Early critical studies of the Gothic are sparse indeed. Nearly every scholar of the Gothic today mentions the pioneering Edith Birkhead, Montague Summers, and Devendra Varma, whose critical tasks in the 1920s through the 1950s, included the identification of Gothic texts as well as an explanation of the genre itself.

Between this early criticism and what might be called an explosion of critical interest in the Gothic beginning in the late 1970s were several important contributors whose approaches suggested avenues of significant study: J. M. S. Tompkins's *The Popular Novel in England: 1770–1800* in 1932, a cultural exploration of the relationships between popular readers' fantasies and the Gothic, among other genres; Leslie Fiedler's psychosocial commentary on the Gothic and American literature in his 1960 *Love and Death in the American Novel;* Paul Frankl's comprehensive historical study *The Gothic: Literary Sources and Interpretations through Eight Centuries,* also in 1960; and Irving Malin's 1962 *New American Gothic,* a discussion of symbolic functions of Gothic devices in contemporary American literature not usually regarded as Gothic. Maurice Levy wrote the first major effort to update the historical survey provided by the earliest critics in *Le roman gothique anglais, 1764–1824,* where he makes interesting distinctions between the Gothic novels of male writers, beginning with Matthew Lewis, and of female writers, starting with Ann Radcliffe. Once Robert D. Hume's article reevaluating the Gothic novel appeared in 1969 and Robert Kiely's fine exploration of *The Romantic Novel in England* in 1972, the study of the Gothic was no longer constrained by the standards of realism.

In fact, a history of critical approaches to the Gothic reveals just how much an appreciation of the genre has benefited from the recent variety of literary theories and approaches to textual analysis. In the 1970s and 1980s there appeared extremely useful genre studies, such as Elizabeth MacAndrew's *The Gothic Tradition in Fiction* (1979) and David Punter's psychological-cultural *The Literature of Terror: A History of Gothic Fictions from 1765 to the Present Day* (1980), as well as studies using feminist, psychoanalytical, reader-response, and cultural approaches to literary analysis. These last are especially enlightening in coming to terms with a genre that relies on, as Punter explains, the fictional truth of the imagination rather than the truth of real experience.[1] Shortly after Coral Ann Howells, for instance, analyzes sensibility and the Gothic heroine in *Love, Mystery, and Misery: Feeling in Gothic Fiction* (1978), Stephen King writes his own informal psychosocial study of the genre in *Danse Macabre* in 1979. While William Patrick Day traces the Gothic as a subversion of the Romantic in his book *In the Circles of Fear and Desire* in 1985, Kate Ferguson Ellis sees the Gothic as a fantasized protest against values of the hearth in *The Contested Castle: Gothic Novels and the Subversion of Domestic Ideology* in 1989. In the same year, Joseph Grixti explores relationship between Gothic fiction and popular audience in *Terrors of Uncertainties: The Cultural Contexts of Horror Fiction*. These and many other Gothic studies provide researchers of the Gothic today with many resources. Bibliographers of the Gothic have also produced at least two comprehensive bibliographies of primary and secondary materials: Frederick Frank's *Gothic Fiction: A Master List of Twentieth-Century Criticism and Research* (1987) and Benjamin Fisher's *The Gothic's Gothic: Study Aids to the Tradition of the Tale of Terror* (1988).

Although elements of the Gothic occurred in all genres of literature long before the eighteenth century, coverage of novels that are predominantly Gothic begins with Horace Walpole's *The Castle of Otranto* in 1764, which was clearly a reaction against the dominant vogue of fictional realism. Stating that the reader's fancy had been "dammed up" in the novel, Walpole planned to move away from the "strict adherence to common life" to arouse the reader's imagination. The means he chose—the supernatural, the dreary castle, the prevailing atmosphere of fear—

inspired many other eighteenth-century novelists, such as Clara Reeve, and influenced the two best-known eighteenth-century Gothic novelists, Ann Radcliffe and Matthew Lewis.

Ann Radcliffe and Matthew Lewis are the Samuel Richardson and Henry Fielding of the Gothic. Just as Richardson and Fielding originated two major traditions in the history of realistic novel writing—the psychological, interior focus (Richardson's *Pamela*) and the more exterior, panoramic scope (Fielding's *Tom Jones*)—Radcliffe and Lewis established two different mainstreams of Gothic fiction with identifiable characteristics still labeled as female and male. Despite the obvious variations and mixtures of these characteristics over the history of the genre, Gothic novels have been typed by gender categories.

Women writers following the Radcliffean tradition have focused on the prolonged pursuit of the pure and passive heroine by the aggressive male villain in a dark, labyrinthine setting that intensifies the anxiety and fear throughout the novel. Usually, all ends well as the threats of the villain, whose powers appear to be supernatural, are never actually realized, and the virtuous heroine, like Emily St. Aubert in Radcliffe's *The Mysteries of Udolpho* (1794), emerges triumphant over her oppressor. This restoration of moral order is accompanied by a return to the rational as well, since the seemingly supernatural elements are reduced to the natural by an elaborate, contrived explanation at the end of the action.

This moral rationalism is not the case with Gothic novels written by men, in the tradition established by Matthew Lewis in *The Monk* (1796) and continued most powerfully in Charles Robert Maturin's *Melmoth the Wanderer* (1820). Though the persecution of the virtuous heroine still drives the plot, the male writer shifts the focus of interest from the heroine threatened by male villainy to the villain-hero, whose evil nature may indeed be aggrandized by his supernatural nature, such as vampirism. The innocent young woman does not stand a chance against this power; unlike her Radcliffean counterparts, she may actually be murdered, or worse, seduced or raped. Lengthy atmospheric descriptions conventional in the women novelists' works are discarded in favor of erotic and violent sensationalism, as the villain indulges appetites only imagined in the women's Gothics: hence the distinction between the atmosphere of psychological terror in the female Gothic novels and that of physical horror in those written by men. The reader is asked to suspend disbelief in the actual and experience the reality of supernatural evil before the blackguard is destroyed at the end.

The varying treatments of evil suggest the traditional preference by women writers for Radcliffean Gothicism. Since the innocence of the heroine is never violated, she upholds and perpetuates the idealized virtues assigned to women in a patriarchal social structure—delicacy, fortitude, and chastity—by means of passive resistance. At the same time, she reveals the anxieties of women in a subordinate social position, particularly those who must endure persecution and imprisonment by men. As many recent feminist critics have pointed out, the nature of evil is equated with male tyranny, with the villain remaining an unsympathetic character whose powers are finally constrained by morality, reason, and social propriety. The tremendous popularity of this genre with women writers and readers in late eighteenth-century England shows that it addressed particularly female concerns. Women dominated by men related to fantasies of victory and freedom that did not require overstepping the ideal codes of behavior. Commenting on the impact of women writers on the late eighteenth-century novel, Tompkins writes that "In their hands the novel was not so much a reflection of life as a counterpoise to it, within the covers of which they looked for compensation, for ideal pleasures and ideal revenge."[2] The extent to which these early Gothics responded to a widespread need among female readers accounts for the popularity of this relatively new genre.

In the Gothic novels written by men, the focus on the villain-hero allows the reader to identify psychologically with the source of evil, as the torment, rebellion, and power of this larger-than-life figure call up all forbidden desires—the beast within, the id, the subconscious. Well argued by psychoanalytic critics of the Gothic as a major   if not the major—source of appeal of the eroticism and sensationalism of the genre, the escapades of the Gothic villain provide a vicarious experience normally taboo in actual life, where these desires are repressed. As Stephen King puts it, the horror scene is "an invitation to indulge in deviant, antisocial behavior by proxy—to commit gratuitous acts of violence, indulge our puerile dreams of power, to give in to our most craven fears."[3]

This subversion of conservative, middle-class values of restraint and respectability was simply too great a leap for women writers to make; their more genteel Gothicism, while revealing discomfort with the status quo, certainly did not appear to be openly rebellious. As a result, the villains of the early Gothic novels written by men have exhibited a power and an evil comparable with the rebels of Romantic fiction and the Promethean figures of Romantic poetry. Early women's Gothics have been more divisive, however, with evil playing a secondary role to the portrayal of exemplary virtue and extensive didacticism justifying the sensational action. Both traditions have depended on well-defined roles of male aggression and female passivity (the moral equivalent of virtue).

Surveying the scene of Gothic fiction today to see what remains of these early characteristics is similar to tracing the influences of Richardson and Fielding in the mainstream of the novel; novelists' technical experiments have blended all kinds of conventions and devices so that the original distinctions are blurred and less meaningful. Clearly identifiable traits of the Gothic—ghosts, monsters, hauntings, and other supernatural threats to humans—have also merged with elements of other genres to form Gothic science fiction, Gothic detective fiction, Gothic erotica, and other hybrids. Vestiges of the gender distinctions are evident in the contemporary pulp extremes of both types: the purely violent Gothics that wallow in grisly gore and the equally shallow Radcliffean Gothic romances now sold widely in retail stores. With few exceptions, Radcliffean Gothicism still dominates the popular Gothic novels written by female writers for female readers. As Janice Radway explains, "Romance reading and writing might be seen therefore as a collectively elaborated female ritual through which women explore the consequences of their common social condition as the appendages of men and attempt to imagine a more perfect state where all the needs they so intensely feel and accept as given would be adequately addressed."[4] Despite modernizations of the female protagonists, the Radcliffean model continues in that the plot hinges on the prolonged terror caused by the male who oppresses the female with threats of imprisonment. Why this plot device continues to attract today's more liberated women readers is the source of some critical debate. Helen Hazen argues that in contemporary women's Gothics, "the tension of the story is that the heroine might be defiled, and the struggle is, without exception, sexual."[5] The interest lies in "how to prevent the occurrence, and also in the temptation to imagine calamity when normal life seems not lively enough from day to day" (Hazen, 41). Disagreeing with some feminist critics, who argue that the portrayal of actual rape prevalent in less romantic fictions and more erotic Gothics is effective in revealing female readers' real fears of male villainy, Hazen states that women do not want to read about the actual event; their fantasies do not entail explicit sexual violence. Accounting for the dominance of the romantic model, she goes further to distinguish between romantic and feminist Gothics, arguing that "Romantic gothics end happily; feminist gothics do not" (44); that is, sexual threats remain unrealized in the more popular romantic fiction.

In discussing the persistence of the Radcliffean model and its contemporary variations, Cynthia Griffin Wolff states that "the specific details are different in modern Gothics, but the pattern is the same: the author assigns interesting talents and a measure of intelligence to her heroine at the beginning of the novel, and these then vanish as soon as the young woman is swept into danger."[6] While Wolff sees female fictional identity in modern Gothics as still dependent on relationships with men, she does note a major difference between eighteenth-century and modern Gothics: today the woman "marries the demon lover" whom she would have been obliged to reject in earlier novels. Wolff sees this difference as appropriate for earlier readers, whose heroines were virtually sexless, and the sexually liberated contemporary audience, where a fictional female's choice "leads not to a rejection of feminine sexuality, but to an embracing of it: what seemed at first menacing is revealed as both tolerable and desirable" (105). In today's more liberated female Gothics, writers may describe actual sexual violence, and acceptable choices of lovers may be expanded to include rakish Lovelace types capable of reformation. Still, the predominant Gothic novel sold over hundreds of bookstore counters to women readers remains more conservative, nonerotic, and Radcliffean.

In stark contrast to these novels, Anne Rice's non-Radcliffean Gothics explore a new vein, just as Mary Shelley's *Frankenstein* transcended the boundaries of female Gothic writers in 1818 and broke down distinctions between the two traditions established by Radcliffe and Lewis. Replacing the images of male tyranny so prevalent in contemporary female Gothics with those more commonly favored by male writers, Rice vividly depicts the horrors of physical violence enacted by supernatural villain-heroes reminiscent of Lewis's Ambrosio, Poe's Montresor, and Stevenson's Dr. Jekyll. In the postmodern world of Anne Rice, the physically horrifying and the morally depraved Gothic villain-heroes are transformed into sympathetic creatures who, like their human counterparts, must confront the existential realities of the late twentieth century. "They are lonely, prisoners of circumstance, compulsive sinners, full of self-loathing and doubt. They are, in short, Everyman Eternal" (Ferraro, 67). Like their great Byronic ancestors, they travel toward destruction, suffering, and renewal. The imprisonment from which they are delivered is not the stifling tyranny of men over women but that resulting from the Blakean mind-forged manacles, their own dependence on self-delusions concerning social institutions and religious myths.

Rice burdens her characters with inescapable physical conditions (vampirism, race, castration) that exaggerate their alienation from humanity and emphasize their need to establish their significance. In *The Vampire Chronicles*, humanizing the vampires' conflicts, their relationships with each other, and their often genderless natures opens up the possibilities of a genre increasingly narrowed by stereotypical conventions over the years. This expansive spirit is apparent in the wide open space and global travel of Rice's Gothics—as compared with the claustrophobic interiors of many female Gothics—and in their persistent eroticism, now a part of the liberating psychological process instead of a forbidden pleasure inherent in the male-female pursuit plot of more conventional Gothics. Since the protagonists achieve their own personal codes of moral choice in a godless universe, the restoration of order typical of female Gothics is pointless. In Rice's contemporary fictional reality, the focus shifts away from the traditional external conflicts depicting moral victories of women over men or human beings over the vampire and toward the psychological struggles of the vampires themselves seeking ways of surviving the conditions of their eternal existence.

Analyzing the cultural appeal of the Gothic, Joseph Grixti argues that the genre is a "type of narrative which deals in messages about fear and experiences associated with fear" (xii). He goes on to list some of these fears: "the discomfort we occasionally feel about our own psyche and about what may lurk in its dark depths; our worries and qualms about our own creations and about the technological advances which might be turning us into helpless robots in a ruthless world; our anxieties about the ways in which our bodies can let us down, about pain, death, and the dead, and about all forms of hostile forces which may at any moment (or so we are told) intrude into our uncertainly patched-up social and personal worlds" (xiii).

While some fears are universal, others may be more intensely felt and shared by a particular group of readers at a given time. It is no accident, for instance, that during the beginnings of outerspace explorations in the 1950s, Gothic films portraying invasions of extraterrestrial monsters were extremely popular, such as *Earth vs. Flying Saucers* and *Invasion of the Body Snatchers,* while in the 1970s films like *Demon Seed* and *The Andromeda Strain* appealed to the audience's "vision of technology as an

octopus—perhaps sentient—burying us alive in red tape and informa-
tion-retrieval systems" (King, 160). Since the most successful Gothic
writers touch the reader's deepest anxieties, analyzing the threat imagined in the Gothic becomes "a process of cultural self-analysis, and the
images which it throws up become the dream-figures of a troubled social
·roup" (Punter, 425). Unforgettable film images that come to mind are
  ꞓ robotic women in *The Stepford Wives* (1975), the bags of human com-
  ﹒st in *Soylent Green* (1973), the schizophrenic Norman Bates in *Psycho*
)60), and the suspended human bodies kept alive in a repository as
resources for organ donations in *Coma* (1978).

Other than the Frankenstein myth, whereby the unlawful creation
unleashed on us can assume many different shapes depending on the
current technology that we fear, perhaps no other Gothic image is as
persistent and powerful and therefore appropriate for "cultural self-
analysis" as that of the vampire. As Grixti points out, "the figure of the
vampire is one whose history is interestingly intertwined with the public
and private concerns of the epochs which popularized and endorsed it as
an objectification of uncertainly understood and disturbing phenomena"
(14). Since the actual supernaturalism of the vampire's existence and the
repeated eroticism of its attacks were considered as improper subject
matter for women writers operating within codes of social propriety and
moral probability, the vampire has been the province of the male Gothic
fantasy perpetuated by male writers. Beginning in the early nineteenth
century, John Polidori's classic forerunner *The Vampyre* (1819) was followed by James Malcolm Rymer's popular penny dreadful *Varney the
Vampyre, or The Feast of Blood* (1840), then Sheridan LeFanu's disturbing
Carmilla (1872), and finally Bram Stoker's great prototype, *Dracula*
(1897).

Though there are too many variations of the vampire myth today to
discuss here, Stephen King's *Salem's Lot* (1975) and Whitley Strieber's
The Hunger (1981) are notable, since both represent extremely successful
combinations of traditional aspects of vampirism and original adaptations appealing to contemporary readers. King's frighteningly credible
Mr. Barlow poses with the British Straker as a reputable antique dealer
and turns a small town in southern Maine into a community of horrors.
Though Ben Mears and Mark Petrie seem finally to destroy Barlow in
the traditional way, with a stake through his heart, and watch his disso-
lution, when they return to inspect the damage, Barlow's teeth are still
alive. Also, Barlow's progeny, made up of familiar townspeople, live on,
as is evident from the numbers of bizarre deaths reported in the local

newspaper. As Ben and Mark leave the town permanently, they realize that the fire they set will dislodge but not destroy all of the vampires. Whitley Strieber's Miriam is a highly intelligent female vampire who allows herself to be examined by her major adversary, Sarah, a doctor researching potential links between genetics and aging. In this confrontation with feminist overtones (men are clearly the weaker characters in *The Hunger*), the best human resources prove to be ineffective, as it is Sarah and not Miriam who is destroyed. Sarah ends up locked inside one of Miriam's trunks in total darkness, listening to the "little rustlings and sighs" that "filled the air around her, coming from other chests" that had lain there in the attic for centuries.[7]

Both King's and Strieber's vampires are ruthless and indestructible; as in many contemporary Gothics reflecting a loss of belief in the powers of establishment forces to overpower evil, their threat persists. They also demonstrate Leonard Wolf's description of the power of Stoker's Count Dracula: "The vampire of greatest interest is, of course, the man or woman of overwhelming ego and energy whose will for an evil life is so great that he will not die or who, when surprised by death, has reacted with a burst of rage against the inevitable and refuses to lie still."[8]

With few other exceptions, the contemporary popularization of the vampire myth has effected a reduction of stature that is similar to the impact of Jane Austen's *Northanger Abbey* on the overdone conventions of Gothics that became clichés between 1780 and 1830 in England. Now a friendly, familiar subject of cartoons, cereal names, and comic films, the late twentieth-century vampire has been defanged into a harmless caricature of his former self that hardly fits Wolf's description of Stoker's Dracula. As Brian Frost observes, "These days, with undead counts and countesses now considered passé, the traditional image of human bloodsuckers—as vicious, self-seeking predators—has undergone a dramatic change. In contemporary horror novels the prevailing trend is to portray vampires as highly intellectual beings living a separate but not entirely incompatible existence alongside the human race, with the pursuance of knowledge (rather than nubile maidens) as their main recreation."[9]

Though this recent demystification of the myth has made it difficult for a serious writer to employ the vampire as metaphor successfully and to overcome critical prejudice, the potential of the myth testifies to the need for careful distinctions. Sylvia Plath managed to demonstrate its power and flexibility to convey serious literary intent in her poem "Daddy" (1963), in which she attempts to free herself from male tyranny and assert her independence. After developing images of Nazi torture, the persona compares the sapping of her vitality by men to the vampire's drinking blood and her throwing off this domination to the villagers' staking the vampire in the heart. Reviewers need not assume, as some do, that any incorporation of the vampire into literature automatically debases the work's merit.

For Rice, the prejudice against Gothic conventions has larger implications. In a 1993 *Playboy* interview, she argued that critics' tendencies to believe that "to be profound a book has to be about the middle class and about some specific domestic problem of the middle class" reflect the triumph of a Protestant vision over the Catholic. Portrayals of the real, interior lives of people working out small problems and achieving moments of awareness is "the essence of what Protestantism came to be in America," a faith in "the less magical, more practical, more down-to-earth," and, for Rice, "the more sterile."[10] She sees her own choice of the unreal and marvelous, the grand lives of supernatural characters, as the result of her being "nourished on" the miraculous stories of Catholic saints, vivid memories she brings to her vampires.

The richness and power of the myth have also been well-established by critical explorations of Stoker's *Dracula,* where the villain-hero becomes an ambivalent Romantic rebel that Victorians both fear and envy. Having commented on the sources of popularity of Stoker's novel with a Victorian audience coping with repression, loss of religious faith, empiric decline, and fear of evolution, David Punter sees the "continuous oscillation between reassurance and threat" as the "central dialectic of Gothic fiction" (423). In Stoker's version of the vampire story, the evil represented by Dracula is finally destroyed and the Victorian values of hard work, duty, and technology reaffirmed. The reader of Stoker's novel and earlier Gothics could take comfort that in the end, the menace would be defeated; virtue would indeed triumph over evil.

Rice's sympathetic and indestructible vampires are more like images of the world-weary Tithonus, who, in Tennyson's poem of that name, caught in the meaninglessness of an eternal existence, sees himself as a "grey shadow, once a man." Instead of creatures to be destroyed, her weary vampires also complain of being consumed by "cruel immortality" and run the risk of their own self-destruction. As such, they exaggerate the senselessness of existence and serve as metaphors for human beings searching for truths to live by.

Joseph Grixti, who takes up the issue of how we evaluate contemporary horror fiction, states: "A number of representatives of the genre reflect considerable artistic, imaginative, and intellectual merit in their application of the conventions of the genre to a searching analysis of human concerns, and in their employment of standard images of horror to convey insights which can form the basis of constructive action. At the same time, the genre of horror fiction can also be said to harbour an increasing amount of popular material which thrives on cliché and which projects images and interpretations of experience which are as hollow and self-enclosed as they are pretentious" (xi). As will become evident in the discussions that follow, the fictional images Rice uses in the four novels that form *The Vampire Chronicles* do hold up a "searching analysis of human concerns," and her technical devices and original handling of Gothic conventions represent a fascinating variation and broadening of the genre's traditions. A serious analysis of her books in *The Vampire Chronicles* is warranted for both of these reasons.

Most unconventional in *The Vampire Chronicles* is Rice's establishment of a vampire community in the first novel of the series, *Interview with the Vampire,* and her consequent development of interrelationships among vampires rather than conflicts between vampires and humans. This shift of focus causes other major departures from the tradition: vampires rather than humans tend to tell their own stories; each has individual traits that distinguish one from the other; they remember centuries of events and live in locations all over the world; they need relationships with one another and belong to small families or groups; they fear destruction from one another more than from humans; they experience loneliness and frustration. The suspense does not hinge on whether or not the humans will outlast the vampires but on whether or not the vampires will survive the aggressive actions of other vampires with power even greater than their own, and whether or not the vampires will mature enough to find ways of enduring the self-annihilating elements built into the very conditions of their undead existence. Vampires learn about their origins and histories, which are grounded in ancient myths that reveal the same enlightening, archetypal patterns of human experience. The need for blood that is both disgusting yet erotic in Dracula becomes less loathsome (yet still highly erotic) in Rice, as the descriptions of blood drinking involve the ecstasy between vampire and vampire. The blood also takes on symbolic overtones of family preservation and pagan rituals of human sacrifice. Human kills are still necessary, but understated so that the reader forgets how the vampire sustains itself.

Her other two Gothics, *The Mummy* and *The Witching Hour,* show her willingness to explore other occult phenomena and supernatural figures, though they do not provide quite the same opportunities for demonstrating originality within a larger literary tradition. Its film-script origin, abundant eroticism, and lack of seriousness turn *The Mummy* into a near spoof of the mummy Gothics. *The Witching Hour,* however, is Rice's most ambitious book. In this novel, perhaps because of the interplay between human and supernatural characters, she conveys the ambivalences of high Gothic and integrates most effectively philosophical issues of free will, predestination, the nature of good and evil, and the relativity of reality. As in her other novels, the use of allusions to familiar literary classics and religious rituals develops layers of meaning and enriches the texts, a device that provides the fine metaphorical structure of her most literary book, *The Tale of the Body Thief.*

Since its origins with Horace Walpole's *The Castle of Otranto* in 1764, Gothic fiction has been associated with the spirit of liberation; in Walpole's case from what he saw as the damning up of fantasy in the novel, to female writers' expressions of male tyranny against women in a patriarchal society, to other novelists' revelations of anxieties and rebellions against repression. Unlike realistic novels, which depict conflicts in the contexts of probability to convey the truths of reality, Gothic novels rely on elements of fantasy and horror to address the truths of imagination (Punter, 408). In other words, the universal significance of such mythic figures as Frankenstein's monster and Count Dracula must be explored like other Romantic images on a symbolic, psychological level. Because of her highly original adaptations of the vampire myths, Rice's vampires have this kind of power and complexity. Louis's counterpart is surely the Romantics' cast-out Cain and Lestat the modern Prometheus. With her own villain-heroes, Rice not only recaptures the richness and dignity of the tradition but perpetuates its spirit of liberation in freeing the genre from its present insignificance and opening up new realms for the vampire.

Chapter Three

Interview with the Vampire

When *Interview with the Vampire* appeared in 1976, it received reviews ranging from extremely enthusiastic to decidedly hostile. Positive reviewers appreciated the philosophical content, which they believed restored a Romantic stature to the vampire. Edmund Fuller called the book a "masterpiece of the morbid,"[1] and Charles W. Gold described it as a "Transylvanian *Tom Jones*," with Louis as the Tom figure taking a journey toward self-awareness and understanding.[2] Yet this same dimension was criticized by other critics, such as Pearl K. Bell, who saw the book as "all talk and no terror,"[3] and Phoebe-Lou Adams, who felt that a Rice vampire "could talk an adder to death."[4] Another reviewer recognized the seriousness of themes, such as the "desire to be an individual, different from anyone else, and simultaneously to be part of a loving, nurturing community," but still felt that the novel was "too superficial, too impersonal and too obviously made."[5] Edith Milton went further to condemn what she saw as sheer hypocrisy: "What makes *Interview with the Vampire* so bad is not that the erotic content is so explicit, but that the morbid context is so respectable."[6]

There was far less debate over the freshness and originality that characterize Rice's handling of the vampire tradition. Taking up the vampire at all distinguishes Rice's Gothicism from that of most of her female contemporaries, who tend to prefer the Radcliffean mode. Rice's Gothic novels differ from those written by most male writers as well, since her protagonist, Louis, and the other vampire figures in the novel become metaphors for human responses to an insignificant existence and depart in just about every way from the traditions established in Stoker's *Dracula*.

Perhaps the most obvious departure is the plot itself, as indicated by the title. In the *Dracula* tradition the story is a human one with human protagonists desperately trying to destroy Dracula; in *Interview with the Vampire* the focus of the story is the vampire himself, who is being interviewed in San Francisco by a young man identified later in *The Queen of the Damned* as Daniel. Louis recounts his adventures, which are organized into four sections. Part 1 begins with his being made a vampire by Lestat in

1791 at age 25 in New Orleans. It traces his tutelage under the sensualist Lestat, the creation of the child-vampire Claudia, and their efforts to destroy Lestat. Part 2 chronicles Louis's travels with Claudia through Eastern Europe on a quest to find out the meaning of their existence as vampires and their struggles with others like themselves. In part 3 they meet the more knowledgeable vampire Armand in Paris, and he answers some of their questions. As leader of the Parisian vampires, he invites them to attend a performance at their theater. A major battle ensues among the vampires, who discover from Lestat that Louis and Claudia tried to destroy him. Claudia is burned to total destruction. After torching the theater and decapitating the vampire enemy ringleader, Santiago, Louis returns with Armand to New Orleans. Less a narration of action and more an epilogue to Louis's story, part 4 explains how he has changed as a result of these experiences and concludes with a reunion between himself and Lestat staged by Armand, who hoped to restore Louis's capacity for feeling. The scene then returns to San Francisco, where the interview concludes and the young man demands to be turned into a vampire. Louis, appalled that the interviewer could make such a request after all he has told him of his own despair, makes a single attack upon him and departs. It is morning when the interviewer wakes and the novel ends.

From the beginning of his transformation to a vampire, Louis has a strong need to justify his existence and a compassion for mortals unique among vampires. Having human traits makes him vulnerable to other vampires and causes him torment. It is guilt over his brother's death that leads Louis to accept Lestat's "gift" of immortal life; he longs to appease his guilt with self-damnation and self-punishment. Nearly transformed, or in a state between the human and the vampire, he experiences a loss of ego and an accompanying sense of the possibilities of a new existence.

Lestat's remorselessness and cruelty parallel Dracula's, but Louis continues to suffer from the stress caused by the conflict between his longing for blood and his hatred of killing. He is "[t]orn apart by the wish to take no action—to starve, to wither in thought on the one hand; and driven to kill on the other.[7] Lestat, enjoying the lingering deaths of his human victims and forcing Louis to participate in or at least watch his killings, tells Louis that peace will come to him only when he accepts his vampire nature: "Vampires are killers! They don't want you or your sensibility!" (*Interview*, 90).

Louis is repulsed by Lestat's insensitivity to human death, particularly after Lestat kills Freniere, the young owner of a plantation nearby, whom Louis tried to save. Louis eventually comes to loathe his ruthless creator and realizes the painful truth that Lestat has nothing to tell him about what it means to be a vampire. He tells Lestat: "I'm confident I shall find vampires who have more in common with me than I with you. Vampires who understand knowledge as I do and have used their superior vampire nature to learn secrets of which you don't even dream. If you haven't told me everything, I shall find things out for myself or from them, when I find them" (*Interview*, 88).

Louis's leaving Lestat is delayed, however, when Lestat, not wanting to lose Louis's help in arranging financial affairs and accommodations, turns a five-year-old child into the child-vampire Claudia, whom he calls their daughter. Knowing that Louis will feel responsible for her welfare, Lestat rightly believes that Louis will stay. Indeed, for 65 years, Louis adores this daughter and tries to teach her about literature and a love of beauty to counteract the influence of Lestat. Under the influence of Louis's sensitivity, combined with Lestat's relish of the kill, Claudia experiences an odd maturation. She decides to sleep alone instead of with Louis, demands to know how she was created, and shows every sign of departing. Unable to bear the thought of being without her, Louis tells her he loves her "with his human nature"; Claudia tells him that she has no human traits, but does have his "passion for truth" (*Interview*, 128); in other words, she, too, must have questions answered about their lives. She says they have both grown beyond Lestat and must destroy him to be free of him.

True to her word, Claudia poisons Lestat, who seems to wither away horribly before their eyes, but is in fact not destroyed. Louis, horrified at what Claudia has done, vows to leave her, which makes her cry. Helpless against this evidence of human anguish, Louis consents to go with her to Eastern Europe, where they hope to learn something about themselves and their origins. Before departing they survive an attack from a vengeful Lestat, leaving him to burn in flames. Louis and Claudia board ship unsure of whether they have finally managed to incinerate Lestat. (Fire, not stakes or crosses, is one of the few ways a vampire may be destroyed in Rice's Gothics.) Louis and Claudia escape together, but their relationship is changed. Her initial willingness to murder Lestat disturbs Louis—for vampires, killing another vampire is the only crime. Despite their mutual commitment to the search for knowledge, he continues in his state of "sublime loneliness" and fear that Lestat will somehow follow them. Louis, in particular, longs to know the purpose of his immortal state; he would be consoled even to know Satan, "to look upon his face, no matter how terrible that countenance was" rather than to remain forever in the "torment of this ignorance" (*Interview*, 177).

The travels of Louis and Claudia among the Transylvanian vampires are amusing to the knowing reader, who places them in the traditional contexts of other vampire fictions, but futile for Louis and Claudia. They learn nothing from these "mindless, animated corpses" dressed in foul rags who prey on the peasants of the countryside. The real substance of their journey lies in Paris, at the Theater of Vampires, where Louis and Claudia go to a play performed by vampires.

The story of the play, which concerns a beautiful young woman who is forced to choose between death and vampirism, foreshadows later developments in the novel. The audience takes great pleasure in watching a tantalizing—and real—vampire kill, unaware that the play is not an illusion. A "sophisticated and perfumed crowd" (*Interview*, 246) whose decadence suggests fin de siècle Paris (Milton, 29), the theatergoers are unable to distinguish real horror from dramatic entertainment. When the play ends, Louis and Claudia follow the vampire-actors downstairs to a kind of subterranean ballroom ghoulishly decorated with frescoes and murals depicting Breughel's *Triumph of Death* and other lurid scenes of the corpses, skeletons, and monsters of Bosch, Traini, and Durer. There they meet Armand, the intellectual Parisian vampire and manager of the Theater of Vampires, who tells them, unhappily, what they wish to know: there is no God, no devil, no moral dimension to their vampire lives. Armand's wisdom distinguishes him from the vampires in the theater above, who "had made of immortality a club of fads and cheap conformity" (*Interview*, 276), from the Transylvanian bestial types, and from the insensitive Lestat.

The meeting with Armand proves fateful in Louis's movement toward knowledge and therefore self-degradation. Shortly after, at Claudia's request, in part because she senses Louis is attracted to Armand, Louis creates a companion for her, a female vampire named Madeleine. Louis initially refuses, and Claudia is furious. She tells him she hates him because he cannot be evil and because her vampiric birth as a child leaves her to suffer "immortality in this hopeless guise, this helpless form!" (*Interview*, 285). Deprived of Claudia's love, which has allowed him to live with his self-hatred, Louis continues to "die," to lose human feeling and become cynical and detached. Creating the vampire for Claudia is an act of supreme evil for Louis, who promised himself that he would never use this power, even to curb his own loneliness. He tells Claudia when it is over that it is he, not Madeleine, who has died: "It will take her many nights to die, perhaps years. What has died in this room tonight is the last vestige in me of what was human" (*Interview*, 297).

Claiming later that he used his power to influence Louis to transform Madeleine, Armand urges Louis to leave Claudia with her and come with him. In a passage that clearly demonstrates Rice's efforts to use her vampire images to reflect serious human concerns, a despairing Armand warns Louis that he must develop a philosophical perspective to cope with the losses and changes that will characterize his eternal life of vampirism: "How many vampires do you think have the stamina for immortality? . . . [I]n becoming immortal they want all the forms of their life to be fixed as they are and incorruptible . . . When, in fact, all things change except the vampire himself . . . Soon, with an inflexible mind, and often even with the most flexible mind, this immortality becomes a penitential sentence" (*Interview*, 308).

When Armand tells him that he loves Louis and needs to revitalize his own contact with the nineteenth century through Louis, whom he sees as the "spirit of the age," Louis replies that he has always been out of touch with his time and has never belonged anywhere. Armand says Louis's fall from grace and faith "has been the fall of a century," that his experience reflects the very spirit of his age, unlike the pleasure-seeking theater vampires: "'They reflect the age in cynicism which cannot comprehend the death of possibilities, fatuous sophisticated indulgence in the parody of the miraculous, decadence whose last refuge is self-ridicule, a mannered helplessness. You saw them; you've known them all your life. You reflect your age differently. You reflect its broken heart'" (*Interview*, 312).

Before he commits himself to Armand and trades one small family relationship for another, Louis has to undergo the loss of Claudia. Returning to her, Louis's learns that she and Madeleine intend to leave Paris. He is saddened by this news but pleased that she has someone else in her life, now that he wishes to be with Armand instead of her. Their honest communication with each other is violently interrupted by an onslaught of the theater vampires under the leadership of Santiago and Lestat, who has returned for revenge, particularly against Claudia. After a grisly battle and his own rescue by Armand, Louis views the charred remains of Madeleine and the ashes of Claudia with great pain: "A cry rose in me, a wild, consuming cry that came from the bowels of my being" (*Interview*, 330).

Rice, commenting on the connections between Claudia and her own daughter, Michele, who died of leukemia when she was nearly six, explains that in the first version of the novel she had Claudia and Louis "happily joining other vampires in Paris" (Ferraro, 74). When asked by the publisher for a stronger ending, however, Rice knew that she was cheating in letting Claudia live, that she had to let her die and let go of her daughter. The book, according to Ferraro, "seems to suggest that mortal death—however final—is better than some kinds of immortality" (74). The intensity of Claudia's death and its impact on Louis demonstrate the power of Gothic images to transform real pain. In a burst of uncharacteristic rage, Louis decapitates Santiago, torches the theater where the other vampires had taken refuge, and turns against Armand, whom he believes allowed the deaths to take place. Even the art in the Louvre fails to provide any "transcendent pleasure that would obliterate pain": "Before," says Louis, "all art had held for me the promise of a deeper understanding of the human heart. Now the human heart meant nothing" (*Interview,* 346).

Despite his later reconciliation with Armand, Louis tells the interviewer at the end of the novel that he never changed after that evening in the Louvre. As he explains, "I sought to learn nothing that could be given back to humanity. I drank of the beauty of the world as a vampire drinks. I was satisfied. I was filled to the brim. But I was dead. And I was changeless" (*Interview,* 349). Louis now sees that the love and goodness he hoped for in eternal life were impossible from the beginning, "because you cannot have love and goodness when you do what you know to be evil, what you know to be wrong. You can only have the desperate confusion and longing and the chasing of phantom goodness in its human form. I knew the real answer to my quest before I ever reached Paris" (*Interview,* 366).

In confirming the awful truths of his own existence, Louis clearly is not just a spirit who represents Armand's nineteenth century but a voice for late twentieth-century readers as well. As Punter explains, "the Gothic vision is in fact an accurate account of life, of the ways we project our fantasies onto the world and then stand back in horror when we see them come to life" (398). The conditions of vampirism represent for the contemporary reader feelings of helplessness in the midst of an awareness of atrocity and a sense of insignificance and alienation in an overwhelming atmosphere of decline. Louis resembles Tennyson's Tithonus, who recognizes the superiority of mortal life over the eternal. Louis has immortality but needs more emotional sustenance than the ecstasy from the kill that he abhors. Louis's journey from relationships with Lestat to Claudia to Armand takes him from physical to psychological and philosophical truths about his existence. Each brings him growth as well as pain.

While the suspense in *Interview with the Vampire* is caused mainly by conflicts among the vampires themselves rather than by human beings' fear of vampire attacks, the reader senses the possibility that the human interviewer may not be entirely safe in the presence of Louis. The reader knows that it is nighttime, that the vampire and the young man are alone, and that through the course of his experience, Louis's human compassion has been lost or diminished. Though Louis reassures him that he intends no harm because he wants his story to be told, the young man has "sweat running down the sides of his face" (*Interview,* 4). At one point in describing Lestat's preferences, Louis tells the interviewer, "A young man around your age would have appealed to him in particular" (*Interview,* 45). Louis interrupts his narrative later to ask the boy, "Are you still afraid of me?" Receiving no answer, the vampire continues, "I should think you'd be very foolish if you weren't" (*Interview,* 105). Throughout the interview Louis tries to put the young man at ease by offering to light his cigarettes and by being generally considerate and affable. The reader, realizing that the interviewer's modern sensibilities make him vulnerable to the lure of pleasure and power and stir his desire to be made a vampire, remains anxious for his welfare until the very end.

Similar to the thematic purpose of the framing device in Mary Shelley's *Frankenstein,* where the sea captain Robert Walton listens to Victor Frankenstein tell of his concern about overstepping God's boundaries in doing research, Rice's interview format further confirms the theme of existential realities. The naive interviewer seems incapable of understanding the meaning of Louis's despair. Relating only to the power and pleasure of vampirism and not the pain, he insists that he be transformed into a vampire. This response testifies to the barrenness of his existence, which compels him to choose vampiric immortality over human life even after all that Louis has told him. The device also modernizes the more conventional Gothic technique of telling a story through a found manuscript, which enables a past tale of horrifying events to be narrated in the first person. Relying on Louis as her single narrator in this novel—unlike the first-person diaries, journals, and minutes narrated by different characters in Stoker's *Dracula*—Rice achieves a concentration that adds to the emotional impact of Louis's experience.

In writing the next two novels in the *Chronicles* and her later Gothics, she experiments with more complicated ways of telling the stories, such as interrupting the present narrations with other characters who recount past events and using multiple narrators to develop simultaneous actions and converging multiple plots. The historical, panoramic scope she achieves later is innovative and ambitious, especially for the Gothic genre, but never quite matches the dramatic intensity of Louis's voice in the *Interview with a Vampire.* Like the young interviewer, the reader is mesmerized by Louis's story and made to feel both comfortable and sympathetic; yet in moments of awful truth, the intensity of the vampire's needs creates a revulsion and horror in the reader that the interviewer—though nervous and fearful—does not share.

Traditionally, vampires need blood to survive. Not only do they sustain themselves by drinking blood, but they derive great pleasure, even erotic ecstasy, from the human kill. Louis himself, attempting to explain the thrill of this experience, tells the interviewer that it is like describing sex to someone who has never had it. The correlation between descriptions of vampiric blood drinking and both homosexual and heterosexual intercourse has been discussed in many studies of the Gothic. Emphasizing the eroticism at the heart of the appeal of the vampire myth, critics describe how the reader indulges in the forbidden pleasures experienced by the predator vampire. In Rice's vampires the androgynous blood exchanges between vampire and vampire broaden their appeal by providing a "gender-free perspective" on the eroticism (Ramsland, 148).

Edith Milton's negative response (cited earlier) to what she sees as the hypocrisy of eroticism disguised by respectability in Rice's novel is typical of critical observations that go back to the beginnings of the genre in the eighteenth century, when reviewers noted the contradictions between stated didactic intentions of Gothic novelists to inculcate virtue and rationalism and the actual sensational events depicted in the novels that encouraged irrationality and emotionalism. David Punter, on the other hand, sees Stoker's *Dracula* as dealing with the liberation of repressed desires, a problem particularly pertinent to late Victorians, and then explains the ambivalence of the novel's appeal, whereby readers engage in the taboo pleasures of Dracula yet take comfort in his destruction at the end. Punter concludes that the "problems of sexuality" are at the root of such tales as Radcliffe's *Mysteries of Udolpho,* Shelley's *Frankenstein,* Stoker's *Dracula,* and their descendants (411). This appeal is based on a kind of negative psychology dealing with the taboo, with the "dreadful pleasure" of emotional ambivalence in which "the mind oscillates between attraction and repulsion, worship and condemnation" (410). James B. Twitchell, too, sees Rice's vampires as exceptions to modern vulgarizations of the myth and argues that the Romantic origins of the vampire are based on its capacity to evoke the ambivalent "attraction/repulsion" response; the vampire can thus be emblematic of incest, power, homosexual attraction, and repressed sexuality.[8]

There is no question that the eroticism of drinking blood constitutes a major appeal in Anne Rice's Gothics, yet the examination of a few passages shows how she integrates this eroticism with other fictional elements. Eroticism in *Interview with the Vampire* is tied up with the torment of Louis, whose thirst for blood must be fulfilled yet whose moral sensibility is revolted by the act of killing. Louis says that despite his trying to live off the blood of animals, "the killing of anything less than a human being brought nothing but a vague longing" (*Interview,* 95), a longing for his former human existence that fades only when he achieves total intimacy with humans in the kill.

Shortly after watching the vampire play, Louis is torn by his own passion for the girl on the stage and his revulsion at the spectacle of the kill. Weakened by this tantalizing performance, he is unable to resist feasting upon Denis, the young companion of Armand:

> But before I could push him away for his own sake, I saw the bluish bruise on his tender neck. He was offering it to me. He was pressing the length of his body against me now, and I felt the hard strength of his sex beneath his clothes pressing against my leg. A wretched gasp escaped my lips, but he bent close, his lips on what must have been so cold, so lifeless for him; and I sank my teeth into his skin, my body rigid, that hard sex driving against me, and I lifted him in passion off the floor. Wave after wave of his beating heart passed into me as, weightless, I rocked with him, devouring him, his ecstasy, his conscious pleasure. (*Interview,* 250)

Rice focuses here on the feelings of the vampire over the human to elicit sympathy for the vampire's dilemma. She downplays the moral horror of vampiric murder, since the willing Denis lives to offer himself another day. She also focuses either on erotic blood exchanges between vampires, such as Lestat's creation of Louis and Claudia, or on other scenes between vampires and humans who, like Denis here and the interviewer later, are eager participants deriving pleasure from their experience.

One of the most erotic passages transpires when Louis turns Madeleine into a vampire companion for Claudia:

She gasped as I broke the flesh, the warm current coming into me, her breasts crushed against me, her body arching up, helpless, from the couch. And I could see her eyes, even as I shut my own, see that taunting, provocative mouth. I was drawing on her, hard, lifting her, and I could feel her weakening, her hands dropping limp at her sides. . . . I gathered her close to me, the blood pouring over her lips. Then she opened her eyes, and I felt the gentle pressure of her mouth, and then her hands closing tight on the arm as she began to suck. I was rocking her, whispering to her, trying desperately to break my swoon; and then I felt her powerful pull. Every blood vessel felt it. I was threaded through and through with her pulling, my hand holding fast to the couch now, her heart beating fierce against my heart, her fingers digging deep into my arm, my outstretched palm . . . until, without will or direction, I had wrenched free of her and fallen away from her, clutching that bleeding wrist tight with my own hand. (*Interview*, 293–94)

Louis's pleasure, however, is tainted with self-loathing; creating yet another creature who must kill to survive is a final act of degradation in his coming to terms with the horror of what he himself has become. Unlike Dracula, whose evil pleasures are finally destroyed, Louis's self-punishment continues, as future pleasures fail to compensate for the knowledge that he is "damned" in "his own mind and soul." More appropriate for a late twentieth-century audience than a Victorian one, Louis's experience implies that the cultivation of pleasure, perhaps a last resort to counteract the hopeless conditions of life, is not enough.

William Patrick Day, in his study of Gothic fantasy, offers a more positive view of vampiric pleasure. He argues that the Gothic, in its "continual transformation of images of suffering into pleasure, its portrayal of the dead end of suffering and the terrors of the pleasure impulse deformed into monstrousness, affirms that the most vital human impulse is the search for pleasure in its fullest and most imaginative forms. The continuing vitality of the Gothic tradition, its extraordinary hold on us, grows from its revelation, through the images of pain, death, and disintegration, of the possibilities of pleasure, life, and wholeness."[9] Lestat achieves this sense of wholeness later, in *The Vampire Lestat,* and embraces even the worst parts of his vampiric nature in *The Tale of the Body Thief,* but Louis remains unable to move beyond personal despair and pain.

Louis is not alone in his departure from vampiric tradition. Rice's main vampire characters—as well as the setting of her novels—distinguish her Gothic fiction. Claudia contrasts with the Parisian vampires, characterized by their ignorance and conformity. The females tell Claudia that she must wear black, that her pastel dress is "tasteless." Watching them play with Claudia's golden curls, Louis notes that all of these vampires had dyed their hair black, an act that gave a disturbing impression of their dullness and conformity. Indeed, Armand confirms that "Their blood is different, vile. They increase as we do but without skill or care" (*Interview*, 267). The vampires' mindlessness and savagery not only distinguish them from Claudia but encourage the reader to sympathize with Louis, whose sensitivity sets him apart.

Defining the characteristics of vampires by placing them within a larger group humanizes them in a new way, as does locating them in actual settings that go far beyond the conventional coffins and castles. Rice's keen attention to place, especially her native New Orleans, has been noted by many reviewers; in fact, her fictional descriptions have been explored in an architectural journey through "Literary New Orleans."[10] While in Paris, Louis recalls that

> New Orleans, though beautiful and desperately alive, was desperately fragile. There was something forever savage and primitive there, something that threatened the exotic and sophisticated life both from within and without. Not an inch of those wooden streets nor a brick of the crowded Spanish houses had not been bought from the fierce wilderness that forever surrounded the city, ready to engulf it. Hurricanes, floods, fevers, the plague—and the damp of the Louisiana climate itself worked tirelessly on every hewn plank or stone facade, so that New Orleans seemed at all times like a dream in the imagination of her striving populace, a dream held intact at every second by a tenacious, though unconscious, collective will. (*Interview*, 221–22)

Louis, who returns to New Orleans at the end of his quest, describes the city's landscape in language that reveals his sadness and aesthetic sensitivity and that supports an epicurean pursuit of pleasure as an antidote to despair: "But this sadness was not painful, nor was it passionate. It was something rich, however, and almost sweet, like the fragrance of the jasmine and the roses that crowded the old courtyard garden which I saw through the iron gates. And this sadness gave a subtle satisfaction and held me a long time in that spot; and it held me to the city'" (*Interview*, 352). In all of her novels, the rich tradition of New Orleans provides a haven where Rice's characters come to terms with their lives.

As the above passage suggests, the settings in *Interview with the Vampire* are not only conveyed with accurate and rich detail but reflect

Louis's states of mind and feelings. Right after his transformation into a vampire and his optimistic determination to explore the mysteries of his new existence, Louis goes out on the gallery of his plantation Pointe du Lac to experience a full moon instead of the sunshine: "The moon was large over the cypresses, and the candlelight poured from the open doors. The thick plastered pillars and walls of the house had been freshly whitewashed, the floorboards freshly swept, and summer rain had left the night clean and sparkling with drops of water. I leaned against the end pillar of the gallery, my head touching the soft tendrils of a jasmine which grew there in constant battle with a wisteria, and I thought of what lay before me throughout the world and throughout time" (*Interview*, 34). This quiet optimism is short-lived, of course; Louis has a characteristically dark vision—a nightmare— projected against a "a great wasteland backdrop" that reflects his own despair.

In the vision, his personal rite of passage takes him across the ocean, "the unconscious, the sea of life" (Ramsland, 173). As he passes aboard ship through the Straits of Gibraltar, his search for truth turns to "bitter flower" when he imagines that the sea tells him his quest is "for darkness only": "I wanted those waters to be blue. And they were not. They were the nighttime waters, and how I suffered then, straining to remember the seas that a young man's untutored senses had taken for granted, that an undisciplined memory had let slip away for eternity. The Mediterranean was black, black off the coast of Italy, black off the coast of Greece, black always" (*Interview*, 181).

In a scene that previews Rice's more extensive symbolic use of Catholicism in *The Queen of the Damned*, Louis's visit to a cathedral short-ly after he and Claudia believe they have destroyed Lestat confirms his own supernatural existence and the utter absence of God's presence. Sitting in the pew, he envisions himself "ascending the altar steps, open-ing the tiny sacrosanct tabernacle, reaching with monstrous hands for the consecrated ciborium, and taking the Body of Christ and strewing Its white wafers all over the carpet; and walking then on the sacred wafers, walking up and down before the altar, giving Holy Communion to the dust" (*Interview*, 156). Despairing at the utter loneliness involved in giving up his belief in God, Louis continues: "The cathedral crumbled in my vision; the saints listed and fell. Rats ate the Holy Eucharist and nested on the sills. A solitary rat with an enormous tail stood tugging and gnawing at the rotted altar cloth until the candlesticks fell and rolled on the slime-covered stones" (*Interview*, 157).

Reminiscent of the landscape imagery in Robert Browning's "Childe Roland" as he searches for the dark tower, the continuing nightmare turns into a funeral procession, in which the skeleton of Lestat changes to the body of Louis's brother and Claudia whispers that he is "cursed from the earth." Since Louis later in the novel describes his grief for his brother as his only true emotion, these visions emphasize the awful truth of his present state by juxtaposing the vampiric deeds he loathes himself for with images of an innocent mortal past. Enraged at the priest, who is ignorant of his anguish and powerless to help him, Louis grabs him "on the very steps to the Communion rail" and violently takes his life.

Since Louis is giving an interview, it is obvious that he has managed to remain a survivor, though his spiritual death belies his physical immortality. True not only for his time but for the contemporary reader's, Louis's "fall from grace and faith" speaks to a prevalent feeling of the "very spirit of the age." At the end of this novel, it is clear that Lestat, too, has not fared so well after surviving the theater fire. When Louis seeks him out in New Orleans, he finds Lestat "stooped and shivering" in a sweltering room with the stench of rotted animals and a coffin with "the lacquer peeling from the wood, half covered with piles of yellow newspapers" (*Interview*, 355). Confronting his creator, who he assumes destroyed Claudia, Louis looks back and feels no hatred or revenge, only a profound sorrow that he is unwilling to admit to Armand. Obviously unable to be mortal yet retaining the capacity for human feeling that set him apart from the pleasure-seeking vampires in Paris, the tormented Louis engages the reader's sympathy, unlike Stoker's Count Dracula. Instead of an evil threat to be destroyed, Louis is a metaphor for the outcast, the Wandering Jew or Cain figure whose despair is intensified by the supernatural conditions of his existence. Answers to Lestat's question of how to endure and Claudia's curiosity about the origins of vampirism remain unanswered for Louis at the conclusion of this novel and in the second novel in the series, *The Vampire Lestat,* where Louis assumes a minor role.

Chapter Four
The Vampire Lestat

Anne Rice published *The Vampire Lestat* in 1985, after her two historical novels, *The Feast of All Saints* and *Cry to Heaven,* and several erotic fantasies written under the pseudonyms of Anne Rampling and A. N. Roquelaure. As with *Interview with the Vampire,* this second novel of *The Vampire Chronicles* received mixed reviews. Nina Auerbach praised the novel for Rice's "chilling originality" in adapting the Victorian vampire myth to reflect a late twentieth-century milieu, yet felt that at times it "chokes on its own excesses."[1] Walter Kendrick saw the book as "fiercely ambitious, nothing less than a complete unnatural history of vampires," with a "post-Orwellian" world starring Lestat as the "ultimate post-modern artist."[2] Sybil Steinberg, disagreeing with Auerbach's observation that Rice's "undead characters are utterly alive" (15), wrote, "Even if Rice's undead don't quite come alive, her rococo imagination delivers an up-scale Rocky-Horror show in fevered prose."[3]

Many critics have noted Rice's lush, ornate style. Criticizing her tendency on occasion for "lugubrious, cliché-ridden sentences that repeat every idea and sentiment a couple of times," Michiko Kakutani compared the baroque atmosphere of the novel with "spending an entire day in a museum."[4] Others noted the wit and humor that lighten the tone of this book and distinguish it from the *Interview.* Auerbach felt that its extravagance is appropriate to Lestat as grand performer, in contrast with the claustrophobic sensibility that accents Louis's despair (15). Rice herself has expressed concerns over the structure of the novel, regretting that it takes so long to get the still-human Lestat to Paris and that the ending lacks a sense of closure (Ramsland, 261). Reviewers continued to comment on Rice's revitalizing the vampire figure, her lending a convincing credibility to Gothic fantasy, and her taking up philosophical issues.

As in *Interview with the Vampire,* the focus of *The Vampire Lestat* is on a community of vampires rather than on vampires among humans, and the narrative is related through vampires rather than through human beings who have confronted vampires. *The Vampire Lestat,* however, is a much lighter book, often edging toward an entertaining campy humor,

as Lestat, more lively than the incapacitated Louis, feels empowered
rather than burdened by the conditions of vampirism. Both characters
seek knowledge, but while Louis's quest is for moral significance and a
way to endure despair when he discovers the amorality and insignificance of his immortal existence, Lestat challenges his fate. Louis is the
long-suffering melancholic; Lestat is the supervampire rebel, the rule
breaker with Dionysian energy and ebullience. This second novel of the
series represents a transition from the intense concentration on one
major protagonist in the *Interview* to the panoramic world of vampire
community in *The Queen of the Damned*.

Continuing with the first-person vampire voice, Rice employs an autobi-
ographical format here instead of the interview. Stunned by his reading
of *Interview with the Vampire,* Lestat tells the reader in a prologue,
"Downtown Saturday Night in the Twentieth Century 1984," that he
did remain underground in a dormant state after seeing Louis in New
Orleans in 1929. In 1984 he was awakened by the "technologically dazzling," "barbaric and cerebral" rock music of a band named "Satan's
Night Out" (*Lestat,* 5). Exploring the world of the 1980s and joining up
with this band to become a rock star, he states his motives in writing an
autobiography. He intends not only to provide information that he was
unable to give Louis earlier but to break all the vampires' rules of secrecy
in order to arouse his fellow supernatural beings and to gain mortal
attention and admiration.

He also explains "a reason even more dangerous and delicious and
mad." Thrilled with the idea of great danger and romantic adventure
and hoping that humans will believe his story when they see him in
action at the concert, he envisions a great battle between humans and
re-energized vampires, which "would be fought in this glittering urban
wilderness as no mythic monster has ever been fought by man before"
(*Lestat,* 16). Katherine Ramsland explains his motives further: Lestat
"sees the power of nihilism and chaos as a means of transition from one
set of values into another. He believes he is setting people free to sub-
tract from their lives a false god and to find good within themselves"
(259). With these Romantic goals in mind, he puts "a fresh disk into the
portable computer word processor" and writes the story of his life that
follows.

Lestat titles his autobiography "The Early Education and Adventures
of the Vampire Lestat" and organizes the events of his life into seven
parts, followed by an epilogue on *Interview with the Vampire* that con-

cludes the autobiography in 1984. In a brief section after the autobiography, he returns to the present to narrate the performance of "Dionysus in San Francisco 1985." In part 1 he portrays his unhappy childhood in an impoverished family of French nobility during the 1770s, where a loving relationship with his mother compensates for his alienation from an ignorant father and brutish brothers. Known for his bravery in hunting, he single-handedly fights a pack of wolves terrorizing the village, becomes further isolated from his brothers, takes up with an acting troupe, and finally runs away with his philosophizing, violinist friend Nicolas de Lenfent to Paris, where they are hired as actors.

The ancient vampire Magnus, seeing Lestat as a proper heir because of his fearlessness in fighting the wolves, turns Lestat into a vampire in part 2, where he explores the powers of his new existence and performs as a vampire on the stage. His mother, on the verge of death, comes to Paris to be with Lestat before she dies, and Lestat turns her into a vampire in part 3. Together they confront primitive vampires similar to the ragged Transylvanian ones in the *Interview*, who have taken the still-mortal Nicolas prisoner. Their leader, Armand, whose knowledge is less valuable here than it was for Louis, explains in part 4 the "Rules of Darkness" by which they live, laws that Lestat sees are ridiculously outdated. Freeing Nicolas and turning him into a vampire at Nicolas's own request, Lestat lures the vampires away from Armand's tyrannical leadership. The vampires are drawn to Lestat because of his bold life-style as well.

Founding the Theater of the Vampires as a refuge for Armand's vampires and for Nicolas at the end of this section, Lestat continues his confrontation with the angry Armand in part 5, which is devoted primarily to Armand's story and the history of his creator, Marius. After a philosophical debate between Armand and Lestat, Lestat and his mother set out on their travels and leave Armand behind to cope with the loss of the empty religious convictions by which he rules his coven: that vampires are "Children of Darkness" created to carry out the evil of Satan. The adventurous mood at the beginning of part 6 is replaced by gloom, however, when Lestat learns of Nicolas's self-immolation and then endures the departure of his mother. Failing to locate Marius for consolation, Lestat lapses into a period of wasting in the earth.

The 1800-year-old Marius finally responds to Lestat's search by calling to him at the end of part 6, and in part 7 Marius fulfills his role as a kind of vampire mentor and reveals to Lestat the great mysteries of vampire origins and lessons of immortality. He recounts the mythic story of his own transformation and then explains the secret rituals surrounding the two first vampires, Akasha and Enkil, "Those Who Must Be Kept," whom he serves as protector. Though Marius allows Lestat to see them, he must never reveal their presence or these mysteries. Marius then encourages him to go to New Orleans to live out his own first vampire life. (In their maturation toward the wisdom of the ancient brood, Rice's vampires live out different roles in different time periods, sometimes retreating to a dormant, buried state for a variety of motives: despair, boredom, frustration.)

The somewhat contrived epilogue is Rice's attempt to account for Lestat's whereabouts between his encounter with Marius here in 1789 and his nearly ruined condition in New Orleans at the end of *Interview with the Vampire* in 1929. Lestat explains that he spent about 70 years of this time with Louis and Claudia. He describes his alienation, even after his reunion with Louis, and affirms his determination to return to the earth. He remained dormant until 1984, when he experienced a vision from Marius and a beckoning call from Akasha. Though at some expense to the reader's credibility, the epilogue does provide dates that link Lestat's past with the present rock-concert performance that follows. The chronology also reconciles the history of this novel with that of its predecessor and prepares for the awakening of Akasha in the next novel in the series, *The Queen of the Damned.* The list of facts and figures deflates the dramatic impact of the concert, however, which the reader has been waiting for since the opening pages.

At the conclusion of both the *Interview with the Vampire* and *The Vampire Lestat,* each of the central characters has undergone a significant change as a result of their separate quests. The wise but miserable Louis wanders away at the end of the *Interview,* but the triumphant Lestat retains his sense of adventure and curiosity. Rice smoothly anticipates the next installment of *The Vampire Chronicles* as Lestat becomes aware of the presence of Akasha and hears her call.

Intent upon creating a more positive impression of himself in his autobiography than Louis conveys during the interview, Lestat acknowledges the love and tenderness he feels for Louis. He proceeds to set the record straight by correcting certain distortions, however. He agrees that Louis captured the atmosphere of their lives together with Claudia in New Orleans, and forgives Louis for "the lies he told, the mistakes he made" and for his "excess of imagination, his bitterness, and his vanity" (*Lestat,* 434). Admitting his own wrongdoing in creating the child-vampire Claudia, Lestat otherwise defends his motives and actions. He says that he kept silent about his powers because Louis "shrank in guilt and self-loathing from using even half of his own." As for enjoying the lingering deaths of his human victims, Lestat justifies himself by asking, "how was he to know that I hunted almost exclusively among the gamblers, the thieves, and the killers, being more faithful to my unspoken vow to kill the evildoer than even I had hoped I would be?" (*Lestat*, 434–35). He recalls other specific scenes from the *Interview* where he seemed particularly vile and confidently tells the reader to "Read between the lines." His self-assurance here is characteristic of his bravado throughout the novel.

Lestat's resilience and resourcefulness are typical of the continuing appeal of the vampire myth. As Brian Frost states, "Perhaps the most remarkable characteristic of the vampire is its ability to adapt to changing social and environmental conditions" (1). Unlike Louis, who never really accepts the contradictions of his vampirism or the losses he experiences, particularly the burning of Claudia, Lestat has a devil-may-care attitude that enables him to be not only an adapter par excellence but a challenger to the status quo. By turning the vampire into a rock star, Rice presents, therefore, an image of rebellion rather than despair in response to a 1980s existential milieu. The orgiastic frenzy inspired by this music provides a necessary emotional high that substitutes for the religion missing in a decade rampantly materialistic, often characterized by Ivan Boesky's remark that "greed is good."

Describing himself as someone who does not engage in moral battles, Lestat confronts the uncomfortable realities of vampirism and explores its mysteries to sharpen his own vampiric powers, enhance his reputation, and stir up some romantic excitement in an otherwise dull and predictable eternal life. While Louis's fate could hardly be regarded as fortunate, Lestat completes his adventures in a state of exhilaration: he has increased his vampiric powers by drinking the blood of Akasha; his earthly fame as a rock star has fulfilled his need for achieving significance and contact with humans; and his San Francisco performance has succeeded in arousing his ancient ancestors and placing him in real danger.

When Marius describes him as an "innocent," Lestat replies that he cannot possibly be speaking of him. "You're guilty of killing mortals because you've been made into something that feeds on blood and death, but you're not guilty of lying, of creating great dark and evil systems of thought within yourself"; "To be godless is probably the first step to innocence," "to lose the sense of sin and subordination, the false grief for things supposed to be lost" (*Lestat*, 333). Lestat responds, "So by innocence you mean not an absence of experience, but an absence of illusions." Marius tells him that innocence is the "absence of need for illusions," it is a "love of and respect for what is right before your eyes."

Lestat displays the attitudes and abilities necessary for survival without illusions throughout his adventures in the prologue, where Anne Rice is at her best in using the first-person vampiric voice to convey humor dependent on departures from traditional vampire fictions. For Gregory Waller, this "play of repetition and difference" with conventions is a "most entertaining and the most significant feature" in popular Gothics.[5] Introducing himself to the reader, Lestat begins the book: "I am the vampire Lestat. I'm immortal. More or less. The light of the sun, the sustained heat of an intense fire—these things might destroy me. But then again, they might not" (*Lestat,* 3). He says that his being six feet tall "was fairly impressive in the 1780s," that he has curly blond hair (hair color being one way to distinguish one vampire from another), and that his "highly reflective" white skin has to be "powdered down" for the cameras. If he is starved for blood, he looks "like a perfect horror." He talks "like a cross between a flatboatman and detective Sam Spade," and when he writes, he may drift into an eighteenth-century vocabulary, which he hopes the reader will take into account if his language is inconsistent (*Lestat,* 4). Once awakened into the 1980s, he can be seen "roaring around New Orleans on a big black Harley-Davidson motorcycle making plenty of noise," wearing "gorgeous black leather clothes," and carrying "a little Sony Walkman stereo" in his pocket so he can listen to Bach's *Art of the Fugue* as he rides along.

Lestat relishes the 1980s' sensuality and love of luxury, qualities he has not seen widespread in human beings since the aristocrats in the 1700s. As he says, "This century had inherited the earth in every sense" (*Lestat,* 8). With less poverty, however, and fewer corrupt humans for him to feed on, he has to "work for a living," that is, to learn to find new victims to sustain himself: "the drug dealers, the pimps, the murderers who fell in with the motorcycle gangs." Lestat notes the "curious innocence" of modern humans, for whom the Christian God is dead: "And no new mythological religion had arisen to take the place of the old." Appreciating this "vigorous secular morality" yet uncertain as to how he will fit in where "[p]ure evil has no real place" (*Lestat,* 8–9), he concludes that "[t]his stunning irrelevance to the mighty scheme of things" is enough "to make an Old World monster go back into the earth" or "become a rock singer."

As his autobiography shows, Lestat's bravado and love of the stage are consistent with traits in his earlier human life, when he and Nicolas shared the misfortune of unhappy family lives and engaged in philosophical conversations concerning the moral nature of the universe. Lestat says he believed then that "music and acting were good because they drove back chaos," chaos being "the meaninglessness of day-to-day life" (*Lestat,* 49). Once employed as actors in Paris, he and Nicolas continue these discussions, Nicolas arguing that they are outcasts who need be concerned only with good or bad art, and Lestat hoping to use the performances to do good. Lestat can live without God or the possibility of an afterlife, but he needs to believe in his potential for goodness.

Once he is whisked away by Marius and transformed into a vampire, however, he believes that his debates with Nicolas are no longer relevant and that good and evil are merely "concepts man has made" (*Lestat,* 114). He will live, instead, regarding the world as a "garden of savage beauty," where "only aesthetic principles can be verified, and these things alone remain the same" (*Lestat,* 124). Once having subscribed to the decadent aestheticism of the late Victorians, suggestive of the late twentieth-century climate as well, Lestat writes: "the last barrier between my appetite and the world had been dissolved." A dominant metaphor here and in *The Queen of the Damned,* the garden image comes up again when Marius reveals the mythic origins of vampirism. Listening to the stories of ancient civilizations who believed that their sacrifice of human blood was a good way to ward off the evils of plague and famine, Lestat observes that the vampires' history "seemed more than ever the story of the Savage Garden . . . where no law prevailed except the law of the garden, which was the aesthetic law" (335). Rice's garden of natural law and beauty that includes lions as well as lambs exists apart from traditional human, ethical, and social systems.

As in *Interview with the Vampire,* the protagonist's few significant relationships with other vampires are the source of his maturation. For much of *Interview with the Vampire,* the "family" that sustains Louis consists of Lestat and Claudia; in *The Vampire Lestat,* Magnus, Lestat's creator, abandons him shortly after Lestat's transformation, so that Lestat creates his own family with his mother and his childhood friend Nicolas. Once she becomes a vampire, Lestat's mother becomes a completely new creature, Gabrielle, whose vampire identity nullifies and transcends her mortal role as mother. Lestat says he relates to her as "*she,* the one I had needed all of my life with all of my being. The only woman I had ever loved" (*Lestat*, 147).

Free of earthly roles, Gabrielle cuts her hair, dresses like a man, becomes a colder, more ruthless killer than Lestat, and develops a philosophical curiosity that moves her away from vampires and humans toward nature, and therefore away from Lestat, who thrives on closeness to mortals. She decides to retire directly to bare soil instead of to a coffin to sleep during the day. The first time, Lestat watches, "staring in disbelief at the emptiness where she had been, and the leaves that had settled as if nothing had disturbed the spot" (*Lestat*, 279). In contrast, Lestat orders coffins for himself and prefers to sleep in the house instead of in the graveyard or church. Lestat sees that they are drifting apart from each other and wonders, "What did I want of her, that she be more human, that she be like me?" (*Lestat*, 295). Shortly after Gabrielle does indeed desert him to set out on her own explorations of nature's truths, and Lestat's loneliness forces him to dig into the earth where he remains alive yet wastes away, a metaphor "of the misery that is everywhere unseen, unrecorded, unacknowledged, unused" (*Lestat*, 313).

Gabrielle does not reappear until the end of the novel, when she returns to protect Lestat during the rock concert. Her ties with the earth, her absolute rejection of gender roles and social values, along with her bold independence, support Nina Auerbach's praise of her as a powerful character (15). The relationships made possible here because of vampirism and Marius's mythical story of the worship of the Great Mother suggest that women are soon to become more important figures in Rice's Gothic fiction.

The transformation of Nicholas to a vampire proves to be more painful for Lestat. Its outcome fulfills Armand's prediction that the humans to whom Lestat gives the "Dark Trick" will never satisfy him: "In silence the estrangement and the resentment only grow" (*Lestat*, 218). During the transformation scene, when he gives Nicolas his blood, Lestat has a horrifying vision of a bird "sailing on through the darkness over the barren shore, the seamless sea" that foreshadows the dark destructiveness of this relationship. The instant Nicolas's mortal life ends, Lestat feels cold and empty, realizing that he *couldn't stand the sight of him now*." Leaving his old friend with the other vampires to run the Theater of the Vampires, Lestat later learns that Nicolas, after being punished by Armand, destroyed himself in the flames of a Sabbat ceremony danced by the actor-vampires. Lestat feels responsible: "It was I who subverted the path his life might have taken" (*Lestat*, 301).

A comparison of Lestat's feelings toward his mother and Nicolas with Louis's toward Claudia and Madeleine in the *Interview* shows how Rice varies Gothic conventions to distinguish her supernatural characters, to lend them some sympathy, and to maintain a focus on the metaphorical power of the vampires as humans. In both books the plots depend on relationships between vampires, with suspense arising from vampires struggling with each other or their own internal weaknesses. Given their outcast state, vampires rely on the companionship and intimacy of a few others like themselves to endure the loneliness of immortal life. Both Lestat and Louis take comfort in these family structures for a time and then experience their loss. While both feel responsible for their "families," Lestat moves beyond the guilt that overwhelms Louis.

Lestat, who accepts the realities of vampirism and savors the excitement of dramatic contact with humans, is not tormented by the act of creating other vampires, as is Louis; he sees it as a way of ending mortal suffering and, in the case of his mother, of continuing a physical relationship with his mother beyond the grave. As Armand's prophecy comes true and Lestat realizes the limitations of these relationships, he boldly breaks the vampire rules of secrecy by leaving messages all over the world to find the ancient vampire Marius, about whom he has heard from Armand. While the process of propagation plunges Louis into despair, Lestat soars upward to achieve contact with the older and more powerful vampires.

Gabrielle and Lestat discuss the potential significance of Marius while they prepare to leave Paris. Gabrielle says that as far as she is concerned, Armand's tale of Marius confirms her desire to get as far away as she can from the insufferable humanity and sorrows of other vampires; it teaches her "that immortals find death seductive and ultimately irresistible, that they fail to conquer death or humanity in their minds" (*Lestat*, 278). Lestat, however, is fascinated by the idea that earlier beings may have "used immortality in a wholly different way." Unable to find Marius and lonely for Gabrielle, Lestat feels shut out from both human and vampire lives and buries himself in the earth, where he experiences a grand awakening by the 1800-year-old Marius.

As Marius lifts Lestat up out of his sandy grave in Egypt, Lestat says that the face he saw "was beyond the realm of possibility. What one of us could have such a face? What did we know of patience, of seeming goodness, of compassion? No, it wasn't one of us. It couldn't have been. And yet it was" (*Lestat*, 316). This reverent description of Marius exem-

plifies the stature that Rice accords to her ancient vampires, whose powers increase with age. Wearing red velvet, Marius has iridescent eyes that
gather "the light from all directions, tiny eyelashes like strokes of gold
from the finest pen." His hair has "thick, white and gold strands mingled in waves fallen loosely around his face, and over his broad forehead.
And the blue eyes might have been brooding under their heavy golden
brows had they not been so large, so softened with the feeling expressed
in the voice" (*Lestat*, 317). In keeping with his godlike stature, Marius
has a great deal to offer Lestat; indeed, Marius's narration in "Ancient
Magic, Ancient Mysteries" occupies the next 150 pages, creating a
smaller novel within the novel.

Marius tells Lestat that he responded to his pleas for understanding
because he shares a kindred spirit with Lestat and identifies with his
needs. Explaining how he was also created "at the end of an era" of
unprecedented changes (*Lestat*, 333), Marius compares his own creation
during the time of Augustus Caesar with Lestat's in the late eighteenth
century: "The point is that you were born on the cusp of the old way of
seeing things. . . . And so it was with me. We sprang up from a crack
between faith and despair, as it were" (*Lestat*, 334). He also says that
they were both chosen for immortality for the same reason: "that we
were the nonpareils of our blood and blue-eyed race, that we were taller
and more finely made than other men" (*Lestat*, 335). Having established
Lestat's worthiness to learn all of the secrets of vampire history, Marius
reveals the subterranean resting place of the Adam and Eve of vampires
for whom he is responsible, Enkil and Akasha. Rice interweaves pagan
myths with the vampiric as Marius tells the story of the origins of the
vampires.

Not a child of Satan, Marius was imprisoned by an ancient Egyptian
tribe called the Keltoi, who had chosen him to replace their badly
burned, ailing "god" upon whom their preservation depended. It was he
who drank human blood in an elaborate ritual of human sacrifice to the
Great Mother for abundant crops. Marius understood that he was to be
the God of Growing Things, the one who fulfilled the part known in
many civilizations under different names of the lover and son, the Dying
God of the Great Mother, the one who would grow to manhood "as the
crops grow, only to be cut down as the crops are cut down, while the
Mother remains eternal" (*Lestat*, 356).

What he did not understand was that he would not die, that the god
whom he was to replace had eternal life. Marius's job was to become the
new god, conduct the ceremony of human sacrifice, and escape to Egypt

to discover why the present god was being stricken "with terrible calamity." He describes how he became a blood-drinking immortal within a tree, an appropriate adaptation of pagan myth, since this transformation ritual is widely known as a symbol of growth, regeneration, and therefore immortality.[6] Marius then narrates stories of human sacrifice and his escape to Alexandria, where he learns more mysteries from the Elder who tells him about the Mother and Father in his keeping. He discovers, for instance, that the tribal god is suffering because Akasha and Enkil have been left out in the sun. The Elder explains that since their blood comes directly from them, "what befalls them befalls us. If they are burnt, we are burnt" (*Lestat*, 378).

In a story that goes back to Osiris and Isis, the "unnatural power" we know as vampirism apparently began with what the Elder calls "an ugly occurrence" experienced by the king, who "made a worship of it, seeking to contain it in obligation and ceremony, seeking to limit The Powerful Blood to those who would use it for white magic and nothing else" (*Lestat*, 377). While *The Queen of the Damned* will provide further details about this "ugly occurrence," the Elder explains that the Mother and Father were stabbed by conspirators and that demons then entered their bodies through the wounds, so that the "King and Queen were New Things. They could no longer eat food, or grow, or die, or have children, yet they could feel with an intensity that terrified them. And the demon had what it wanted: a body to live in, a way to be in the world at last, a way to *feel*" (*Lestat*, 384).

So as to "sanctify and contain what was done by mystery, or else Egypt might become a race of blood-drinking demons," the King and Queen "girded with the symbolic and the mysterious what could not be allowed to become common, and they passed out of the sight of mortal men into the temples, to be worshiped by those who would bring them blood. . . . Innocents, outsiders, evildoers, they drank the blood for the Mother and for the Good" (*Lestat*, 386).

Sensing that the Elder intends to destroy her, Akasha asks Marius to take her and Enkil out of Egypt. Marius wraps them in linens and encases them as mummies, but his way is barred by the Elder, who is finally done in by Akasha herself. Marius, rewarded by the ecstasy of Akasha's powerful blood to heal his wounds, succeeds in taking them out of Egypt and devotes himself to their care.

Marius's history illustrates that humans originally perceived the blood-drinking immortals as servers of the good. He explains that it was only during the end of the Roman Empire that they were seen as demons by the Christians: "It was useless to tell them as the centuries passed that their Christ was but another God of the Wood, dying and rising, as Dionysus or Osiris had done before him, and that the Virgin Mary was in fact the Good Mother again enshrined. Theirs was a new age of belief and conviction, and in it we became devils, detached from what they believed, as old knowledge was forgotten or misunderstood" (*Lestat*, 404).

Marius concludes his tale by stating that the real perversion of their original nature was "accomplished when the Children of Darkness came to believe they served the Christian devil, and like the terrible gods of the East, they tried to give value to evil, to believe in its power in the scheme of things, to give it a just place in the world" (*Lestat*, 404). In fact, as Marius says, vampires "have never had a true purpose. We have no place" (*Lestat*, 405).

Lestat initially promises Marius he will keep his knowledge of the history of vampirism secret, but he breaks his vow. Believing he is doing good, Lestat reveals all of these mysteries to mortals by writing his autobiography and performing in the rock concert. His first act of disobedience is to descend to the tomb of Those Who Must Be Kept on his own and play Nicolas's violin. He does indeed awaken Akasha, the oldest and most powerful, and experiences the ecstasy of drinking her blood, which gives him supervampire powers and bonds him to her. At this moment, she becomes everyman's Oedipal fantasy, replacing the mother-lover relationship with Gabrielle. Unfortunately, Lestat also arouses Enkil, who nearly destroys him but for the arrival of Marius. Eventually, Marius sends a strengthened but saddened Lestat away. In spite of his new powers, Lestat senses that his needs make him "somehow kin to every mortal man" instead of an "exotic outcast" (*Lestat*, 430). Longing to belong somehow, he dreams of a union with the mother figure Akasha.

After connecting his relationship with Louis and Claudia from *Interview with the Vampire* to this narration of Marius at the end of his autobiography, Lestat explains how he is awakened from his earthly sleep in New Orleans by a vision of Akasha, as he imagines her calling to him. In a passage that anticipates *The Queen of the Damned*, Lestat hears Akasha's thoughts and learns of her intention to return to the world and claim him as her companion: "I long for one with the strength to roam it fearlessly, to ride the Devil's Road through its heart" (*Lestat*, 449). The progression of Lestat's companions from Nicolas to Gabrielle, to Armand and Marius, and then to Akasha (his intimacy with Louis having been fully portrayed in *Interview with the Vampire*) marks his increase in stature. Not only does he gain awesome physical powers, but in his fearless search for significance he animates the ancient figures who provide him with the philosophical perspective necessary for his survival as a vampire. In Rice's adaptations of vampirism, to be older is to be more remote from the vulnerability of human feeling; with age comes wisdom.

Lestat does indeed awaken to orchestrate his most daring performance, the 1985 rock concert. Reminiscent of the spectacular exhibition stunts in the Theater of the Vampires in Paris, the San Francisco concert also provides a startling image of fin-de-siècle aestheticism, where intense physical pleasure infuses life with vitality. Taking center stage and seeing his "mortals glorified and frenzied already as they perched amid the endless wires and silver scaffolding," Lestat gloats, "This was a human experience made vampiric, as the music itself was vampiric" (*Lestat*, 467). As their Dionysus, he hears the "convulsions" of the audience and feels exhilarated by the intensity of physical sensations. Rice connects the orgiastic rhythms of this moment with the ceremonies of the past: "What was it about this sound? It signaled man turned into mob—the crowds surrounding the guillotine, the ancient Romans screaming for Christian blood. And the Keltoi gathered in the grove awaiting Marius, the god" (*Lestat*, 467).

As Ramsland explains, the Dionysian myth serves several purposes in that the god represents both the eternal spirit of passion and energy worshiped by the Greeks in frenzied rituals and Nietzsche's human "overman," who has the courage to face a world without meaning and set up new ethical standards. Conveniently, he is also the god of the theater (258). Today's flamboyant and charismatic rock stars are the descendants of Dionysus, whose performances seem to satisfy universal thirsts for the communal, irrational, ecstatic experience in a time when no "mythological religion" has taken the place of the old (*Lestat*, 8). Several critics have noted the resemblance of Lestat to David Bowie, who achieved fame as a rock star in the 1970s. Rice's own comments on Bowie's appeal in a 1983 *Vogue* article shed light on her intentions here. She praises the "androgynous allure" that enables him to abolish "gender tyranny" in his film performances and emphasizes the importance of gender transcendence that characterizes her vampires: "if we can preserve that earlier complexity, that mingling of masculine and feminine we hear so exquisitely in the boy soprano, we can have the endless possibilities of it all."[7]

Not only do Bowie's androgynous traits fit the traditional eroticism of the vampire, but the antiestablishment messages of rock music contribute to the vampire's freedom from conventional moralities and the power of this subversive appeal. Making points that could describe Lestat as well as Bowie, Rice states: "Whirling on the very edge of the culture, the great rock singers of our time personify our laments, our fears, and our dreams. They are the fantasy figures of the romantic artist vision, set free to evolve on record and in live performance exactly as they please" ("Gender," 434). Rice's transformation of Lestat into a modern rock-music idol is another inspired stroke by which she connects her hero with the Dionysian mythic past while at the same time reestablishing the relevance of the vampire image to contemporary readers.

As the concert concludes, Lestat is attacked by other vampires who, feeling threatened by his exposure of their secrets, attempt to destroy him. Lestat manages to escape with the assistance of Gabrielle and Louis and some powerful force that appears to be incinerating their vampire pursuers. Once the danger is over, Lestat receives an unspoken message from Marius, warning him that his music has awakened Akasha and that they are all in danger. Though Lestat has achieved a momentary sense of power, the novel ends suspensefully at sunrise, when he begins his rest and feels "a hand suddenly close" on his own.

The suspense created here is typical of Rice in that she sets up tension among vampires rather than between vampires and humans. Lestat's existence is threatened by Armand's white-faced Parisian vampires, by the ancients, and especially by Akasha. He has little reason to fear humans, who, despite their ability to destroy vampires, remain foolishly incapable of believing in their existence.

While Rice's flashbacks to ancient times open up endless possibilities for future narratives, the first-person intensity that keeps the reader emotionally involved with Louis in *Interview with the Vampire* is diminished here when the action shifts to Marius and his conversation. Like the interviewer, Lestat is a learning listener throughout Marius's story, and the ancient vampires that Marius describes are important to the impact of the rock concert later. But the relationship between Marius and Lestat lacks the delicate tension that exists between Louis and Daniel, the young interviewer. Later, in the first section of *The Queen of the Damned,* Rice develops concurrent plots through different points of view to create an effect that sustains suspense when she moves adroitly from one character's perspective to another.

An emphasis on the vampires themselves also intensifies the eroticism in *The Vampire Lestat,* which emanates more from exchanging vampire blood than taking human life. As a result, the vampires remain sympathetic creatures and the blood ensures a physical, familial bond. Lestat drinks Magnus's blood in a very erotic scene during his own transformation; he has an orgiastic union with his mother during hers; and his pleasure culminates when he drinks from Akasha: "nothing else existed but our mouths locked to each other's throats and the relentless pounding path of the blood. There were no dreams, there were no visions, there was just this, *this*—gorgeous and deafening and heated—and nothing mattered, absolutely nothing, except that this never stop" (*Lestat,* 423).

Eroticism also becomes the subject of humor as it pertains to conventions of vampire tales. When Lestat tries to piece together the myths of vampire origins, he remembers that when Isis found the dismembered body of Osiris, she located all but one part of his body: "the part that Isis never found, well, there is one part of us which is not enhanced by the Dark Gift, isn't there? We can speak, see, taste, breathe, move as humans move, but *we cannot procreate*" (*Lestat,* 289).

It is the old-fashioned Armand who believes that the drinking of blood is similar to Christian Communion. This parallel suggests the deeper, forbidden appeal of vampirism in addressing the fantasies of contemporary readers, who, like their pagan ancestors, experience a religious ecstasy in the rock concert and in the vampire's blood-drinking rituals. While Rice exploits this connection more fully in *The Queen of the Damned,* for Lestat, drinking blood is an act wherein "the spiritual and the carnal" come together: "Holy Communion it seemed to him, the Blood of the Children of Christ serving only to bring the essence of life itself into his understanding for the split second in which death occurred. Only the great saints of God were his equals in the spirituality, this confrontation with mystery, this existence of meditation and denial" (*Lestat,* 266).

Lestat decides from the beginning of his vampire existence that the notion of a Christian God is insignificant: "He was part of some dull and dreary realm whose secrets had long ago been plundered, whose lights had long ago gone out" (*Lestat,* 80). Unlike the climactic cathedral scene in *Interview with the Vampire,* where Louis's anguish compels him to murder a priest, an emboldened Lestat goes into a church, climbs over the Communion rail, and takes out the consecrated wafers as if to confirm God's irrelevance. "No, there was no power here, nothing that I could feel or see or know with any of my monstrous senses, nothing that responded to me" (*Lestat,* 99). Later, when he and Gabrielle are fleeing from the Parisian vampires, he gives her an emerald crucifix to wear, knowing that it will frighten these primitive and superstitious beings. He also takes her with him into the church, where they hide under the altar. While Gabrielle is uneasy, Lestat says, "Gibberish and nonsense. God isn't in the House of God" (*Lestat,* 166). Ironically, in his mortal youth he despaired of his inability to believe in the existence of God; now that he is a vampire, he discredits Catholicism to validate his own daring and power.

Rejecting the false morality and empty grandeur of the Christian temples, Lestat is overwhelmed by the Greek island dwelling of the god-like Marius, as he embraces the aesthetic codes of vampirism. Creating an Elysian effect, Marius's opulent refuge is a palace of art resplendent with Grecian urns, oriental rugs, and startlingly realistic murals painted in a mixture of styles. The scene demonstrates Anne Rice's powerfully vivid descriptions of place and establishes suspense for Lestat's introduction to the great mystery Armand referred to earlier. From this elegant eighteenth-century salon a stairway descends deeper and deeper into the earth, opening onto the grand chapel of Those Who Must Be Kept. Ramsland points out that stairways and subterranean rooms have psychological significance in Rice's fiction, as they lead toward awareness, descents "into the unconscious, where the most profound and secret knowledge exists."[8] In this instance, Lestat discovers the origins of his identity as a vampire. Awed by such beauty, the breathless Lestat admires paintings of "Egyptian palm trees, the yellow desert, the three pyramids, the blue waters of the Nile," as the air comes down "through deep shafts in the rock above" and stirs "the flames of the ever burning lamps, ruffling the tall green bladelike leaves of the lilies as they stood in their vessels of water giving off their heady perfume" (*Lestat,* 337). This lush Grecian paradise is the appropriate altar for the royal Akasha and Enkil, as Rice's vampires surround themselves with beautiful art objects to appreciate rather than religious icons to worship. The scene reflects the aesthetic truths of the philosophical savage garden that they live by.

The uniqueness of Rice's Gothic settings is also apparent in her handling of the more conventional settings of dark forests, crypts, and hidden coffins. Unlike the civilized elegance of Marius's home, the filth and stench of the subterranean sepulcher that houses the Parisian vampires, for instance, emphasize the primitivism of these creatures. The places where Rice's vampires choose to rest during the day often convey their emotional states, such as when Lestat hides his coffin inside cottages to be closer to humans or when he literally returns to the soil if he feels degraded: "The earth was holding me. Living things slithered through its thick and moist clods against my dried flesh" (*Lestat,* 447). Although conventionally solitary in their eternal lives, Rice's vampires are also social beings who take part in unusual crowd scenes, such as the Parisian Theater of the Vampires, the Keltoi ceremonies, and the San Franciscan rock concert, which underscore the sense of vampire community.

They also like to travel. The adventures of Lestat, Armand, and Marius occur all over the globe and move back and forth in time, with the sensuality and materialism of the present emphasized as the most comfortable milieu for Lestat. In conveying the modern scene, Rice is particularly effective in including small details that lend realistic credibility to fanciful situations: Lestat complains about the "stench of chemicals and gasoline" and the "drone of air conditioners and the whine of the jet planes overhead"; he explains how he found a lawyer to help him "procure a legal birth certificate, Social Security card, and driver's license." As in *Interview with the Vampire,* the two cities of San Francisco and New Orleans provide the contemporary settings, New Orleans suggesting again a kind of damp wilderness and dark lawlessness appropriate for the existence of vampires. Lestat describes how he walks unnoticed "among the crude little bungalows that spread out to the ramparts, peeping through windows at gilded furniture and enameled bits of wealth and civilization that in this barbaric place seemed priceless and fastidious and even sad" (*Lestat,* 429). San Francisco, though "almost Venetian" in its "somber multicolored mansions and tenements rising wall to wall over the narrow black streets" (*Lestat,* 455), is old-fashioned enough to accommodate the ageless vampires, yet liberated and avant-garde as a site appropriate for the rock concert.

True to his restless nature, Lestat does not remain in San Francisco for long. Though Rice may have felt the need for more closure at the end of this novel, the final view of Lestat is as consistent with his rebellious character as Louis's despair is with his character. Rather than an ending, the rock concert proves to be a beginning, an opportunity for new experience since Lestat accomplishes his purpose of stirring up the universe of vampires. In an earlier conversation with Marius, Lestat explains to some extent the resilience and energy that define his nature. He says that "We dream of that long-ago time when we sat upon our mother's knee and each kiss was the perfect consummation of desire. What can we do but reach for the embrace that must now contain both heaven and hell: our doom again and again and again" (*Lestat,* 430). Strengthened by the self-

knowledge he has gained from Marius and his adventures, Lestat understands that for him the essence of survival comes not from searching for
the meaning of a vampiric existence but from discovering ways to feel
intensely alive. Never content to remain on the sidelines, the rebel Lestat
will need to reach out again to embrace Akasha in *The Queen of the
Damned*.

Chapter Five
The Queen of the Damned

In 1988 Anne Rice published the best-selling *The Queen of the Damned.* The critical reception was again mixed, though not entirely for the same reasons as it was for *Interview with the Vampire* and *The Vampire Lestat.* The differing responses to the blend of philosophical content and sensational Gothic adventure persisted: Laurence Coven, for example, noted that "Rice's vampires are natural philosophers. Their immortality serves to heighten those concerns which have beguiled and befuddled humans for centuries."[1] Sybil Steinberg criticized Rice's "philosophical overkill."[2] Eric Kraft, seemingly prejudiced against the vampire literary tradition in general, wrote that "the book itself wallows in gore while preaching peace" and that Rice's gifts as a writer "are wasted on vampires."[3] Michael Rogers argued that "Rice is doing for the vampire genre what Dashiell Hammett did for that of the private detective—raising it from the dregs of the penny dreadful to the heights of A fiction."[4]

Lindsy Van Gelder praised the novel for the satiric appeal of the vampires, who are also "living (or at least undead) metaphors for the modern human condition; angst-ridden, alienated creatures who are powerful against everything but their own violent appetites."[5] Negative assessments, even in the more positive reviews, derived less from the erotic content criticized in the first two novels and more from Rice's tendency toward repetition or "overwriting." Walter Kendrick, an avid fan of the *Interview* and *The Vampire Lestat,* was disappointed to find this book verbose, sluggish, and boring and believed that the 200-page historical flashback did not work.[6] Another reviewer commented on the seemingly unnecessary complexity of plot elements, mentioning that Rice's novel "rambles and perambulates and diffuses itself, leading the reader to wonder what the point is, other than to chill and entertain with layers of vampire goings-on."[7]

As these new observations indicate, the structure of *The Queen of the Damned* represents quite a departure from the first two novels in the series. Instead of an intense concentration on the adventures of one main character (Armand's and Marius's tales in *The Vampire Lestat* lead in this direction), the novel displays a panoramic scope of multiple plots and characters layered in simultaneous strands of action told by interior vampire monologues in the omniscient voice and by Lestat in the first person. Continuing to adapt the vampire literary tradition, Rice focuses on warring factions among vampires rather than on their pursuit of humans. She therefore abandons in yet another way the traditional plot of humans terrorized by an outer threat, since the anxieties in *The Queen of the Damned* involve vampires threatened by a force in their own global community. Moving back in time, Rice tells a history of vampire origins that reads like the violent and instructive legends of primitive folklore and pagan myth, stories that inform the present action and prepare for the climactic gathering of powerful first vampires at the end of the novel as they confront Akasha and decide whether or not to intervene in the future of the human race.

The ambitious mythic-saga approach taken in this novel meets Joseph Grixti's criteria for effective Gothic fiction in that the power of these new images encourages a "searching analysis of human concerns." In tracing vampire histories and linking them with pagan beliefs, Rice legitimizes vampirism as another myth. Primitive tribes constructed stories of the supernatural to account for natural events and performed ceremonies to plead for survival against the cruelties of natural phenomena, and so Rice also ties vampirism to human needs and fantasies. In *The Queen of the Damned,* a community of vampires is divided between the forces of good and evil: Maharet's desire to protect the freedom of the human family to play out its own destiny versus Akasha's wish to establish a new fascist world dominated by women with a new religion based on herself as the god.

A prologue to the five major sections in the form of an ominous "Proem" introduces the vampire Marius reading a declaration that calls on all vampires to destroy Lestat, along with his followers, for threatening the survival of vampires by revealing their secrets. Amused by Lestat's bravado yet anxious to learn what the other vampires' intentions are, the wise Marius philosophizes on human beings' devotion to Lestat. Ironically, they refuse to believe that Lestat is a vampire because they have made their greatest strides toward morality and tolerance by discarding religious beliefs in favor of secular truths "embedded in the physical." Marius decides that he has been away from Those Who Must Be Kept for too long, so he returns to their resting place "miles from the nearest outpost of the modern world, in a great frozen snow-covered waste" (*Queen,* 22), where he is shocked to discover that Akasha has awakened from her dormant state and destroyed Enkil. The terrified Marius is then trapped by Akasha, who brings the icy tomb down on him, the glass "piercing his flesh like so many daggers." After watching her depart, he drops down into a "giant crevasse," where the ice crushes his bones and buries him. Before losing consciousness he cries out to Lestat: "*Danger, Lestat, beware. We are all in danger*" (*Queen*, 29).

In part 1, "The Road to the Vampire Lestat," various groups of characters set out for Lestat's performance in San Francisco on "All Hallow's Eve." Their separate stories are held together not only by their common goal to attend the concert but also by their experiencing the same violent, mysterious dream of red-haired twins in a sacrificial ceremony, a persistent nightmare that foreshadows the mythic revelations and confrontations with Akasha that transpire in the second half of the novel, after the concert. Moving from the archaeologist's discovery of similar drawings of the twins "buried in the mountain caves of Palestine and Peru" in chapter 1, chapter 2 takes up the lonely young vampire Baby Jenks, as she cycles her way to San Francisco to join up with other members of a rock group called the Fang Gang. En route to the concert, she and another vampire, whom she refers to as "the Dead guy," are mysteriously incinerated by an unidentified supernatural presence.

As the spirit of Baby Jenks ascends toward a reunion with the mother she had murdered, the action shifts to a Himalayan setting in chapter 3. Here the ancient vampire Pandora, created by Marius, feels the horror of being irrelevant to anyone, "utterly unconnected," and senses the danger of an awakening Akasha. She goes to Azim, a 1,000-year-old vampire ruler who is conducting a grisly orgy of human sacrifice at his mountain temple "from which no worshiper ever departed alive" (*Queen*, 61). Azim tells her of his dream of the twins and the distant warnings he has heard from Marius in his icy tomb. After participating in the sacrifice and drinking the blood of the acolytes who thrust themselves at her, Pandora ascends into the clouds to begin her journey to the other side of the world to help Marius.

In chapter 4 Rice returns to Daniel, the human interviewer from the *Interview*, who also dreams of the twins. He is sick and penniless in Chicago and longs for Armand's return. Both he and Armand know of vampire covens mysteriously incinerated and realize that some destructive force is placing the vampires in danger; nonetheless, Daniel chooses to become a vampire rather than die as a mortal, and Armand grants his request. Daniel awakens as a vampire in San Francisco, where Armand hopes to see Lestat and to defend him if necessary.

In chapter 5 the narrative shifts from the newly created Daniel to Greece and the ancient vampire Khayman watching a group of young vampires suddenly explode in flames. After a brief confrontation with a female supernatural presence later identified as Akasha, Khayman recalls events centuries ago when, as a human royal steward to the king, he was commanded by Enkil and Akasha to rape the two red-haired young women Maharet and Mekare, whose contacts with spirits threatened the royal couple's sovereignty. As he is also having dreams of their existence, Khayman wonders if indeed the predestined hour has come for him and the twins to fulfill their curse against their persecutors and exact revenge. He sets out for San Francisco, hoping that indeed the "first brood" of vampires will know victory over Akasha.

Finally, the last of part 1, chapter 6, turns from the ancient Khayman to the young mortal with spiritual powers named Jessica, descended from Khayman's rape of Maharet. Because of her special talents, such as reading people's thoughts and seeing ghosts, Jesse is recruited by a member of the Talamasca, a group that researches supernatural phenomena. She is given a copy of *Interview with the Vampire* and told that it is not fiction. After researching the New Orleans locations mentioned in this book, Jesse picks up a copy of *The Vampire Lestat*. She begins to sense connections among her dreams of the twins, some bizarre events that took place during her summer at her "aunt" Maharet's compound in the Sonoma mountains of California, and the legends described by Lestat in his novel. Her intention in going to San Francisco is to discover her past; she is sure that when she sees Lestat, she will have "the answer to everything."

Each of these disparate groups convenes at the concert in part 2, described from the multiple perspectives of Daniel, Khayman, and Jesse. Young vampires come into contact with ancient ones, ancient vampires uneasily approach one another, and vampires mingle with humans. Khayman is struck by the ignorance of both the younger vampires, who do not realize that Akasha has awakened and destroyed many vampire covens, and the mortal concert-goers, who fail to grasp that the concert is not illusion, but reality. He observes that Mael, the ancient Druid vampire priest who created Marius, has been sent to the concert by Maharet to protect Jesse. Upon actually touching Lestat's flesh on the stage, she realizes the truth of the supernatural, which she longs to reveal to David Talbot of the Talamasca, but one of the angry vampires breaks her neck and she is rushed to the hospital. The action then turns to Daniel worshiping Lestat as the concert erupts into chaos, with both vampires and mortals mobbing Lestat and with Akasha incinerating the vampires pursuing him. In the end, Khayman observes Akasha's abduction of Lestat from Gabrielle and Louis, as Maharet turns Jesse into a vampire rather than lose her to death.

In part 3, "As It Was in the Beginning, Is Now, and Ever Shall Be . . . ," the narrative shifts back and forth between Maharet's telling of the story of the twins that characters have been dreaming about throughout the novel and Akasha's rampage of destruction. Maharet tells an assembly of vampires that includes the first brood—or first generation—the tale of ancient pre-Egyptian civilizations linking the twins with Akasha and Enkil and explaining the creation of vampires introduced by Marius in his talks with Lestat in *The Vampire Lestat*. Since Maharet's narration is interrupted at suspenseful points by shifts to Lestat and Akasha, the facts are somewhat slow to emerge.

Maharet and her twin sister, Mekare, were raped and mutilated under order of the king and queen, Enkil and Akasha, 6,000 years ago in a grisly public scene. Members of a peaceful civilization with different beliefs and rituals, Maharet and Mekare were good witches who inherited their mother's special abilities to contact spirits in nature, with whom they lived in harmony. Enkil and Akasha, rulers of the Kemet civilization, summon them to appear before them, and Maharet and Mekare refuse. During the procession and feast honoring their dead mother, armies of the Kemet civilization descend on their village, slaughter their people, burn their dwellings, and take Maharet and Mekare away to the king and queen. Akasha, clearly the dominant ruler, demands to know about their special powers. Upon learning that the twins have no contact with great gods, Akasha humiliates and punishes them with the public rape by Khayman. Once released, Maharet and Mekare wander back to their village, where Maharet bears Khayman's child, Miriam, and they live briefly in peace.

They are pursued again, however, as Khayman explains that the evil spirit (whom the reader knows as Amel) has continued to torment Enkil and Akasha and invaded their bodies: "He has changed the very substance of their flesh" (*Queen,* 316). Maharet and Mekare return with Khayman to go before the changed Enkil and Akasha, who ask them questions about what has happened to them. Though she has never heard of such a thing happening before, Mekare reasons that the evil spirit Amel, having tasted human blood and wanting the power of a physical form, plunged into their bodies: "And so the fusion of blood and timeless tissue was a million times magnified and accelerated; and blood flowed through all his body, both material and nonmaterial" (*Queen,* 368). When an enraged Akasha learns that the only way to rid themselves of this evil spirit is to destroy the body, she accuses them of lying and condemns them to be tortured. Mekare is to have her tongue cut out because of her "evil lies and discourse with demons," and Maharet is to have her eyes removed because of the evil she has seen and tried to make them believe. Then they are both to be burned alive.

The first part of this punishment is accomplished. They are not burned, however, but transformed into new beings by Khayman, whose mortal nature had been changed by Akasha and Enkil. Understanding that he is perpetuating evil, Khayman nonetheless wants Maharet and Mekare to have the power to become equal enemies of Akasha. Eventually, Maharet and Mekare are placed in separate stone coffins and cast adrift in oceans to the east and west. Since their separation centuries ago, Maharet has kept careful track of the "Great Family" of humans descended from her daughter, Miriam. With the help of archaeologists whose research she has supported, she has also tried to find her sister, Mekare, who Maharet now believes is awake and en route to fulfill Mekare's defiant curse to Akasha: "You are the Queen of the Damned. . . . Your only destiny is evil, as well you know! But I shall stop you, if I must come back from the dead to do it. At the hour of your greatest menace it is I who will defeat you!" (*Queen,* 375). Since the first brood of vampires are but "blossoms on a single vine," the challenge is how to destroy Akasha without ending their own eternal lives. Meanwhile, Akasha has been on a violent rampage during Maharet's narration of vampire history, so it is clear that the time is at hand for Mekare to appear.

Several chapters in part 3 are narrated in the first person by Lestat, who recalls the first time he drank from Akasha 200 years ago and learns that despite her destruction of many children of darkness, she has spared those whom he cares for: Louis, Gabrielle, Armand, and others. Akasha says she resurrected herself to rule as she was meant to rule, as a new god to be worshiped in a peaceful world without starvation, poverty, and violence—a world dominated by women: "All males save one in a hundred should be killed, and all male babies save one in a hundred should also be slaughtered immediately" (*Queen,* 277). Men will be allowed to return to their normal ratio only when women's ways have prevailed. Hoping to appeal to Lestat's daring and his desire to do good, she chooses him as her new prince and says that he will now have the "purity of a righteous cause" he has long wanted.

Drawn to the ecstasy of loving her, afraid of her power, and revolted by her massacres, the torn Lestat nonetheless knows that Akasha's gender-cleansing plan is evil. Although Lestat is unable to deter Akasha from her intentions, he does manage to convince her to consult with the other ancient vampires, whom they join at Maharet's compound at the end of this section.

In a philosophical discussion more reminiscent of the fallen angels' council in Milton's *Paradise Lost* than the suspenseful action of Gothic novels, the brief part 4, entitled "The Queen of the Damned" and narrated by Lestat, consists of Akasha arguing for her brave-new-world plan with the other vampires, who try to persuade her to give it up. Marius does not agree with Akasha's cynical observations about the decline of the human race and her violent resolutions for solving the world's problems. Presenting evidence that the human race is evolving toward something better, he believes that the vampires have forfeited the right to intervene in human lives and must not alter the course of human destiny. Akasha attempts to sway their views by exploiting their sense of irrelevance and loneliness. She promises them a renewed sense of purpose and significance. Marius reminds her that in her new religion mortals will be worshiping superstitious lies: "Have we not had enough of them? And now, of all times, when the world's waking from its old delusions. When it has thrown off the old gods" (*Queen*, 406).

Maharet shows how religion has been the cause of wars, persecutions, and massacres. At a time when modern humanity is nearly free of superstitions, Maharet continues, Akasha wants to begin it all again to glorify herself: "You would bring a new religion, a new revelation, a new wave of superstition and sacrifice and death." The discussion ends in a standoff, with Akasha turning to Lestat and asking if he intends to betray her by joining the others. Knowing that he is against her, she threatens to kill him. Maharet warns that if she tries, they will all attack her. As Akasha pleads again with Lestat to come with her, the missing twin, Mekare, finally enters the room and exacts her revenge. She decapitates Akasha with shards of broken window glass. As Akasha writhes on the floor in an attempt to restore herself, Lestat and the other vampires experience her pain. Mekare consumes the heart and brain of Akasha to avoid the destruction of all the others. The section ends with Mekare staring forward, "expressionless, uncomprehending, the living statue," and Maharet declaring, "Behold. The Queen of the Damned" (*Queen*, 417).

Part 5 is a kind of postscript narrated by Lestat, who is now at Armand's villa in Miami with most of the vampire group. The whereabouts of Maharet and Mekare are unknown, and there is much speculation by the vampires about the implications of Mekare having consumed the heart and brain of Akasha: "Had any of *her* survived in Mekare?" (*Queen*, 425). Marius tries unsuccessfully to get Lestat to burn his new book, *The Queen of the Damned*, but convinces him to go to New Orleans to retrieve Louis. As Lestat relives the scenes of his immortal life with Louis, his old spirit returns and he thinks of a new way to get human attention. He demonstrates the special powers that Akasha gave him by picking up Louis and flying away to London, where he mischievously contacts David Talbot, the British leader of the Talamasca. From David's tutoring of Jesse earlier in the novel, it is clear that he knows what vampires are and believes in them. Ever resilient and ready for action, Lestat finds amusement in David's discomfort and playfully offers him immortality. When Talbot declines, Lestat leaves his phone number in case Talbot changes his mind. The novel ends with Lestat in a light-hearted mood, being scolded by Louis for breaking the vampire rules yet again.

As this summary of the action shows, *The Queen of the Damned* represents a departure not only from the traditional Gothic conventions in vampire fictions but also from Rice's own creation of a single villain-hero evolving toward self-awareness. In this third chronicle she assembles a large number of characters, establishes an overall pattern to their actions, and weaves pagan myths with the vampiric to encourage broader, archetypal interpretations of the text. As Northrop Frye explained years ago, stylized characters of Romantic novels "expand into psychological archetypes. It is in the romance that we find Jung's libido, anima, and shadow reflected in the hero, heroine, and villain respectively. That is why the romance so often radiates a glow of subjective intensity that the novel lacks, and why a suggestion of allegory is constantly creeping in around its fringes."[8] Reassigning the specific gender associations of these different types, Rice makes use of their potential impact in setting up the central conflict of the novel.

Maharet's narration of Enkil and Akasha's persecution of Maharet and Mekare during pre-Egyptian times builds on the story of vampire origins begun by Marius in *The Vampire Lestat* and includes many of the happenings common to mythic experience: fertility ritual, abduction, rape, dismemberment, separation, and transformation. Throughout the novel the characters who experience dreams of the twins mention their red hair, which Frazer in *The Golden Bough* connects with the color of ripe corn. One of the rites in worship of Osiris, the corn spirit, was the burning of a human victim and scattering his ashes over the fields to fertilize them and ensure abundant crops.[9] Though Maharet and Mekare are the red-haired twins reminiscent of the good corn-spirits Osiris and Isis, in Rice's adaptation of the myth, the king and queen take on "the identity of Osiris and Isis, and darkened those old myths to suit themselves." Enkil became the "God of the underworld," the king who could appear only in darkness, the queen "became Isis, the Mother, who gathers up her husband's battered and dismembered body and heals it and brings it back to life" (*Queen*, 380). Maharet reminds the vampires of Marius's earlier story of Enkil and Akasha's creating blood gods, their taking blood sacrifices of evildoers, and the blood gods' rising up against Enkil and Akasha and fighting among themselves until finally the king and queen were entombed in the earth, where they have sat like stone statues for 6,000 years.

The awakened Akasha, referred to by Maharet as "Mother," is clearly a perversion of Isis, who is one manifestation of the great goddess. Instead of a "beneficent queen of nature" or a "tender mother," as Isis is regarded in myth (Frazer, 444), Akasha is the terrible mother who ensnares and devours her offspring (and her own mate, Enkil) to enhance her power. Her true opponent, or the other side of the great goddess in the novel, is Maharet, who exhibits nurturing traits of the good mother in wishing to protect the Great Family of her human descendants.

The action of the novel fulfills the prophecy of the mysterious dream of the twins experienced by so many characters: the overthrow of the demonic terrible mother, Akasha, by the apocalyptic good mothers, Maharet and Mekare. Maharet and Mekare were originally associated with nature, with a peaceful and harmonious civilization: "Ours was a land of serenity and beauty, of laden fruit trees and fields of wild wheat free for anyone to cut with the scythe. Ours was a land of green grass and cool breezes" (*Queen*, 288). Akasha's realm, however, is materialistic and artificial. Maharet describes a "sprawling city of brick buildings with grass roofs, of great temples and palaces built of the same coarse materials, but all very fine" (*Queen*, 298). Even the people in their realm have an element of fakery about them: "And their painted eyes tended to unnerve us. For the paint hardened their stare; it gave an illusion of depth where perhaps there was no depth; instinctively, we shrank from this artifice" (*Queen*, 299). Maharet and Mekare are similar to many twins in myth in representing "beneficent deities." They do not within themselves reflect "counterbalancing principles," such as good and evil or light and dark (Cirlot, 337), however. Instead, they are together the counterbalancing anima to Akasha's evil shadow, made immortal for this purpose by Khayman. When the vampire group led by the first brood of

vampires—primarily Maharet and Khayman with Mekare returning to
become the actual avenger—manage to destroy Akasha, they restore the
positive principles of the great goddess that point toward human survival rather than destruction.

The classical female figure from a sterling silver punch bowl on the
novel's dust jacket suggests the important role of female vampires in *The
Queen of the Damned* and—given that the vessel or bowl is a common
symbol for the essence of the feminine,[10]—their associations with archetypal female principles. Males take a backseat to females in this novel:
Enkil is easily done in by Akasha, and the ancient vampires Khayman,
Mael, and Marius seem rather helpless compared with Akasha, Maharet
and Mekare. Ironically, Akasha sees what she regards as destructive male
traits epitomized in Lestat but fails to recognize them in herself: "I love
you because you are so perfectly what is wrong with all things male.
Aggressive, full of hate and recklessness, and endlessly eloquent excuses
for violence—you are the essence of masculinity; and there is a gorgeous
quality to such purity. But only because it can now be controlled" (*Queen*,
336). Akasha's egotistical lust for power and philosophical rationale for
her violence against men have perverted her natural role as mother.
Maharet tells her later that her thought (traditionally male) has dominated her compassion (traditionally female), creating an unnatural
imbalance. Ramsland sees the ossification of Akasha's flesh as symbolic
of this perversion: "In her centuries-long dormancy, while her body ossi-
fied, her mind fed on the concept of absolute perfection—an idea formed
by what she was becoming" (300). Appropriately, when Akasha is
destroyed by Mekare, she is decapitated first. In other words, Mekare
strikes out at the head, the real source of Akasha's evil.

     In the end, the victory of Maharet and Mekare over Akasha has inter-
esting implications concerning gender, reflecting perhaps Rice's own
departure from certain feminist positions. Since not all males will be
killed, there will be no domination or control by either sex or gender
principle, despite the acknowledged negative role men have played in
human history. The vampires will remain marginal, passive creatures
while humans live out their lives. In other words, they will adopt the
female principle embodied in Maharet. Abdicating the female role, however, the vampires will not create more of their own kind, even to
assuage their desperate loneliness, so they also exemplify the female
capacity for self-sacrifice. Because they manage to stop Akasha and to
resume their cosmic insignificance in human destiny, no new religions

will establish false values to obscure the truths of a godless secular morality—always valued by Rice—or to provide fresh motives for massive violence. Somewhat incapacitated here by his contradictory feelings toward Akasha, Lestat learns the errors of his own schemes for establishing his personal significance on a smaller scale. Unable to make a real difference, he will have to resort to new sources of self-justification in *The Tale of the Body Thief,* the fourth novel in the *Chronicles.*

The future of vampires and humans remains uncertain in *The Queen of the Damned* because of Mekare's ingestion of the heart and brain of Akasha. Earlier in the novel, Maharet and Mekare were engaging in a ceremony whereby they would consume the heart and brain of their dead mother, believing they could perpetuate her conscience and spirit in themselves. At the end of the novel, the ritual has a different purpose. Mekare consumes Akasha's organs to prevent the destruction of all vampires that are physically dependent on Akasha's remaining alive. Yet she clearly takes into herself an evil power. The vampires survive as a result of her action, but the issue arises as to what the absorption of the terrible mother into the good mother will mean for vampires and the human race.

In addition to interweaving pagan myths with the vampiric, Rice also includes Christian elements to unify the various shapes archetypal images have taken over the centuries. Although Ramsland mentions that Rice was inspired by a map in the book *Lost Cities of Africa* in naming Akasha (1993, 8), the name as a variation of the acacia flower might be regarded as both pagan and Christian. The pink and white blossoms of the acacia were sacred to the Egyptians because of their duality; that is, the shrub itself was connected with the paradoxical complexities of the red-and-white principle: death and immortality, passion and purity, destruction and rebirth; the thorn represented the mother-goddess Neith (Cirlot, 3, 57, 322). The thorn that came to symbolize "the ideas of existence and non-existence, ecstasy and anguish, pleasure and pain" for pagan civilizations later became representative of the duality of death and resurrection in Christ's crown of thorns worn on the cross (Cirlot, 322).

Akasha intends to set herself up as the god of a new religion for humans to worship and to give Lestat special powers with her blood so that he may rule with her as her prince. She is also the blood-mother of all the vampires, but a mother who has been infused with a demonic rather than holy spirit. She is thus associated with imagery of both God and the Virgin Mary, and Lestat with the Christ figure. When she rescues him and does not destroy him along with the others at the concert, she tells him: "For a century I watched you suffer, watched you grow weak and finally go down in the earth to sleep, and I then saw you rise, the very image of my own resurrection" (*Queen*, 236). An inverted image of God, Akasha intends to create an Eden, but in fact perverts nature and sets up an antiparadise.

For Lestat, whose childhood was marked by unanswered prayers and alienation from his family, the relationship with Akasha satisfies his desires to feel totally alive and a part of life, the very same needs that drove him to become a rock star. The concert described in *The Vampire Lestat* is the modern counterpart of pagan rituals of human sacrifice and idol worship, only without the actual sacrifice. Lestat becomes the anti-Christ figure for the humans who need him: "The blood ran in tiny rivulets down his white face, as if from Christ's Crown of Thorns" (*Queen*, 204). For the vampires in the audience, Lestat is the rebel who has turned against them and must be destroyed for revealing their secrets. They watch for the right time to attack and destroy him. For Daniel, Lestat is a Christ figure because he expresses the feelings of all the outcast, especially the vampires: "Lestat was Christ on the cathedral cross. How to describe his overwhelming and irrational authority?"

Ultimately, of course, despite his deep attraction, Lestat rejects Akasha, thereby confirming her role in the novel as the terrible mother. Likewise, Jesse's acceptance of Maharet supports Maharet's position as the moral opponent of Akasha. In the erotic yet maternal blood exchange that occurs when Maharet gives Jesse eternal vampiric existence after a vampire breaks her neck at Lestat's concert, Jesse senses that she has found "her eternal place" at last, that her life and research into vampires have been leading her toward the destiny of Maharet. Later, as she sees once again the great electronic map tracing Maharet's human family, Jesse feels "perhaps the finest love she had ever been capable of": "it seemed for one moment that natural and supernatural possibility were equal in their mystery. They were equal in their power. And all the miracles of the immortals could not outshine this vast and simple chronicle. The Great Family" (*Queen*, 391). Jesse feels a "terrible pain" at the thought of a supernatural force intervening in human lives, as Akasha threatens both the human and vampiric families nurtured by Maharet.

Traditionally in the Gothic, vampires represent the dark physical threat outside to be overcome by humans or the more ambivalent psychological forces within. Mythically they are representatives of the terrible mother associated with the darkness, the earth, and the appetite for human blood: "Among all peoples the goddesses of war and the hunt express man's experience of life as a female exacting blood" (Neumann, 149). In pitting good vampires, who wish to protect the human race, against the bad ones, who threaten it, Rice uses her vampires as larger metaphors for humans who, like Lestat, must confront the truths of their lives and weigh the choices available (such as those represented by Akasha or Maharet) in finding a decent way to survive. Despite the temptation to have a sense of purpose with Akasha as his mother-lover forever, Lestat must reject the ideas she offers and find other outlets for coping with his inevitable insignificance. His readers sympathize with the issues of the human condition that his vampirism exaggerates.

As Rice greatly enhances and expands the fictional world of the vampire community, she reworks traditional conventions associated with the vampire nature and also devises new and refreshing characteristics befitting her modern creations. As in *The Vampire Lestat,* old vampires are clearly stronger, wiser, and less dependent on human blood to survive than younger vampires. Both Akasha and Khayman can go for years without drinking human blood and can incinerate other vampires, which Khayman inadvertently does when he tries to approach the younger group. In a kind of explosive nuclear impact, the horrified Khayman watches as "[o]ut of him, a power seemed to leap as if an invisible tongue. Instantly it penetrated the hindmost of the fleeing trio, the female, and her body burst into flame (*Queen,* 118). While Akasha goes on her rampage incinerating other vampires en route to Lestat's concert and later slaughtering males, it stands to reason that the killing abilities and the drinking of human blood will be downplayed in the portrayal of good vampires like Maharet, whose 6,000 years are marked by her nurturing of the family and no mention of her taking mortal lives.

Like their nineteenth-century predecessors, Rice's vampires may be destroyed by sun and by fire, so they are still creatures of the night, but they are no longer vulnerable to crosses and other religious symbols, since these items have no real significance. Rice's vampires also create mirror images since they are more firmly grounded in the flesh. Standing before a looking glass, Lestat notes the signs of his physical change and increased powers under the influence of Akasha: "I'd been bleached by Akasha's blood, but I hadn't become smooth yet. I'd kept my human expression" (*Queen,* 326). Rice's modern vampires also adapt to contemporary life-styles and choose trendy clothes, ride motorcycles, leave phone numbers, watch television, and respond to high technology.

Armand, for instance, marvels over his gold watch: "Think of that thing flashing its digits inside a coffin during the day" (*Queen*, 99); Khayman hears "people laughing and talking" in the planes that fly overhead.

Rice's technique of integrating these ancient vampires who adapt to modern times and interrelate with both Louis and Lestat, the main figures of the first two novels in the *Chronicles*, also serves to expand her supernatural world by elaborately intermingling the past with the present. Within the overall simplicity of the central plot that builds toward the confrontation between Akasha and the other vampires led by Maharet and Mekare, Rice tells complex stories to establish connections among these characters' present purposes and their past histories. Particularly effective is the first part of the novel, "The Road to the Vampire Lestat," where she builds suspense by introducing in separate chapters characters who are experiencing the ominous dreams of the twins and preparing to set out for the concert.

Waiting for the concert to begin in part 2, the reader realizes from Lestat's introduction that the "cataclysm" and "disaster" are not the concert itself but the greater danger that the concert initiates, which turns out to be the awakened, obsessed Akasha. As Lestat explains at the beginning, to reconstruct the events before the concert, he will have to let the reader "slip into the minds and hearts of other beings" by using the "'third person' and 'multiple point of view'" (*Queen*, 8). In fact, the omniscient storyteller moves freely from one character's story to those of others.

Speaking to us via interior monologues or first-person dialogue, Rice's characters distinguish themselves by their peculiar turn of phrase or distinct habit of observation. Baby Jenks, for instance, speaks in contemporary slang when she contemplates Lestat: "I mean he was a rock star, for Chrissakes. Probably had his own limousine. And was he ever one adorable-looking guy, Dead or alive! Blond hair to die for and a smile that just made you wanna roll over and let him bite your goddamn neck!" (*Queen*, 44). By contrast, the ancient Marius is connected with a more sophisticated vocabulary and dignified tone: "He loved these eloquent modern expressions. He loved the sudden shift of her luscious breasts as she'd shrugged, and the lithe twist of her hips beneath the coarse denim clothes that made her seem all the more smooth and fragile. An incandescent flower" (*Queen*, 21). Maharet, too, has Marius's more formal manner as she narrates the suspenseful story of her past. Lestat, the only character who speaks entirely from the first-person perspective, remains consistently informal with understated, often comical language: "To paraphrase David Copperfield, I don't know whether I'm the hero or the victim of this tale. But either way, shouldn't I dominate it?" (*Queen*, 8).

The omniscient perspective of part 1 continues during the concert in part 2, broken up with narratives by Khayman, Daniel, and Jesse further intensifying the suspense. Each of them views events from an entirely different perspective that is limited compared with the reader's overview. Once the climactic concert is over and Akasha is on the scene, most of the second half of the novel is taken up by a technically complicated part 3, which alternates the first-person voice of Lestat, who is now with Akasha, with the voice of the omniscient narrator, who observes the assembly of vampires as they listen to Maharet's narration of the twins. The intention here would seem to be to create suspense through the same kind of simultaneous action that works so well in part 1. In the first section, however, the source of tension originates from the introduction to different characters and stories rather than from an alternation between two sets of characters, with one group focused on a single tale. The reader does receive signals foreshadowing Mekare's return and appreciates the real threat of Akasha after witnessing her violence, but the pre-Egyptian tales of Maharet and Mekare are tedious and needlessly repeated later by Akasha.

This method of holding off the climax with intrusions into Maharet's narration of the past also becomes transparent when the vampire-assembly chapters end on particularly suspenseful points in Maharet's narration. At the end of chapter 2, for example, Maharet says that she and her sister were witches: "We talked to the spirits and the spirits loved us. Until she sent her soldiers into our land" (*Queen*, 260). Chapter 4 concludes with Maharet's having gotten to the point where their "brief year of happiness with the birth of Miriam was past now—and the horror that had come out of Egypt was reaching out to engulf" them once more (*Queen*, 317), just as Marius envisions Mekare en route: "He heard the feet begin their relentless tramp again; he saw the feet caked with earth as if they were his feet; the hands caked with earth as if they were his hands. And then he saw the sky catching fire, and he moaned aloud" (*Queen*, 320). Returning to the first person of Lestat, the brief parts 4 and 5 pick up the pace again, despite the philosophical debate that leads to the destruction of Akasha by Mekare.

This violent resolution of conflict hinges to a great extent on the revelation of ancient myths and the fulfillment of prophecies. By incorporating these myths into the vampire genre and then making distinctions between good and bad and old and young vampires, Rice also takes the meaning of traditional blood drinking beyond the erotic. For example, Maharet's drinking of Jesse's blood, while it has an erotic component, serves the purpose of saving Jesse from death, not fulfilling Maharet's lust for blood. The transfusing of eternal-life-giving blood emphasizes the maternal function over the paternal, implying the prevalence of the good mother over the terrible, Maharet over Akasha. Whereas Akasha gives her blood to Lestat only to increase her own stature and power through him, Maharet's blood preserves the flesh in Jesse, as it "anchors" her "soul to substance forever." Rice's transformation of Daniel, who is also dying, is intensified by her depiction of him as the religious suppli- cant at the altar of immortality receiving the body of Armand: "'Drink, Daniel.' The priest said the Latin words as he poured the Holy Communion wine into his mouth" (*Queen*, 105). Reminding the reader of the timeless sacramental significance of the blood, Daniel visualizes the twins' bloody ritual at their mother's burial ceremony and sits up, "crushing Armand to him, drawing it out of him, draught after draught. They had fallen over together in the soft bank of flowers. Armand lay beside him, and his mouth was open on Armand's throat, and the blood was an unstoppable fount" (*Queen*, 105).

While these sensual unions are between members of the same sex, Lestat also experiences the sublime ecstasy of drinking from Akasha's "fount." These androgynous intimacies transcend family roles as well as gender distinctions. Maharet is a mother-figure to Jesse as Akasha is to Lestat, since she has replaced his true mother, Gabrielle. As Rice's biog- rapher points out, the vampires' blurred sexual identities account for a major source of their appeal: "Becoming a vampire involved a merging of like minds in a way prohibited to people with fundamentally different perspectives. Female readers strongly identified with Louis, and later with Lestat, because Anne provided for them a means to experience male qualities that society prizes so highly without a loss of the female-orient- ed perspective" (Ramsland, 148–49).

Sexual encounters are less frequent, however, than are the large, vio- lent scenes of human sacrifice and massacre. Beginning with Baby Jenks's murder of her parents and her own incineration, through Pandora's participation in Azim's blood-drinking orgy in the Himalayas, Akasha's burning of vampires at Lestat's concert and her killing of males, the rape and mutilation of Maharet and Mekare, to Mekare's beheading and dismemberment of Akasha, *The Queen of the Damned* is a violent novel where grisly details of group atrocities are more frequent than the sensuality of intimate vampire penetration. These epic-like episodes may also appeal to the worst tastes of readers, but the historical context of violence suggests a larger significance. Maharet's central story, which she describes herself as having the "hard purity of mythology," shows the timeless needs of humans to engage in violent battles and conquests to protect the communal beliefs that ensure their survival. Understanding ancient ceremonies and conflicts, however violent they may be, sheds light on the archetypal significance of all rituals, from the pagan gatherings on the hill to the masses of youths descending on San Francisco for the rock concert. In addition, the vampiric perspective affords the disinterested analysis that comes from their having lived through centuries of changing cultures and observed various religious systems give way to the secularity of the twentieth century.

Lestat, for instance, says that he loves killing males for Akasha, "as men have always loved it in the absolute moral freedom of war" (*Queen*, 269), because he believes for a time that she justifies what he is doing. He awakens in an awful place where "mortals lived in misery, babies crying in hunger, amid the smell of cooking fires and rancid grease." These are the signs of true war, "Not the debacle of the mountainside, but old-fashioned twentieth-century war" (*Queen*, 275). Continuing with hideous descriptions of disease, misery, and poverty, Lestat asks Akasha where they are. In effect, as she tells him, the location is irrelevant: "Calcutta, if you wish, or Ethiopia; or the streets of Bombay; these poor souls could be the peasants of Sri Lanka; of Pakistan; of Nicaragua, of El Salvador. It does not matter what it is; it matters how much there is of it" (*Queen*, 276). Lestat observes, "This was the ragged edge of the savage garden of the world in which hope could not flower. This was a sewer" (276).

These human atrocities are pervasive and certainly more harmful to humans than Maharet's brand of vampirism, yet Lestat later sees that Akasha's self-serving objectives are far worse. Her observations testify to the human capacity for violence on a massive scale, along with the cleverness to structure political systems to justify or ignore it. Modern mortals retain their savage natures but are also "technologically astute" as they seek to satisfy the same desires for power and domination. The overall pattern that unifies the struggles of the past with those of the present and relates the vampires' history to that of humans is the universal confrontation with the great goddess figure and all of the destructive forces that she symbolizes. The outcome, in this case the destruction of Akasha, is less a victory than a moment of true awareness, since the ending of the novel leaves room for the forces of Akasha to continue in

Mekare. The survivors, however, see the need to restrain their power and
protect one another as the "exquisite monsters" in the savage garden.

The broad canvas of action in *The Queen of the Damned* once again
demonstrates Rice's adaptations of setting apparent in the first two novels of the series, as she continues to move away from the conventional
scenes of vampire novels. Almost entirely removed from graveyards and
subterranean crypts, the vampires in this novel are very active and hardly ever seen asleep in coffins. Their adventures range worldwide, from
the arctic to San Francisco, from the Himalayan mountains to Haiti.
Rather than the frozen depths appropriate for Akasha's tomb, they prefer warm climates and elegant surroundings, which they furnish with
artistic treasures. Reminiscent of Marius's Grecian paradise, Armand's
home in southern Florida reflects "the skilled mixture of old and new.
Elevator doors rolling back on broad rectangular rooms full of medieval
tapestries and antique chandeliers; giant television sets in every room.
Renaissance paintings filled Daniel's suite, where Persian rugs covered
the parquet. The finest of the Venetian school surrounded Armand in his
white carpeted study full of shining computers, intercoms, and moni-
tors" (*Queen,* 92).
    Maharet's home hidden in the Sonoma mountains of California is "at
the end of an impossible unpaved road, to begin with; and its back
rooms had been dug out of the mountain, as if by enormous machines"
(*Queen,* 140). Ramsland sees this setting as symbolic of "hidden powers
and mysteries about to be revealed" (303). As magnificent as Armand's,
the compound has "every convenience. Aerials high on the mountain
brought television broadcasts from far and wide. There was a cellar
movie theater complete with projector, screen, and an immense collection of films," along with an enormous library and observatory. Clearly
comfortable creating convincing ornate settings of the present and the
primitive tribal civilizations of the past, Rice nonetheless returns the
reader to her favorite New Orleans, as Lestat goes there at the end of the
novel to retrieve the melancholy Louis.
    The last glimpse of Lestat and Louis is in London, where the beams of
the car light up "the regal face" of old buildings, "revealing the gar-
goyles, and the heavy arches over the windows, and the gleaming knock-
ers on the massive front doors" (*Queen,* 441). Sensitive to architectural
details and the aesthetics of his surroundings, Lestat's observation that
these grand old dwellings "invite the spirits of the dead to come back"
looks forward to the haunting history of the Mayfair witches in *The*

Witching Hour and the returning spirit of Lasher rather than the indomitable vampire Lestat in the grand antebellum mansion in New Orleans.

The prevampire existence of Maharet and Mekare as witches in touch with the cycles of nature also suggests new interests to be developed in Rice's later books. Stating that there have always been witches, Maharet tells the vampire assembly that "there are witches now, though most no longer understand what their powers are or how to use them. Then there are those known as clairvoyants or mediums, or channelers. Or even psychic detectives. It is all the same thing. These are people who for reasons we may never understand attract spirits. Spirits find them downright irresistible; and to get the notice of these people, the spirits will do all kinds of tricks" (*Queen*, 279). Motivated apparently by "hatred and jealousy of the flesh," the evil spirit Amel, who invades and transforms the physical bodies of Enkil and Akasha, anticipates the relationships between Lasher and the Mayfair family. Maharet wonders about the spirit's retaining the body after death: "I thought as many a man or woman has thought before and since that maybe it was a curse to have the concept of immortality without the body to go with it" (*Queen*, 311). Speculations on the nature of life, death, and immortality are thus in place, along with two members of the Talamasca, who research these issues further in *The Witching Hour*, especially Aaron Lightner, and Lestat's friend David Talbot, who will play a much larger role in *The Tale of the Body Thief*.

Maharet also introduces the subject of Rice's next novel, *The Mummy*, published just one year after *The Queen of the Damned*. She tells the other vampires that the whole custom of mummifying the dead began when Enkil and Akasha banned the cannibalism of civilizations who ate their dead rather than "commit one's ancestors to the earth." The king and queen decreed that the bodies be wrapped and "displayed for all to see, and then placed in tombs with proper offerings and incantation of the priest" (*Queen*, 287). Maharet, who has contact with spirits of the dead, believes it is better that humans forget their bodies in death so that they may "relinquish their earthly image" and "rise to the higher plane." She continues, "If anyone had told us that this custom of mummification would become entrenched in that culture, that for four thousand years the Egyptians would practice it, that it would become a great and enduring mystery to the entire world—that little children in the twentieth century would go into museums to gaze at mummies—we would

not have believed such a thing" (*Queen*, 287). Shifting her central characters from vampires to mummies and then to witches in her next two
novels, Rice explores new images of the occult yet continues to develop
concerns that have always fascinated the many readers who enjoy
"Ligeia," "The Fall of the House of Usher," "The Raven," "Ulalume,"
and other works by her grand Gothic predecessor Edgar Allan Poe—the
contacts between the living and the dead, the possibilities of reunion
after death, and the potentialities of humans' extending the life of the
body beyond the grave.

Interweaving pagan myths with vampiric images in *The Queen of the
Damned* lends credibility to the vampire, whose existence is no less fan-
tastic than the primitive beings that earlier civilizations believed in to
explain natural phenomena and mysteries and to impose order on their
lives. This context tends to trivialize human-made religions and magnify
the importance of facing realities and appreciating the beauty and violence of life as it is rather than finding false meaning in new religious
beliefs. Unlike traditional vampires, who are consumed by lust and
marked for annihilation, Rice's undead creatures are fortified with the
knowledge of eternity and the awareness of the accidental, amoral
nature of their very existence that involves them in philosophical dilem-
mas. Their responses to their vampirism are very human: Louis, for
instance, remains unable to conquer his despair, while Lestat has the
appealing energy and determination to act and to make a difference.
Both retain a great love and longing for the human life they have lost;
Lestat, in particular, tries to establish a meaningful place in connection
with the mortal world. In her next two novels, *The Mummy* and *The
Witching Hour,* Rice will reverse the special fictional vantage point provided by vampire protagonists and focus on the humans' responses to
the supernatural. *The Tale of the Body Thief* is the logical continuation for
Lestat in the *Chronicles;* his obsession with human life results in the ultimate rebellion against his vampiric nature and actual experiment to
return to a human form.

Chapter Six
The Tale of the Body Thief

Published in 1992, two years after *The Witching Hour, The Tale of the Body Thief* immediately rose to the top of the *New York Times* best-seller list, where it remained well into 1993. As usual, critical reception was divided, though most reviewers applauded Rice's suspenseful storytelling and her movement away from the lengthy interruptions of present narratives with past histories and from the large casts of characters in *The Queen of the Damned* and *The Witching Hour.* David Gates, for instance, referred to the "Mozartian" *Interview with the Vampire* and the "Wagnerian" vampire books, *The Vampire Lestat* and *The Queen of the Damned,* and noted that in this novel "those boring vampire elders keep their distance."[1] Ralph Novak called the novel an improvement over the earlier *Chronicles* for being "blissfully devoid of tedious meditations on the foolish arcana of the occult."[2]

While Novak criticized Rice for her departures from vampiric lore, Roz Kaveney praised the ways in which contemporary writers—Rice among them—lend significance to the vampire myth as a way of examining "possible balances between the demands of humaneness and the siren call of a dominating sexuality."[3] Walter Kendrick, too, acknowledged Rice's revitalization of the vampire tradition, stating that her monsters "are sexy, powerful and above all dangerous."[4] Novak found a "religious avoidance of wit," but Gates noted the comic relief provided by Lestat's reactions to being human. While some critics judged this book as the best vampire novel thus far, Michael Rogers found it "disappointing," the "weakest" in *The Vampire Chronicles,*[5] an assessment echoed by Walter Kendrick, who said the novels of the series were "careening down a steep, sad slope" (Kendrick 1992, 55). Kendrick lamented the loss of "unfashionable gorgeousness" of Rice's prose, yet a *Publishers Weekly* reviewer saw the "lushly evoked settings" as luring readers into "the enchanting world of her anguished and deeply sympathetic hero."[6]

With passing references to homosexuality and bisexuality, reviewers of this novel tended not to dwell on the issue of eroticism, now recognized as characteristic of Rice's Gothic fiction. In focusing on descriptions of action and character, critics also tended to omit the discussions of philosophical themes and innovative stylistic approaches that earlier reviewers emphasized. As a result, critical reception seemed limited.

Technically, *The Tale of the Body Thief* is very different from *The Witching Hour,* Rice's previous novel, and from *The Queen of the Damned.* Perhaps reacting to critical objections toward narrative complexities created by lengthy interruptions into the past, rapidly shifting multiple plots, large casts of characters, panoramic travels, and settings covering centuries of civilizations, Rice returns to the straightforward plotline of the single first-person protagonist that was so effective in the *Interview.* Yet *The Tale of the Body Thief* is original. Here, for the first time, she relies on the Faustian myth historically vital to the Gothic, along with William Blake's poem "The Tyger," to revitalize the vampire and to explore philosophical themes.

The novel takes its title from the central action between Lestat and Raglan James, who knows how to invade others' bodies with his presence or soul and convinces Lestat to make an exchange with him. Against the advice of his two friends, the vampire Louis and the human David Talbot, Lestat, still frustrated with the insignificance of his vampiric existence, goes boldly ahead with the switch and finds himself betrayed by James, who fails to return at the appointed time to return Lestat's body. Lestat realizes the stupidity of what he has done, deplores the physical limitations of being human, and longs to return to his vampiric state. Despite the loyalty and affection of Mojo, a German shepherd he adopts, and a brief love affair with the nun Gretchen, Lestat's human existence is marked not only by comic clumsiness but by real humiliation and suffering because of ill health. Seeing the sunlight is just not worth it.

In his desperation to recover his vampiric body, he seeks out Louis and asks him to make him a vampire. When the typically contemplative Louis refuses to bring any human, even his own creator, into the evils of the vampiric state, Lestat turns to David Talbot. David agrees to put his Talamascan knowledge of the occult to use, including soul travel, so that the novel turns into a suspenseful adventure mystery wherein Lestat and David locate Raglan James aboard the *Queen Elizabeth II.* Taking on amusing combinations of famous Gothic names, such as Sebastian Melmoth, Stanford Wilde, Dr. Stoker, and Sheridan Blackwood, they come up with an intricate plan to force James out of Lestat's body. About three-quarters of the way through the novel, they accomplish their mission. But James then steals David Talbot's body and convinces Lestat that he wishes to be made a vampire. Lestat, amazed at David's complete change of character, realizes none too soon after drinking the blood (but fortunately before giving his own) that the man he thinks is David is in fact James. The real David shows up safe and sound later in the much younger body of James.

Before completing the above action, Rice takes the overjoyed and triumphant Lestat to the rain forest of South America he had visited in his human state. There he fulfills his promise to visit Gretchen, with whom he had a sexual relationship while human, in his true vampiric state. Working as a nurse in the mission of St. Margaret Mary, Gretchen rejects him completely and believes that whoever he is, he is lying to her. Mystified by her revulsion and her miraculous experience of stigmata when she takes refuge in the chapel, Lestat comes to terms with his vampirism again in the jungle that clarifies the lessons of Rice's savage garden. Only loosely connected with the body-theft plot, Lestat's rebirth comes right after Gretchen's mystical experience and prepares for the larger outcome of the novel, his betrayal of David Talbot, whom Lestat turns into a vampire against his will. The significance of this final action is unclear, as is the motivation and complete change in Lestat (who at the beginning of the novel hunts down a killer of old women and respects David's wishes), without a careful look at the context or frame provided by the meditations of Lestat and his conversations with David Talbot before the theft plot begins (about 120 pages or so into the novel). Not an end in itself, the body-stealing adventure is a means for Lestat to affirm his vampiric self and to justify the evil force he represents in the universe.

In his prologue to the novel, Lestat states: "This is a contemporary story. It's a volume in the Vampire Chronicles, make no mistake. But it is the first really modern volume, for it accepts the horrifying absurdity of existence from the start, and it takes us into the mind and the soul of its hero—guess who?—for its discoveries."[7] The devil-may-care Lestat makes it clear that this action will not involve the quests for meaning typical of *The Vampire Lestat* and *The Queen of the Damned* but rather adventures from which discoveries come about accidentally. He casually mentions, however, that two dreams continue to bother him: the scene of Claudia's dying in the hospital for orphans centuries ago and David's efforts to defend himself against a charging tiger in a mangrove forest (*Thief,* 7–8).

Visions of Claudia's presence recur like flutterings of medieval angels serving as voices of conscience in a morality play, in this case to show Lestat's lingering guilt over creating the child Claudia as a vampire. His remorse is an influential factor in his friendship with the human David Talbot. David's trust in Lestat is based on mutual love and respect; in fact, Lestat keeps asking him if he would like to become a vampire as a kind of joke, based on the definite understanding that Lestat would never violate David's beliefs. Lestat's nightmare, reminiscent of Francis Macomber's experience in Hemingway's story, depicts a cruel and fanged tiger bearing down on David, who finally shoots it only yards away. The scene foreshadows danger for David and change in Lestat, who does indeed take David's life and transform him into a vampire at the end of the novel.

Ironically, the visions of Claudia end when Lestat's conscience is clear and when he realizes the purpose of his nature, not just by giving up his vampiric body for awhile but by moving beyond and outside the human realm to a primeval state in nature. It is a Romantic transcendence. After seeing Gretchen's goodness and her sacrificial role in serving humans, he then relates to the energy and power of the wild beasts of the jungle:

> Mindless and endlessly vigorous is the cycle of hunger and satiation, of violent and painful death. Reptiles with eyes as hard and shining as opals feast eternally upon the writhing universe of stiff and crackling insects as they have since the days when no warm-blooded creature ever walked the earth. And the insects—winged, fanged, pumped with deadly venom, and dazzling in their hideousness and ghastly beauty, and beyond all cunning—ultimately feast upon all.
>
> There is no mercy in this forest. No mercy, no justice, no worshipful appreciation of its beauty, no soft cry of joy at the beauty of the falling rain. Even the sagacious little monkey is a moral idiot at heart. (*Thief*, 344)

Images of insects as "winged, fanged, pumped with deadly venom" and feasting on humans are clearly vampiric, and these are the creatures that are "dazzling in their hideousness and ghastly beauty."

The juxtaposition of what Lestat calls his "rebirth" into the darkness of his own free will (*Thief*, 412) in the rain forest with the flowing blood that confirms Gretchen's martyr-like purity suggests the very pattern of Blake's poem, referred to in Lestat's prologue. After describing the dream, Lestat hears a voice saying, "Tyger, tyger burning bright" (*Thief*, 7). Blake's poem is intended as a counterpart to "The Lamb" in its speculation on the source of good and evil in the world. It is comfortable to see God as the creator of innocence symbolized by the lamb, but not so easy to realize that God may also have created the evil, passion, and energy represented by the tiger. Though the question "What immortal hand or eye / Dare frame thy fearful symmetry?" remains unanswered, the word "symmetry" implies a purpose for the tiger as well as the lamb—for Lestat as well as for Gretchen. In keeping with her views on androgynous sexuality as a transcendence of gender roles, and secular, personal morality as freedom from restrictions created by social institutions, Rice's adoption of Blake's liberating Romanticism suggests a similar growth for Lestat as a vampire. As David Punter observes in exploring Gothic terror in the Romantic poets, "Terror in Blake is always to do with distortion, whether it be the distortion which an all-dominant faculty of reason imposes on the passions, or the distortion of a social and sexual code which destroys the human body and pollutes the mind with repression" (102).

Rice includes at least a dozen references to the tiger that point toward Lestat's ultimate acceptance of his vampirism and its consequence: his taking David's life. Shortly after their philosophical discussion concerning the immortal power of Rembrandt's art, Lestat experiences the dream again: "*Tyger, tyger* . . . David in danger" (*Thief,* 40). Still searching for answers to the moral mysteries of life, David later counters Lestat's idea that death is awful and final: "Somebody formed the fearful symmetry, Lestat. Somebody had to. The tiger and the lamb . . . it couldn't have happened all by itself" (*Thief,* 68).

In attempting to convince David of his evil nature, Lestat links the philosophical speculations of Blake's poem with the other predominant literary allusion in the novel: "I've told you I'm the very devil. The devil in your *Faust,* the devil of your visions, the tiger in my dream!" (*Thief,* 413). In addition to the repeated mention of David's reading Goethe's *Faust* in the context of understanding the role or purpose of God's creation of the devil, the inclusion of Gretchen (a character in *Faust*), a "compact" between Lestat and Raglan James, the vision David has of a dialogue between God and the devil that is clearly an adaptation of the famous debate at the beginning of *Faust,* and perhaps even the appearance of the German shepherd Mojo, Rice uses the Faustian myth in multifaceted ways to explore the meaning of Lestat and David's relationship. While Lestat obviously becomes the devil who exacts a great price from David, who, like Faust, has been enticed by the prospect of knowledge, Lestat is in his compact with Raglan James the Faust who triumphs as a renewed vampire. As with the Blakean tiger, the Faustian motif is adapted to Rice's vision of existential reality, since the "saving" of Lestat means his assuming his true predatory nature.

Associations between the Faustian myth and the Gothic are not new. Typically, they are related to scientists like Frankenstein, who lose sight of humanity in their obsessive desires and ambitions. Faustian ambitions can be seen behind the grandiose schemes of Rice's Akasha in *Queen of the Damned* and the unnatural goals of Lasher and the scientific curiosity of Rowan Mayfair in *The Witching Hour.* With Lestat, however, Rice's innovation is bringing the myth to vampirism—to Lestat's desire for human life, along with David's human quest for immortality. David Punter discusses three powerful Romantic symbols of the Gothic that provide "living evidence of the terror at the heart of the world": the wanderer, who attempts to change his destiny with someone to end his perpetually outcast state; the vampire, who represents "the perverse union of passion and death"; and the seeker after forbidden knowledge, usually the means to eternal life (Punter, 114–20). While the "survival of death is clearly a root motif in all three symbols" (and surely a major source of their popular appeal), all involve defiance and rebellion, "transgression of boundaries between the natural, the human and the divine" (Punter, 120).

These powerful Romantic motivations come together in the rebel Lestat, as he changes through the course of the novel from seeing himself as Faust in the body-switch plot and then as the devil (or Mephistopheles) in the larger action concerning David. He begins his story in a suicidal state, rebelling against his vampiric powers and believing that he is beyond redemption: "The evil of one murder is infinite, and my guilt is like my beauty—eternal. I cannot be forgiven, for there is no one to forgive me for all I've done" (*Thief,* 14). Though he likes Goethe's "Romantic optimism" in saving Faust (*Thief,* 34) and enjoys David's speculations on the imperfection of God and the physical nature of the devil, he sees his own damnation as irreversible: "But what good would one act of mercy be in the face of all I've done? I'm damned if there is a God or a Devil" (*Thief,* 73). He discusses spiritual questions with David, but basically sees David's concerns as a waste of time: "I'm finished with all such quests. I look to the world around me now for truths, truths mired in the physical and in the aesthetic, truths I can fully embrace" (*Thief,* 79). Raglan James's offer is the perfect opportunity; instead of being "Cain forever seeking the blood of his brother" (*Thief,* 197), he finds a human eager to give up his mortal life. This act, however, is just as risky, rebellious, and perverse to vampirism as Faust's is to humanity. The human Lestat is, like Faust, cut off from his peers— in Lestat's case, vampires. He must depend on humans when Louis and Marius refuse to come to his aid.

Also like Faust, except for the inversion of the natural and supernatural states, the experience of getting what he wants leads to new perspectives (or his "truths") on what he formerly saw as the limitations of vampirism. He tells Gretchen that in addition to wanting to walk in the sun, he changed bodies with a mortal man to "test a belief": "That being mortal again was what we all wanted, that we were sorry that we'd given it up, that immortality wasn't worth the loss of our human souls. But I know now I was wrong" (*Thief,* 233). Instead of having Lestat abuse and destroy the innocent Gretchen to show total depravity, Rice has Lestat internalize the lesson of Gretchen's life in contrast to his own. He simply cannot feel her need for self-abnegation, which he connects with his own vampiric need for blood, a deep pleasure from pain (*Thief,* 247–48). Indeed, the blood that flows later from Gretchen's palms asserts her spirituality, just as Lestat's drinking the blood of David confirms the vampiric needs of the flesh. Moving toward his realization later in the rain forest that completes his self-affirmation as a vampire, Lestat tells her, "My strength, my will, my refusal to give up—those are the only components of my heart and soul which I can truly identify. This ego, if you wish to call it that, is my strength . . . . nothing . . . not even this mortal body . . . is going to defeat me" (*Thief,* 251). Lestat's assertions here are not all that different from those of the angels in Goethe's *Faust,* who carry Faust's immortal part to heaven at the end of the play:

> Saved, saved now is that precious part
> Of our spirit world from evil:
> "Should a man strive with all his heart,
> Heaven can foil the devil."[8]

Unprepared for Gretchen's total revulsion toward him as a vampire, Lestat realizes in the rain forest, where essence of nature takes precedence over human speculation, that her recognition of his being as an evil force is part of his vampiric salvation: "Something had been saved at that moment. The dark damnation of Lestat had been saved, and was now forever intact" (*Thief,* 356). He knows that hallucinations of Claudia will end because they are connected with the human conscience that he displayed at the beginning of the novel in regretting his inability to be redeemed and in his longing for the human experience. Lestat's damnation is a Faustian salvation; both triumph because of their rebellious aspirations. Instead of being carried off by angels, whom he feared at the beginning of the novel would take him down into hell (*Thief*, 25), the changed Lestat describes a parallel ascent: "I raised my arms towards the stars, swimming so brilliant beyond the clouds, and I went up, and up, and up until I was lost in the song of the wind and tumbling on the thinnest currents, and the joy I felt in my gifts filled my entire soul" (*Thief*, 396).

Lestat may delight in the restoration of his vampiric power and transcendence, but for the reader attached to his human qualities and the character of David Talbot the response may be less than enthusiastic. In a sense, David's experience with Lestat is similar to Wagner's in the play, especially in Christopher Marlowe's version of the Faust legend. Like the servant Wagner, whose conjurings parallel those of his master on a lower level, David goes through a similar process of wanting to know more, underestimating the risks of getting this knowledge, and presumably paying a heavy price. He tells Lestat that he has the ability to call up spirits, but has not yet "cracked the secrets of the universe" (*Thief*, 67), an attempt he makes through rereading *Faust* and being a friend of Lestat. Now approaching the end of his life and wishing to return to his youth, David reminisces about his younger days as a fearless hunter drawn to danger and excitement, to the tiger. Sensing David's regret that his life as a Talamascan is now so far removed from this vitality, Lestat rightly considers "that there was obviously a danger in his knowing me" (*Thief*, 63). Yet David refuses to see Lestat as dangerous, despite Lestat's early warnings.

Lestat feels "closer to him than ever before" when he realizes that they are both men of action, that David had "always found his greatest pleasure in the hunt," especially for the Bengal tiger (*Thief*, 86). In an irony too obvious to miss, Lestat goes on to describe how David always drew "very close to the beast before he fired his gun," so that "he had almost been killed more than once" (*Thief*, 86). In his older years, David's "emphasis was now entirely upon the invisible—upon the perception of inner strength and the battle with the forces outside" (*Thief*, 87). Lestat senses their kindred natures in their similar thirsts for "ever greater spiritual experience" (*Thief*, 88), clearly the motivation for David's attraction to Lestat, coupled with his intense curiosity.

As it turns out, David's friendship with Lestat fulfills many needs, including a return to the excitement of physical danger in getting Lestat's vampiric body back from Raglan James. David is completely in charge of showing Lestat how to close his thoughts so that James cannot read them and how to make his soul transcend the body; in general, he plans the extremely complicated arrangements aboard the *QEII*. In the process of these machinations, it is obvious that David has not entirely come to terms with the vampirism of his friend, as he mentions the possibility of Lestat's staying in a human form and their destroying the vampire. Lestat notes "the sadness in [David's] face, the concern, the obvious moral confusion," when Lestat refuses to remain human (*Thief,* 324).

Having succeeded in returning Lestat to his vampiric body, David undergoes a parallel restoration in that he gets to replace his worn-out old body with that of the younger Raglan James, who forced an exchange in order to trick Lestat into turning him into a vampire. Knowing David's moral convictions, Lestat regrets being the cause of David's never being able to get his old body back, since James has died of injuries suffered from Lestat. David's reaction is rather curious, however, as he tells Lestat, "It was *Faust,* Lestat. I'd bought youth. But the strange part was . . . I hadn't sold my soul!" (*Thief,* 376). In other words, he got something he wanted without having to pay the moral price. Consistent with this honest but self-serving perspective, David fights to the end in resisting Lestat's attack and his second transformation. As he drinks David's blood, Lestat can hear David's heart pounding "with rebellion, recrimination, you betray me, you betray me, you take me against my will" (*Thief,* 415). In the end, however, David forgives Lestat and, in a surprising admission, explains that he wanted vampirism: "You've given me the gift, but you spared me the capitulation. You've brought me over with all your skill and all your strength, but you didn't require of me the moral defeat. You took the decision from me, and gave me what I could not help but want" (*Thief,* 427).

Lestat, too, claims victory at the end, seeing his triumph as "the greedy wicked being in me" conquering weakness. As he writes, "There had been the opportunity for salvation—and I had said no" (*Thief,* 430). Finally accepting his true nature, Lestat presumably comes to an end of his rebellion against the insignificance of vampirism. As with many of Rice's protagonists, he completes his tale with a sense that "a new era was beginning" (*Thief,* 430). Since the appealing vulnerability of Lestat has always come from his human traits (to the extent of taking on a human form in this case) rather than the vampiric, however, this fourth novel in the series suggests a closure of Lestat's quests as a humanized vampire, or perhaps a future shift to other members of the vampire community who remain nearer to mortals and discontent with their vampirism.

Unlike David, who seems ultimately pleased with his transformation, Louis is still pained by his vampirism and is the most human of them all. A minor character here with little influence on Lestat's decisions, he remains extremely appealing. He has refused Lestat's offer to drink his more powerful blood many times (*Thief,* 105). Not the Promethean rebel either, Louis reprimands Lestat for always demanding attention and wanting to conquer someone or something. He says, "But there is no way to triumph. This is purgatory we're in, you and I. All we can be is thankful that it isn't actually hell" (*Thief,* 111). While Lestat has tried to find ways to make his presence known as a rock star, as a companion of the ancients Marius and Akasha, and now as a mortal, Louis has depended on his anonymity to get by (*Thief,* 112).

When Lestat is trapped in James's human body and begs Louis to turn him into a vampire, Louis's reaction comes as no surprise: "I wouldn't do it no matter how great your misery, no matter how strongly you pleaded, no matter what awful litany of events you set down before me. I wouldn't do it because I will not make another one of us for any reason under God" (*Thief,* 264). For Louis, Lestat's decision to return to vampirism is unfathomable. Yet he suffers because he loves Lestat and needs his love. Attempting to seduce him, Lestat senses "the predatory glaze that covered his eyes. But what was stronger than his thirst? His will" (*Thief,* 266). Louis's struggle is a miniportrait that builds on his major role in *Interview with the Vampire;* his ambivalence continues to endear him to the reader, especially as it reflects and exaggerates fin-de-siècle anxieties.

Raglan James, while clearly an important character because of his impact on Lestat, is nevertheless underdeveloped as a character in his own right, primarily because the reader sees him through Lestat. As tempter of Lestat he could be regarded as a Mephistopheles, and as signer of the pact he might also be seen as another Faust, yet the Faustian imagery is not connected with him as it is with Lestat and David. Neither an intellectual nor a compassionate man, he is clever and courageous in attracting Lestat, skilled with mysterious powers of soul travel, and obsessively materialistic. He tells Lestat he is "a thief in every respect. I don't enjoy something unless I bargain for it, trick someone out of it, or steal it. It's my way of making something out of nothing, you might say, which makes me like God!" (*Thief,* 127).

The limitations of James's character are accented by the attributes of Mojo, the magnificent dog he abuses and leaves behind. While Lestat's relationship with James remains superficial despite their inhabiting each other's bodies, Lestat does develop a deep affection for Mojo, who is based on Rice's own shepherd, according to Ramsland (355). Mojo's attraction to Lestat transcends the physical identities of vampire or human. When Lestat as a vampire first meets the dog, he is "vaguely thrilled by the fierce intelligence gleaming in his dark almond-shaped eyes" (*Thief*, 152). Amazingly, Mojo shows no "instinctive aversion" to Lestat's supernaturalism. Reasoning that the dog's name must have something to do with voodoo, Lestat decides that Mojo is "a protective charm" (*Thief*, 153) and a "good omen" that takes him back to his days as a young man with his own loyal dogs helping him fend off the wolves.

Mojo's presence as a fellow beast in the savage garden and his instinctive choice of Lestat over James justify his larger purpose in the novel. He becomes a reflection of Lestat, who marvels over the dog's "fierce stamina and his great gentleness." Lestat asks, "Had ever a beast looked so frightening yet been so full of calm, sweet affection?" (*Thief*, 391). Given the Faustian overtones, Mojo's paradoxical nature might also be viewed as a light-hearted inversion of Mephistopheles, who appears to Faust as a dog and disguises his evil in a harmless poodle form. Though later Lestat is entirely willing to transform David cruelly against his will, when he awakens to find Mojo licking the blood-tears away from his face, he says, "No. That you must never do!" Badly shaken, Lestat continues, "Never, never that blood. That evil blood" (*Thief*, 395). Mojo compensates for Louis's rejection of Lestat and for Lestat's alienation from the vampire community because of his rebellious deeds.

Gretchen, of course, operates in a moral framework and thoroughly rejects Lestat as a vampire. As innocent as Goethe's Gretchen in *Faust*, though modernized and strengthened with common sense and intelligence, Gretchen is devoted to a life of self-denial. In response to Lestat's philosophizing about the irrationality of her religious beliefs, "she said calmly that it didn't matter. What mattered was doing good" (*Thief*, 220). In keeping with her practical benevolence is her choice to have a sexual relationship with Lestat. She describes her chastity as a "destructive obsession" that interferes with her missionary work (*Thief*, 240). As she explains, "I had an abhorrence for my virginity—of the sheer perfection of my chastity. It seemed, no matter what one believed, to be a cowardly thing" (*Thief*, 234). In Rice's adaptation of the Faustian myth, Gretchen's goodness is a temptation to Lestat in his human state. In choosing not to follow her path of redemption, he ultimately saves himself as a vampire.

Consistent with Rice's emphasis elsewhere on secular morality and individual choice, Gretchen's reward is earthly, in the here-and-now, instead of the heavenly redemption afforded to Goethe's Gretchen. It is equated with a physical ecstasy that is appropriate to the existential nature of the universe, where experience itself is more important than its essence. It is also parallel but not superior to the intensities of vampirism. After coming to terms with Louis and bringing an end to these adventures, Lestat goes into a New Orleans church and lights a candle. As he recalls the great darkness of the rain forest, "the scent of blood coming from the wounds in Gretchen's hands," and the adventures of his human and vampiric life, including the wickedness of his creating Claudia, he decides that he is not lighting the candle for Gretchen, that is, for his belief in moral human goodness, but for himself, for "the devil who stood here now, because he loved candles, and he loved the making of light from light. Because there was no God in whom he believed, and no saints, and no Queen of Heaven" (*Thief,* 405).

Once again, images of Catholicism are adapted to intensify vampirism and existentiality. They are also linked to Blake's tiger "burning bright / In the forests of the night": "Yes. For the Vampire Lestat, that little candle, that miraculous tiny candle, increasing by that small amount all the light in the universe! And burning in an empty church the night long among those other little flames" (*Thief,* 406). Gretchen's life affirms the lamb, but Lestat's energy and passion are equally justified. Ironically, Gretchen wonders if God sent Lestat into a human body to be saved for the "[s]ame reason that Christ did it," for redemption (*Thief,* 235). Although Lestat suffers in his human form and pleads with Louis, "Take me off this cross" (*Thief,* 267), his redemption is an amoral inversion of Christ's. David's salvation, too, comes from his rebirth as a vampire and his escape from old age and death, from the "paltry thing, A tattered coat upon a stick" imaged in Yeats's "Sailing to Byzantium" that serves as the novel's frontispiece. Since David rises above the moral scruples that have prevented him from embracing vampirism, he illustrates the ambivalent popular appeal of the vampire. According to Punter, the satiation of the vampire's desires "would involve social disaster, as well as transgression of boundaries between the natural, the human and the divine" (120), yet like David, the reader finds the survival of death and the pleasures of eternal life irresistible.

Consistent with her other novels in the series, the drinking of blood continues to be the greatest pleasure of vampiric existence and a major source of eroticism, particularly the exchange of blood between vampires. Nothing in the book compares with the scene of David's transformation, which comes after a buildup of repressed sexual attraction between the two men. Having weakened David to the point of death with three attacks, Lestat narrates how David begins to respond by devouring Lestat's blood:

> The violent spasm shot through him. His back arched against my arm. And when I drew back now, my mouth full of pain, my tongue hurting, he drew up, hungering, eyes still blind. I tore my wrist. Here it comes, my beloved. Here it comes, not in little droplets, but from the very river of my being. And this time when the mouth clamped down upon me, it was a pain that reached all the way down to the roots of my being, tangling my heart in its burning mesh. . . . On and on he pulled, and against the bright darkness of my closed eyes I saw the thousands upon thousands of tiny vessels emptied and contracting and sagging like the fine black filaments of a spider's wind-torn web. (*Thief,* 418)

With language depicting an ecstatic oneness involving Lestat's pain as well as pleasure, this vampiric exchange stands out all the more because of the contrasting descriptions of earlier vampire kills and less satisfying, sexual relationships that Lestat has with women during his human existence.

When he stalks and kills the strangler of women, Lestat senses "the heat, the fullness, the sheer radiance of the living blood," but the eroticism of the passage is downplayed by the emphasis on Lestat's emptiness: "The fountain opened; his life was a sewer. All those old women, those old men. They were cadavers floating in the current; they tumbled against each other without meaning, as he went limp in my arms. No sport. Too easy. No cunning. No malice. Crude as a lizard he had been, swallowing fly after fly" (*Thief,* 22).

Unique to *The Vampire Chronicles* and certainly to vampire fiction are the awkward sexual encounters of Lestat operating as a man but still thinking as a vampire. With the restaurant worker whom he thoughtlessly rapes, Lestat is just getting used to the idea of having a body. He goes to the bathroom for the first time and watches with amazement his own erection. Aroused by thoughts of her blood as he embraces this woman, Lestat wonders, "Where was the pounding intensity of drawing near the victim, of the moment right before my teeth pierced the skin and the blood spilled all over my tongue?" (*Thief,* 188). Unable to control himself despite her violent struggles against him, he takes her. He finds the whole experience "paltry and common," "overwhelmingly dismal," not only because of his abuse of her but also because the "pleasure itself had been nothing" compared with that of vampirism. Once again the bad odors, the stickiness, and the lumpy mattress arouse distasteful rather than pleasurable sensations.

Sex with Gretchen proves satisfying, though here again, other sensations undercut the eroticism. Now more controlled and considerate, Lestat complies with Gretchen's request to end her virginity. Despite the description of physical pleasure, the tone is more analytic than erotic, as he consciously does what she wants to give her pleasure. When it is over, he says, "I don't think that it was union. On the contrary, it seemed the most violent of separations: two contrary beings flung at each other in heat and clumsiness, in trust and in menace, the feelings of each unknowable and unfathomable to the other—its sweetness terrible as its brevity; its loneliness hurtful as its undeniable fire" (*Thief,* 238). These thoughts lead to comparative speculations on his relationships with vampire women, especially his mother, Gabrielle, and her obvious preference for the vampiric state over the human. For now, Lestat assumes that, like David, Gretchen "would never ask for the Dark Gift or accept it" (*Thief,* 239). Not just a source of eroticism, Lestat's physical encounter with Gretchen, with the sense of loneliness and separation and the atypical roles they play with each other here—her indulgence and his restraint—contrasts with the fulfillment and oneness of his vampiric blood exchange with David and lead toward his finding a place in the savage garden.

As in her other Gothics, Rice uses setting to complement the characters' emotions and discoveries. The rain forest is Lestat's Romantic church, a wilderness of nature outside of human time and civilization, where the vampire can experience his own affinity with the deadly insects that are "dazzling in their hideousness and ghastly beauty" (*Thief,* 344). Less extreme than the jungle are the warm climates that humanized vampires typically prefer in Rice: New Orleans, Miami, and the Caribbean. Planning a trip with Lestat toward the end of the novel, David (still in James's body) describes the pleasures of the tropics: "You've never heard such music as you will hear in that garden in Barbados, and oh, those flowers, those mad savage flowers. It's your Savage Garden, and yet so tame and soft and safe!" (*Thief,* 377–78). Contrasting with the cold wind and snow from which Lestat suffers in Georgetown, where the climate reflects his alien and unnatural state in a human body, the southern locales provide a kind of midrange of human civilization and primitive lawlessness comfortable to the vampire.

Despite the cold spell connected with James's arrival in New Orleans, the language used by Lestat in describing Rice's favorite city continues to suggest vampiric affinities with the survival of nature in the urban scene: "Here and there one finds a stretch of street so overgrown one can scarce believe one is still within a city. Wild four-o'clocks and blue plumbago obscure the fences that mark property; the limbs of the oak bend so low they force the passerby to bow his head. Even in its coldest winters, New Orleans is always green" (*Thief,* 104). At the end of the book, when he returns to New Orleans, Lestat is happy once again to see the bananas' "graceful knifelike leaves" in New Orleans (*Thief,* 424).

More civilized than the southern settings and opposite to the savagery of the rain forest is the artificial luxury aboard the *Queen Elizabeth II,* where a human, frightened, and most vulnerable Lestat confronts Raglan James. Seeing that James is entirely at ease, Lestat writes, "These public rooms with their plastic and tinsel represent some pinnacle of elegance, and he is silently thrilled merely to be here" (*Thief,* 330). Lestat watches James's inability to appreciate and utilize his vampiric powers and recognizes his own major error in wanting to become human. He muses on the inappropriateness of the vampire in this artificial setting: "Did I seem the same wasteful fool to those who had known me and condemned me? Oh, pitiful, pitiful creature to have spent his preternatural life in this of all places, so painfully artificial, with its old and sad passengers, in unremarkable chambers of tawdry finery, insulated from the great universe of true splendours that lay beyond" (*Thief,* 331). Lestat's recognition of self-delusion shows the extent of his character change.

True to Romantic traditions, his salvation is found not in the "sourceless modern gloom" (*Thief,* 114) of the human or social realm but in the burning bright "forests of the night" where the tiger thrives. In a provocative way, Lestat's experience is similar to that of the persona in Yeats's poem "Sailing to Byzantium," which Rice cites at the beginning of the novel to evoke the theme of the brevity of human life and the eternity of art. In resuming a human body, Lestat experiences the sufferings of mortality expressed by Yeats's persona; but through vampirism, Lestat achieves the victory over old age and death longed for by the persona through the world of art. While the persona imagines being gathered into "the artifice of eternity," suggesting the loss as well as the gain of art's preservation of life, Lestat renews his vitality as a vampire through the experience of being human. Since David, too, manages to escape being "fastened to a dying animal," his experience parallels Lestat's and provides another variation on the ambivalence of vampirism as an antidote to mortality. In the nonvampiric Gothics, Rice will further explore these themes with human beings' efforts to preserve the body after death in *The Mummy* and spirits' invasions of human bodies in *The Witching Hour.*

Chapter Seven

The Mummy or Ramses the Damned and The Witching Hour

After the publication of *The Queen of the Damned* in 1988, Anne Rice turned away from *The Vampire Chronicles* to write two Gothic novels not in the vampire tradition, *The Mummy or Ramses the Damned* in 1989 and *The Witching Hour* in 1990. While shifting from vampires to other figures of the occult—mummies, witches, and spirits—these two books nonetheless take up key issues raised by vampirism: the contact between the living and the dead and the quest for immortality, especially how to sustain the human form beyond the grave. The action in both books builds on the origins of physical immortality described in the story of the good witches Maharet and Mekare and their struggle with Akasha in *The Queen of the Damned*. Instead of a bad spirit invading the body and turning humans into vampires who then require blood for sustenance, a miraculous elixir maintains Ramses in *The Mummy,* awakens Cleopatra from the dead, and provides eternal life for several humans. In *The Witching Hour,* where elements of science fiction blend with the Gothic to create more credibility than in *The Mummy,* the fusion of spirit with matter is achieved through the conception of a human fetus. The light-hearted conflict in *The Mummy,* with its tenuous causation and contrived outcome, make the novel difficult to take seriously; in *The Witching Hour,* however, the history of human-supernatural interactions and the tortuous plot that gradually entangles Michael Curry and Rowan Mayfair raises real questions about free will, predestination, and, finally, the nature of moral sensibility.

Unlike *The Vampire Chronicles,* where romantic elements account for a very small part of the larger conflict, in these novels the choices involved in love relationships are central, with the human protagonists finally indicating a preference for supernatural lovers: Julie Stratford dismisses her unofficial fiancé, Alex Savarell, for the mysterious Ramses in *The Mummy,* and Rowan Mayfair leaves her husband, Michael Curry, for the demonic Lasher in *The Witching Hour.* Both Julie and Rowan are strong and intelligent, but Rowan's character is far more developed and her decisions more integral to the central themes of the novel. Although their fates hinge on outcomes with men, Julie and Rowan are new types of protagonists for Rice, since they afford examples of human women rather than female vampires. Instead of focusing entirely on supernatural figures who narrate their own adventures, these two novels are more firmly grounded in human characters and their relationships with the supernatural. The stories are told from a human perspective, either by an omniscient voice with interior monologues for the human protagonists or, as demonstrated in *The Witching Hour,* by first-person histories and reports written by humans. Little suspense is involved in *The Mummy* after Ramses' awakening, since the ancient ruler turns out to be a friendly rather than threatening character. *The Witching Hour,* however, creates real suspense as it traces the 300-year history of the devilish Lasher and his horrific confrontations with humans.

Critical reception of the two novels supports distinctions in substance. In general, reviewers noted the superficiality of *The Mummy,* whether in its "flimsy conflict" or the missed opportunities for satiric commentary on twentieth-century values.[1] Several critics complained about its "lifeless prose,"[2] yet were amused by its campy use of the mummy genre.[3] According to Susan Ferraro, the underlying cause of these criticisms was that Rice began the project as a filmscript. When she and her collaborators could not get along, she abandoned the film and turned the idea into a novel. Ferraro quotes Rice as saying she created the book "just to spite them," she was "so furious" (77).

On the other hand, Rice told Ferraro she hoped *The Witching Hour* would be a great book, her "Gothic epic" (Ferraro, 77). It has received the more typically mixed reviews characteristic of *The Vampire Chronicles.* Critics mentioned the larger themes raised, such as regeneration through destruction and the question of free will.[4] The negative comments focus not on superficiality but on a tendency toward overwriting that has also been observed in assessments of *The Queen of the Damned.* While Rita Mae Brown described Rice's baroque style as "ornate" and "sensual," Patrick McGrath found the book "bloated" and repetitious.[5]

The Mummy

The Mummy takes a lighter and much less philosophical approach to the supernatural than Rice's previous books. Divided into two parts, *The Mummy* begins conventionally enough, with the famous British archaeologist Lawrence Stratford and his Egyptian assistant, Samir, discovering the tomb of Ramses the Great. Lawrence deciphers the hieroglyphs on the stone, which translate as: "In the year of the death of the Great Queen Cleopatra, as Egypt becomes a Roman province, I commit myself to eternal darkness; beware, all those who would let the rays of the sun pass through this door."[6] This information mystifies Lawrence because Cleopatra died 1,000 years after Ramses' reign. Lawrence's continued reading informs him that Ramses claims to have taken a "cursed elixir" that rendered him immortal, against the warnings of a Hittite priestess. While Lawrence is reading, he notices very odd changes in the mummy. "Why, even the hands seemed fuller. And one of the rings had almost broken through the wrapping" (*Mummy*, 24). Awhile later, "the whole figure looked fuller! And the ring, it was plainly visible now as if the finger, fleshing out, had burst the wrappings altogether" (*Mummy*, 26).

Unfortunately for Lawrence, his wastrel nephew, Henry, who comes to Egypt for money, does not share his enthusiasm for the discovery of Egyptian antiquities. Henry is intent on getting his uncle to sign a paper liquidating more of the family company's stock so that Henry can have yet another supply of funds. When Lawrence refuses, Henry spikes his coffee with some of the poison they had discovered in the ancient jars in the tomb. Upon leaving the tomb to announce Lawrence's sudden collapse, Henry imagines that the "grim, loathsome thing in the linen wrappings" is staring back at him. The scene then shifts to Lawrence's two relatives, who receive the news of his death: his brother, Randolph (who is also Henry's father), and Lawrence's daughter, Julie.

In tribute to Lawrence, the mummy and artifacts are moved to the Stratford home in London and put on display. When Henry visits his cousin Julie there and learns that she, too, is fed up with his demands for money, the mummy awakens just in time to save Julie from accepting a cup of poisoned coffee. In a classic reenactment of countless movie scenes, Julie watches as the mummy, "moving with a weak, shuffling gait, that arm outstretched before it, the dust rising from the rotted linens that covered it," attempts to strangle Henry, who flees in terror to the home of his mistress, Daisy. The mummy of Ramses the Great tells Julie that Henry murdered her father and now intends to kill her. Stunned by his physical beauty and regal bearing, Julie becomes sexually aroused rather than terrified. Attempting to suppress these feelings, she welcomes the handsome king into her home, provides him with all amenities, and secures the identity of "Mr. Reginald Ramsey" for him. She also agrees to accompany him to Egypt, where he feels he must

return to come to terms with his past and his reawakened passion for
Cleopatra before he can continue with his new life.

Meanwhile, Elliott, a former lover of Julie's father and the father of
her boyfriend, Alex, now a partially crippled, aging man, has heard
about Ramses' magic elixir and become obsessed with obtaining it.
Elliott dreams of the possibility of eternal life. As part 1 ends with the
whole group (Julie, Ramses, Elliott, and Henry) aboard ship to Egypt,
the reader is faced with the following: how will revenge be exacted
against Henry for the murder of Lawrence? what will come of Ramses'
strangely rekindled passion for Cleopatra? what role will the elixir play
in the fates of the various characters?

Part 2 takes place in Alexandria and Cairo, with steamer trips along
the Nile so that Ramses may revisit his ancient past. Having broken off
with Alex, Julie consummates her love with Ramses, who has extraordinary sexual prowess. Having been successful in testing the miraculous
potency of the elixir by resurrecting a mummified hand aboard ship,
Ramses later revives the mummy of Cleopatra in the Cairo Museum, as
Elliott looks on. After the skeletal horror that is Cleopatra wanders away
into the darkness, Ramses is arrested by museum authorities.

Elliott then picks up the vial of elixir, follows Cleopatra, and offers her
refuge at the apartment of Henry's mistress. As the terrified Henry tries
to shoot her, Cleopatra crushes him to death. When Elliott pours the
elixir on Cleopatra's wounds, her skin miraculously heals and her infamous beauty returns, along with her ravenous lust. (One effect of the
elixir is the desire to make love "perpetually.") She then seduces Elliott
and embarks on a sexual rampage, attacking and raping a series of
young men fatally attracted to her beauty and killing them by breaking
their necks. While she is on her deadly tour through Cairo, Lawrence's
death is poetically avenged. In an extraordinary coincidence, Samir's
cousin turns out to be an unscrupulous dealer of fake mummies and
relics for tourists. Always happy to find a corpse, he drops the dead
Henry into a vat of chemicals. A merchant on the street later offers
Elliott a "great bargain," which he says is the mummy of a great king.
As Elliott moves closer to examine the mummy wrappings, he sees
"beneath that thick veneer" the face of Henry Stratford.

Meanwhile, the narrative has been shifting back and forth between
Cleopatra's exploits and the efforts of Julie, Ramses, and Samir to evade
legal authorities investigating the murders. Ramses leaves Julie to find
Cleopatra and administer more of the elixir to heal her wounds. When
she asks him why he brought her back from the dead, he tells her: "I

wanted you to be with me, the way you are now" (*Mummy,* 339), a desire that does not say much for his supposedly deep love for Julie. Even after their love making, the hot-tempered Cleopatra is still angry with Ramses for not sharing the elixir with her former lover, Antony. She gashes Ramses' neck with a piece of glass and sets off to kill again.

Conveniently, she meets up with Alex, who, eager to fill the void created by Julie, makes passionate love with Cleopatra, though he has no idea of who she is or the danger he is in. Meanwhile, Elliott, wanting to save Ramses for his own reasons, fabricates a story for the investigators that pins all of the crimes onto Henry. All of the characters have a final confrontation at the Opera House in Cairo, where they go to see a performance of *Aida.* Cleopatra tries to kill Julie in the powder room in revenge for Ramses' unwillingness to give Antony the elixir. Cleopatra flees with Alex, and Ramses pursues them in a car chase that ends with Cleopatra's car being stuck on the railroad tracks. While Alex escapes to flee the oncoming train, Cleopatra is trapped in the car when it explodes. Later, a saddened Julie, having refused to take the elixir herself, travels along with the despondent Alex on board a ship to London. It looks as if the former lovers might renew their relationship at this point, except that the naive Alex pales in comparison with the immortal Ramses in Julie's eyes. Distraught over her loss of Ramses and dismayed at the prospects of life with Alex, Julie considers jumping overboard, but Ramses reappears to offer her eternal life once again. This time she accepts and drinks down the tumbler of elixir. As they resume their love making, Elliott, too, drinks the elixir, uttering "a soft cry intended for no one, merely the smallest, most spontaneous expression of his joy" (*Mummy,* 431). Finally, the charred Cleopatra, who had been taken to a Cairo hospital, revives and promptly seduces a young doctor.

The Mummy provides a variation of the situation of many mummy films and stories that Rice pays tribute to in the dedication of her novel. Typically, the awakened and usually misunderstood monster avenges himself on the humans who exploit him or returns from the dead to claim something or someone that rightfully belongs to him; he then wreaks havoc on the guilty, greedy parties. Finally, he returns to his tomb, often with the help of courageous human protagonists. A sense of closure is usually provided at the end, when the mummy is destroyed if he is truly monstrous or when he is returned to the dead if he is the victim of foul play. Ramses' coming to life, his resurrecting a mummified hand and ghoulish Cleopatra, her crushing Henry to death and stalking other young men stand out as scenes intended to evoke conventional horrors of the genre.

In Sir Arthur Conan Doyle's "The Ring of Thoth," one of the mummy stories Rice alludes to in the dedication, a student of Egyptology, John Vansittart Smith, is alone at night in a museum room full of Egyptian artifacts and mummy cases. He sees an attendant named Sosra unwrap a mummy and embrace the preserved body of a female. From the story Sosra narrates to Smith, it is clear that the wandering Sosra has paid the high cost of securing immortality with a potion, since he has been eternally separated for centuries from Atma, the woman he adores. For Sosra, his "accursed health" has been worse "than the foulest disease."[7] Finally recovering the ring containing the antidote that will end the curse of eternal life, Sosra accomplishes his objective by drinking it down. In the newspaper the next day Smith reads how the authorities discovered Sosra's body "lying dead upon the floor with his arms round one of the mummies" (Doyle, 263).

Perhaps for a more contemporary audience, Rice discards the moral lesson of the elixir and turns the horror and gloom of this romantic plot into a lighthearted fantasy, since the elixir enables the lovers Ramses and Julie to go off happily together into immortality. Since Ramses resumes his handsome human form and finds a new love, why should he return to the tomb? Unlike the Faustian vampires or traditional mummies who pay a high price for eternal life, Julie and Elliott have nothing to lose by taking the elixir. The only apparent danger is having the elixir get into the wrong hands, as "whole peoples" could render themselves immortal and thereby endanger "the very rhythm of life and death" (*Mummy,* 319). This prospect remains undeveloped, however, since Samir does not want the potion, and Elliott's ambitions are not so great. Despite her assertion that this "secret must be destroyed utterly," Julie debates only briefly with herself later about taking the potion before she returns happily into Ramses' arms. In omitting serious reflections on the quest for immortality, *The Mummy* resembles the 1992 film *Death Becomes Her,* a satiric send-up of the perennial preoccupation with finding a way to remain young and beautiful. Going far beyond face lifts, tummy tucks, lip injections, surgical extractions, and the like, the female protagonists resort to an expensive potion that guarantees immortality, with some major physical touch-ups necessary from time to time that make for comic effect.

The characters in *The Mummy* are far less complicated than the introspective and philosophical vampires who attempt to come to terms with the meaninglessness of their immortality, the origins of vampirism, the essence of moral choice, and the nature of the contemporary reality in which they find themselves. Rather, they resemble the more simplistic characters of popular television movies. The stupid Henry, for instance, is motivated entirely by greed; Samir is the typically noble servant who has a true understanding of Egyptian culture and undying loyalty to Ramses. As an intelligent woman, Julie has the potential to become a strong character, but under the influence of her love for Ramses she fits the stereotypical model of women in modern Radcliffean Gothics. As Cynthia Wolff explains, "the author assigns interesting talents and a measure of intelligence to her heroine at the beginning of the novel, and these then vanish as soon as the young woman is swept into danger" (102). While Cleopatra is a shallow version of Akasha as the prototype of the cruel, egotistical woman, Alex, who nods off during serious plays and remains awake for Gilbert and Sullivan, is capable of satisfying a women in bed but is otherwise pitifully naive. He tells Cleopatra, for instance, that his friends have nothing to do with the murder and mayhem detailed in the Cairo newspapers and that the whole "foolishness about stealing a mummy from the Cairo Museum" [who happens to be Cleopatra] is "hogwash."

Ramses' potential as a source of social satire and commentary is sacrificed to his less provocative role as ideal mate for Julie. He conforms to the more popular romantic-hero type, as he combines imperial command with intelligence, handsomeness, and extraordinary sexual capability. After educating himself quickly by devouring many books and magazines along with huge quantities of food, Ramses has little to say about the differences in culture between past and present. Apart from noting the persistence of poverty and the foolishness of Karl Marx, he has no time for philosophizing, since he must try to undo the terrible mistake of awakening Cleopatra.

Perhaps the most potentially interesting character in the book is the ailing Elliott Savarell, the Earl of Rutherford, who, though still in love with his wife, has managed to attract the love of nearly everyone else. The former lover of Lawrence Stratford, he also had a brief fling with Henry. Risking danger to help Cleopatra and rising to the occasion of her seduction, he earns the gratitude of Ramses, who decides that he is worthy of the elixir. Ramses sees Elliott as "the man whose advice would always have been good for him, the man for whom he felt a deep and uncertain affection that just might be love" (*Mummy*, 392). Elliott's desire for the elixir motivates him, but he is never willing to go as far as Henry to achieve his own ends. The marginality and quiet wisdom of his character, afforded by ill health and age, remain undeveloped here but remind the reader of the greater philosophical perspective afforded by Rice's vampiric males in the *Chronicles*.

Without this perspective, there is little room in the novel for the characters to engage in internal struggles. Evolution of character does not drive the plot, as it does in other Rice works: Louis's struggle with his vampirism throughout the *Interview*, Lestat's challenge to humans and vampires alike in *The Vampire Lestat*, and his transformation leading to an acceptance of vampirism in *The Tale of the Body Thief*. The terror in *The Mummy* comes in scenes characteristic of the mummy genre, especially the mummies of Ramses and Cleopatra coming to life, with Cleopatra as the grisly monster unleashed on unsuspecting humans. Before getting enough elixir, her eyes bulge "from their half-eaten sockets. White rib bones gleamed through a huge wound in her side. Half of her mouth was gone, and a bare stretch of clavicle was drenched in oozing blood" (*Mummy*, 262).

The eroticism of Rice's *Chronicles* persists in *The Mummy*, but, apart from the heightened sexual needs and powers of Ramses and Cleopatra, the sexual encounters are rendered more ordinary without the vampire context and the sacramental significance of blood. When Ramses consummates his love for Julie, he leads her to his tent in the Egyptian desert. After he undresses her, she tells him to "Batter down the door," as she is a virgin. "He went through the seal. Pain; a tiny sputtering pain that burnt itself out in her mounting passion immediately. She was kissing him ravenously; kissing the salt and heat from his neck, his face, his shoulders. He drove hard into her, over and over again, and she arched her back, lifting herself, pressing herself against him" (*Mummy*, 230). While Lestat's union resulted in his gaining special vampiric power from Akasha, Julie's loss of innocence is simply a part of loving Ramses. Unconvincingly modern for a 1914 female protagonist, Julie's sexual pleasure anticipates the much stronger sexuality of Rowan Mayfair in *The Witching Hour* and reflects the unadorned eroticism more typical of Rice's erotic books than *The Vampire Chronicles*.

In another departure from the *Chronicles*, the narrative focuses almost entirely on the present and not on the past. Instead of moving her characters back and forth in time and locating them in countries all over the world, Rice limits her settings primarily to London and Egypt. Rather than creating a mood that accents the sensibility of character, the scenic details provide the concrete visualization of a film script with the placement of characters on the set. For instance, when Lawrence is attempting to decipher the hieroglyphs in Ramses' tomb, "He turned back to the jars on the deck. The sun was making the little room an inferno. Taking his handkerchief, he carefully lifted the lid of the first jar before him. Smell of bitter almonds. Something as deadly as cyanide" (*Mummy*, 22). The emphasis on placement of characters and articles in rooms, along with gestures and movements of characters while they are speaking, results in a visual or set-direction effect that lacks the resonance of the larger spaces and time periods of the vampire books.

The Mummy shows Rice's flexibility in moving away from vampires to other supernatural beings that appeal to many contemporary readers—perhaps the same readers whose attendance in massive numbers turned the King Tut exhibit into a cultural phenomenon when it toured the United States in 1979 and 1980. As Gothic images, however, the mummies of Ramses and Cleopatra do not invite Grixti's searching analysis of human concerns raised by Rice's vampires or reflect her originality in restoring Romantic stature to the supernatural.

The Witching Hour

The action of *The Witching Hour* is deeply immersed in the past as it pertains to the present and creates a feeling of prophecy that the outcome fulfills. The omniscient perspective is mixed with first-person voices that develop simultaneous stories converging toward a climactic outcome, the overall pattern of the plot structure inviting allegorical interpretations. It thus resembles the richly layered *Queen of the Damned* more than the one-dimensional *Mummy*. Unlike *The Queen of the Damned*, whose plot has a definite resolution in the defeat of Akasha (evil) by Mekare (good), the conflicts in *The Witching Hour* create interrelated and complex themes left interestingly unresolved. The plot, gradually unveiling more and more coincidences that suggest the protagonists—Rowan and Michael—are pawns in the hands of a large destiny, raises issues of free will and predestination. In addition to posing typically Gothic questions about the nature of the supernatural and its relationship to the human, the triangular relationship with Rowan caught between Michael and Lasher also sets up a kind of Hawthornian conflict of head and heart. Rowan gives up her life as a surgeon, where intellect presides over emotion, to become involved in a consuming love relationship with Michael, where the heart dominates. Finally, she is drawn into an irresistible yet ambivalent union of head and heart with Lasher, which she achieves only by coming to terms with her past and assuming her predestined role in

the Mayfair family. While the outcome seems to provide mystical fulfillment and satisfaction for Rowan, her development is clouded by our
knowledge of the dark history of Lasher, the evil means by which he
accomplishes his ends, and the cruel abandonment of Michael, who loses
both wife and child.

The fulfillment of the Mayfair destiny is told in four sections, with
part 1, "Come Together," referring primarily to Rowan Mayfair and
Michael Curry and the events that link their destinies. The narrative
opens with Dr. Larry Petrie reminiscing over the case history of a former
patient in New Orleans, Deirdre Mayfair, and feeling guilty that he was
unable to do more for her. He recounts to Aaron Lightner, a member of
the Talamasca group that researches occult phenomena, an encounter he
had with a mysterious man who knocked the syringe out of his hand
when he tried to give Deirdre the drugs that kept her sedated. Aaron
tells Petrie there was nothing else he could have done for Deirdre. With
suspense clearly established through Petrie's experience and Lightner's
acknowledgment of bizarre happenings in the Mayfair family, the action
shifts to Michael Curry in San Francisco.

Still recovering from his near death in a drowning accident, Michael
keeps reliving his disaster at sea and his rescue by Rowan Mayfair to
understand why he has strange new telepathic powers in his hands.
Relying on alcohol to dull these sensations and hang onto his sanity, he
recalls his childhood in New Orleans, when he often observed a mysterious man loitering around a Garden District mansion. The action then
shifts to Father Mattingly, whose recollections of Deirdre's school days,
her mother's death, Deirdre's own confession as a child, and rumors of
the family's witchery from his parishioners add further credence to the
Mayfair mysteries. From Father Mattingly in New Orleans the story
returns to Rowan Mayfair in San Francisco. As the only descendant of
Deirdre Mayfair, Rowan was given up for adoption to another Mayfair
named Ellie and her husband, Graham. Rowan signed a paper after
Ellie's death promising never to return to New Orleans or to have anything to do with her relatives. Rowan has special telepathic talents. The
same power that caused her to kill three people unintentionally through
her anger has also helped her to make uncanny medical detections that
enable her to be an excellent neurosurgeon. Totally committed to her
work, she nonetheless finds an outlet for her sexual appetites in random
and rough sexual encounters with men who want no commitment.
Finally, Michael manages to meet with Rowan, who he hopes will be
able to shed some light on what happened when she rescued him from

the water and took him aboard her yacht, the *Sweet Christine*. Their attraction for one another is immediate, and their intimacy includes not only sex but a sharing of their deepest fears. Michael explains that he wears gloves to protect himself from the visions that occur whenever he touches something; Rowan confesses to Michael that she is haunted by her own "terrible potential for evil."

Still without an explanation for the visions he has had since the rescue, Michael wrenches himself away from Rowan and flies to New Orleans to discover their meaning. Trailed by Aaron, Michael revisits the house that fascinated him as a young boy, where he has a vision of the same strange man from his childhood in a keyhole doorway. This same man simultaneously appears to Rowan in her house in San Francisco. Finally, Aaron identifies himself to Michael, and through his research on the Mayfair family they see connections between Michael's visions of the New Orleans house, which belongs to the Mayfair family, and his boat rescue by Rowan.

As Aaron continues to explain the Talamasca's involvement in the history of the Mayfairs, Rowan learns of her mother Deirdre's death in New Orleans. Carlotta Mayfair calls with the news, not intending to tell Rowan but her adopted mother, Ellie, who, unbeknown to Carlotta, is dead. Rowan is stunned not only at the news of Deirdre's death but at the fact that Ellie never told her that Deirdre was her mother. Moreover, she is angry that Ellie made her sign an agreement to stay away from the Mayfair family no matter what pretexts they used to establish contact. Rowan decides to break her promise and attend Deirdre's funeral, asking that the coffin not be closed until she gets there, a request that does not please the elderly Carlotta. Rowan is shocked to realize that she saw the male apparition just after the moment her mother died. This first part ends with Rowan's preparations for departure to New Orleans, while Michael sits down in the Talamascan retreat house and begins to read the voluminous files on the Mayfairs.

It takes most of part 2, "The Mayfair Witches" (and approximately one-third of the entire novel) for Michael to read through the documentation on the Mayfairs, which dates back to 1689. In between the Talamascan first-person accounts, the omniscient voice occasionally provides glimpses of Rowan's efforts to reach Michael, her leaving her post at the hospital, her bizarre orgasm created by an unseen lover on the plane, and her attendance at her mother's wake and funeral. It is difficult to do justice to the specifics of the files, as the 300-year history is crammed with genealogical details that include full-blown characterizations of the first Mayfair witches and their descendants, as well as their relationships with the same mysterious spirit of Lasher as gleaned from all kinds of sources and speculations. Despite the variety of Talamascan reporters who have established contact with the family, and the distinctions among the witches and family members themselves, a recurrent pattern emerges from the experiences recorded after the initial invocation of Lasher by the Scottish Suzannah of the Mayfair in the seventeenth century.

This spirit is called Lasher by Suzannah for the first time because of his animation of matter—the wind he sends "that lashes the grasslands, for the wind that lashes the leaves from the trees." Ironically, Suzannah learns the magic of witchcraft that creates Lasher from a witch-trial judge, who reads her a book, *Demonologie*. Lasher becomes a loyal servant who does her bidding and brings her riches. Suzannah's daughter, Deborah, who is also tried for being a witch, tells Petyr van Abel, the man recording the history, that Suzannah was unlearned and did not know how to control Lasher, whose punishment of Suzannah's enemies revealed her as a witch. While Deborah mistakenly thinks that she has Lasher under control, the question comes up again and again as to what the limits of Lasher's powers are, what his intentions are, and whether or not he can be destroyed. These questions are extremely significant, since Rowan is the present Mayfair who has yet to come into her full inheritance. Throughout the history, Lasher serves one witch who is the direct female descendant of the one before; she wears the famous emerald necklace that Lasher procured for Deborah and controls the vast wealth and holdings of the Mayfair estate accumulated over the centuries. When a Mayfair witch dies, there is always a storm created by Lasher, who moves on to the next female heir.

Danger awaits intruders like the Talamascan Petyr van Abel, Stuart Townsend, and Arthur Langtry, whose efforts to separate Lasher from his current Mayfair witch and disrupt the incestuous perpetuation of the family end in their violent deaths. Each reporter includes as many sources as possible to establish authenticity. Schoolteacher-nuns, friends, other relatives in the family, and lovers of the Mayfairs, like Julien's Richard Llewellyn, all provide similar descriptions of weird, violent, and grisly scenes, some of which are referred to again in the present, such as the human heads and other preserved body parts kept in jars and the dolls made out of the flesh and bones of Mayfair corpses.

Michael concludes his reading of the history with a description of Deirdre's pathetic life in mental institutions and an up-to-date report on

Rowan's past, including her telekinetic abilities. The past and the present action now converge, with Michael clearly understanding the menace of the Mayfair legacy but not his role in it. He wonders whether he is exercising his own free will in choosing to do good or simply fulfilling his part in a scheme predestined since his childhood. While he attempts to figure out the significance of his ominous visions of the keyhole doorway and the number 13, Rowan goes to visit Carlotta at the Mayfair house after the funeral. Having gone to great lengths—including murder—to resist the power of Lasher, Carlotta provides yet another perspective on the family and fills in important missing links in the Talamascan coverage. She, too, raises the issue of human choice, as she tells Rowan that she has the power to choose not to be a Mayfair witch and to resist Lasher.

Unable to control her fury over what she sees as Carlotta's unspeakable cruelty to her mother, Deirdre, and grandmother and the murderous lengths she went to in fighting off Lasher, Rowan once again demonstrates her telekinetic power to kill. Rowan's anger shifts to terror when she realizes what she has done and becomes aware of sounds in the house. She puts on Deirdre's emerald that is now part of her legacy and challenges Lasher to appear. As she waits for him, she senses that the life she has made for herself in California is only a "detour in the dark gleaming path of her destiny," which is here in this house and in her identity as a Mayfair. A face and form begin to take shape and then to fade; as she pleads for the figure to return, the dark form coming through the doors turns out to be Michael.

Suspensefully delaying the confrontation between Rowan and Lasher that the whole action has been building toward, the narrative focuses instead on more practical concerns. Michael and Rowan compare notes on the Mayfair history and its meaning for them, explore the house, and decide to renovate it as their home, despite the grisly discoveries of Stuart Townsend's decayed body rolled up in a carpet and the hideous jars of human heads. Rowan also gets to know her relatives, meets with the Mayfair attorneys to discuss her legacy, and asserts her intention of investing some of her vast fortune in a foundation for medical research. Mixed within the upbeat plans for their future are ominous signs pointing in another direction: Michael's visions that convince him of Lasher's intentions to become human, the recurrent sounds of a baby crying, and, most important, Rowan's cold and aloof moods.

This blend of realistic details concerning Rowan and Michael's happiness and supernatural phenomena attesting to Lasher's presence creates tantalizing suspense in the shorter part 3, "Come into My Parlor." House renovations and November wedding plans continue, while Lasher uses flowers mysteriously to get Rowan's attention and attempts to put the emerald around her neck during a dream. Michael continues to speculate about the meaning of his recurring visions, such as when the dead Mayfairs visit him in the newly renovated pool. Still believing that his visions are good and that his role is to break the chain of Lasher's control over the Mayfair witches, Michael does solve the puzzle of the number 13 and the doorway. He does not know how it will happen, but feels certain that Rowan is somehow intended to be the doorway for Lasher to make his passage from the spiritual world to the human, since she is the thirteenth Mayfair witch. But Rowan is convinced she is strong enough to resist Lasher and muses to herself that 13 means bad luck for him.

In part 4, "The Devil's Bride," Rowan's confidence proves ill-founded. The happiness of her wedding day, enhanced by the realization that she is pregnant, is overshadowed by the sudden appearance of Lasher just after midnight. After Michael and Rowan return from their Florida honeymoon, Michael flies to San Francisco to settle his affairs. While he is away, Rowan and Lasher become intimate. Lasher's explanations of his lonely existence enlist Rowan's sympathy. Like Mephistopheles tempting Faust, he arouses her scientific curiosity by telling her he has the secrets of immortality. He also gives her immense pleasure as a lover. By the time Michael returns home, Rowan loves both Michael and Lasher, and she longs for Lasher's kiss right after Michael has left her bed.

Despite Michael and Aaron's joining forces in an effort to defeat Lasher, Michael's visions, Rowan's talents as a Mayfair and her research interests as a surgeon, and the Talamascan histories all culminate in a graphic outcome, whereby Lasher violently aborts the fetus in Rowan's womb on Christmas Eve and takes it for his own human form. When she discovers his true intentions, Rowan invokes her telekinetic powers to thwart him, but he is too strong for her. Observing the grotesque newborn-man before her, she instinctively tends to its needs and offers yet another meaning to the doorway: "This was a new door all right. It was the door she'd glimpsed a million years ago in her girlhood when she'd first opened the magical volumes of scientific lore" (*Hour,* 937).

Before Rowan leaves the country with Lasher, Michael returns to fight him and ends up nearly dead in the pool. Once again he experiences visions of the Mayfair spirits, who tell him that now they will be able to return from the dead and that his role all along has been to return Rowan to New Orleans and impregnate her in order to save them. Left alone in the house to reflect in a diary upon what has happened, Michael persists in his belief that these spirits lied and that he was intended to keep Rowan away from Lasher, an interpretation of events that Aaron clearly does not share. Michael ends the book affirming his beliefs in the capacity for human goodness and free will, vowing to remain in the house and wait for Rowan to return.

While Michael's faith in the tendency of humans to choose good provides "the only true moral force in the physical world," the 300-year history of the Mayfair witches proves otherwise: even Rowan feels that she is fulfilling her destiny. Michael's stubborn assertion that free will is the wellspring of human dignity is challenged in the context of the Mayfair history, in which Lasher's demonic power prevails. This same secular morality is relished by Lestat in *The Vampire Lestat* and affirmed by Maharet in *The Queen of the Damned*, where her intention to let the human race evolve in its own way without supernatural interference wins out over the schemes of Akasha.

Rice relates this universal theme to issues of science and morality in the same way that writers like Mary Shelley and Nathaniel Hawthorne, whose works are echoed here and there in *The Witching Hour*, did before her. In a sense, Lasher's "birth" recreates Frankenstein's monster, and Rowan's fascination with it is similar to Victor Frankenstein's and to that of the overreaching scientists in Hawthorne, whose heads dominate their hearts. Lasher's mutation to human form speaks to the contemporary reader's fear of science, especially research on genetic manipulation, fetal tissue, and organ donation. Aaron sees Lasher's intentions as immoral because they are unnatural, a perversion of nature. He tells Michael, "it's a struggle between normal life and aberration. Between evolution on the one hand and disastrous intervention on the other" (*Hour*, 915). In fact, Lasher's intentions may be more immoral than Aaron imagines. Lasher has during the whole history of his involvement with the Mayfair witches promoted incest in the family. It appears that in entering the body of Rowan's fetus—thereby becoming her son as well as her lover—he has achieved this goal. In a way, Rowan's fate illustrates what Stephen King calls a Jamesian theme in Gothic fiction, "the idea that ghosts, in the end, adopt the motivations and perhaps the very souls of those who behold them. If they are malevolent, their malevolence comes from us" (246).

Rowan is an independent woman in Rice's fiction, a person who has the strength to put her powers to good use in her neurosurgery. As she confides to Michael, "I'm a doctor today because I am trying to deny that power, I have built my life upon compensation for that evil!" (*Hour*, 182). Her real fear is that she is "a person who could really do harm. A person with a terrible potential for evil" (*Hour*, 199). A thoroughly liberated woman, Rowan has inherited not only the Mayfair witchery but also the sensuality and strength of will characteristic of the ancestor whom she most resembles, Mary Beth, who lived from 1872 to 1925. In the Talamascan history, Aaron reports how Mary Beth was undisputed head of the household and built an enormous fortune with investments all over the world. He also writes that "we have more stories about her sensual appetites than any other aspect of her." He continues, "one can see that she behaved more like a man of the period than a woman in this regard, merely pleasing herself as a man might, with little thought for convention or respectability" (*Hour*, 449). Rice's eroticism is more integral here than in *The Mummy*, because it characterizes the independence and daring of the Mayfair witches, particularly Rowan.

When Michael enters her life, she finds not only sexual gratification but a love relationship that arouses her deeper emotional needs. Once she discovers who she is and meets her relatives, she feels a real sense of belonging that she has never had in her life. She tells Michael later on, "Two days ago I was a person without a past or a family. And now I have both of those things. The most agonizing questions of my life have been answered" (*Hour*, 695). The woman who "had never wanted babies" is joyous when she does become pregnant. Responding to Michael's wondering whether she should see a doctor and when she will feel the baby inside her, Rowan brings the professional's perspective to her pregnancy: "It's a quarter of an inch long . . . It doesn't weigh an ounce. But *I* can feel it. It's swimming in a state of bliss, with all its tiny cells multiplying" (*Hour*, 849).

This scientific side of Rowan is ultimately what makes her vulnerable to Lasher, though at first he exploits her sexual appetites. Under Lasher's sexual sway, Rowan has no guilt, no sense of betraying Michael. Lasher also appeals to Rowan's sympathy by telling her how lonely he has always been and how much he wants to become human. Finally, without explaining exactly how he intends to achieve this end, he arouses her passion for science: "Imagine, Rowan, when the mutation is complete and I have a body, infused with my timeless spirit, what you can learn from this" (*Hour*, 876). In the gruesome scene when he takes Rowan's baby from her womb, Rowan's revulsion changes to excitement as her Faustian desires are realized: "I need a microscope. I need to take blood samples. I need to see what the tissues really are now! God, I need all these things! I need a fully equipped laboratory" (*Hour,* 936).

Michael, meanwhile, though far more substantial than his counterpart, Alex Savarell, in *The Mummy,* is no match for the supernatural Lasher. Michael has the sensitivity, the substance, and the sexuality Rowan has never found in any man, but he still cannot satisfy her desire for vast scientific knowledge. Michael's role is more like Maharet's in *The Queen of the Damned,* in that his secular morality and belief in the human capacity for goodness represent the moral polar extreme to the rational schemes of Lasher, who manipulates his human pawns for his own selfish ends. In their triangular relationship, Michael represents Rowan's loving, emotional side as a woman, while Lasher symbolizes her egotistical rationality as a scientist. Seeing Michael and Lasher as projections of Rowan's internal self is invited when Rowan's vision of Lasher's first actual appearance fades into the real form of Michael, as she stares "into the confusion of light and shadow." Michael's name is chosen carefully; Rowan comments on his being her archangel, and on Christmas Eve Aaron gives Michael an old silver medal of St. Michael, the archangel who drives the devil into hell. Unlike his namesake, Michael does not, of course, emerge victorious after his battle with Lasher in this novel.[8] Philosophically, however, his determination to believe in free will, despite all the evidence to the contrary that Lasher has planned the events of his life from his childhood through his impregnation of Rowan, affirms a persistent and natural human attitude that is good.

The Witching Hour focuses on the more traditional Gothic fear that humans have of the supernatural rather than on the supernatural characters themselves, as in the *Chronicles.* Lasher differs from Rice's vampires in that he does not engage the reader's sympathies. His claims to feeling outcast and lonely over the centuries seem all too transparent compared with his long history of manipulating human beings for his own purposes. Born finally as a human child, he is truly monstrous; a horrified Rowan sees the thing lying on its back, "its man-sized head turning from side to side with its cries, its thin arms elongating even as she watched it" (*Hour,* 933). While the large head may symbolize Lasher's unnatural role as rational schemer, the descriptions of Lasher first as "it" or "the creature" and then as "he" point out Rowan's own changing point of view, as her revulsion turns to scientific curiosity and she moves to help him survive.

Instead of focusing on a single figure moving toward self-awareness as in the *Interview* and *The Vampire Lestat,* Rice builds first toward the union between Rowan and Michael and then Rowan and Lasher by continuing the narrative strategies of *The Queen of the Damned*. Once again, the omniscient voice shifts easily from one group of characters to another—early in the book from Father Mattingly's visit to Deirdre, to Michael's childhood, to the memories of Rita Mae, a childhood friend of Deirdre Mayfair, and then to Rowan's professional life—and develops simultaneous, converging stories that create suspense because the reader sees mysterious connections that the characters do not.

Within the omniscient voice, interior monologues capture the feeling of a first-person immediacy, as when Aaron asks Rowan if she would like to go up to the coffin to see her mother, Deirdre: "Yes, please, take me up. Please help me! Make my legs move. But they were moving. He had slipped his arm around her and he was guiding her, so easily, and the conversation had started up again, thank God, though it was a low respectful hum, from which she could extract various threads at will" (*Hour,* 594). As in Michael's interpretations of visions and his diary at the end, the monologues also develop a Jamesian relativity of perspective that contributes to the issue of free will and predestination, since the character's view not only provides credibility but leaves open the possibility of misinterpreting events.

While the historical myth of *The Queen of the Damned* is provided by Maharet's lengthy first-person narration within the omniscient voice, here the Talamascan recorders lend authenticity to the supernatural. Typically, the more formal, passive voice contributes to the objective tone, as in the case of Petyr van Abel's death: "In spite of extensive head wounds, Petyr was easily and undeniably identified by van Clausen, as well as by Charlotte Fontenay, who rode into Port-au-Prince when she heard tell of it, and was violently disturbed by Petyr's death, and 'took to her bed' in grief" (*Hour,* 372). Detailed references to abundant sources and dates establish credibility.

These conscientious and copious accounts do result in repetition, despite the wonderful inventiveness, variety, and completeness of the stories described within each Mayfair generation. The recurrent pattern is as follows: the Talamascan establishes contact with a Mayfair family member or witch at some peril to his own life; he traces the often incestuous parentage of the present witch; he experiences and records the occult phenomena that occur during her childhood and schooldays; he describes her relationships with other members of the family; he follows her life through marriage, children, and death; and, with the exception of Aaron Lightner, he meets his own violent end because he poses a threat to Lasher. Shortening the genealogical history of the Mayfairs would have avoided this repetition, but the past pertains to the present not only in sustaining suspense and developing the question of human choice but in rounding out the portraits of the heiresses to the legacy. For example, Carlotta's explanations to Rowan are even more revealing because of the questions raised in the reports; Rowan's personality is clearer because of her likeness to Mary Beth Mayfair and her difference from Stella, Antha, and Deirdre; Michael's visions are all the more difficult to interpret because of the reader's speculation on the motivation of the dead Mayfairs who appear, such as Deborah or Julien.

The central source of Gothic anxiety throughout arises from the overall movement toward the union of Rowan and Lasher. Rice tantalizes the reader with Rowan's sensations of being watched and signs of Lasher's presence: his violation of her as an invisible lover on the plane, his rustlings in the house, and his leaving flowers about. In an echo of Hawthorne's "Rappaccini's Daughter" that supports the image of Lasher as a perversion of nature, Rowan sees a lurid-looking iris in the garden as it springs up "savage and shivering, a hideous mouth of a flower, its stem snapping back now as though a cat darting through the brush had bent it down carelessly" (*Hour,* 769). Once he actually appears, the source of anxiety is how Rowan will respond to Lasher and how she will fit into his still mysterious plan.

As the book's climactic outcome illustrates, Rice sustains traditionally Radcliffean terror yet also delves into the graphic horror characteristic of Matthew Lewis. *The Witching Hour* contains not only violent murders and grisly deaths but also haunting episodes and images that together strengthen the impact of the grotesque, the unnatural, the perversion of nature that certain Mayfairs have become under Lasher. Particularly unforgettable are the dolls of Mayfairs made by other family members (assisted by Lasher) from flesh, bone, and blood taken from the dead. There are also ghastly jars and bottles of human specimens in "blackish, murky fluid," which Michael explores while in a trance, after he has touched the dolls. While Rowan (symbolically as a Mayfair) has breathed in the stench of the jar storage area "and swallowed it, because there was no other way to tolerate it" (*Hour,* 650), Michael opens the jars, gags on the fumes, and holds up the contents. Hearing the threatening voice of Lasher "from the dead mouth that talked," Michael realizes that these slimy heads somehow resemble Lasher and tries to destroy them: "He snatched at another, smashed it against the wood of the shelf, so that the greenish remains slid down soft and rotten, like a giant greenish egg yoke onto the floor, oozing off the skull that emerged dark and shrunken as he caught it and held it, the face just dripping away" (*Hour,* 723). As the reader later learns, the heads represent Lasher's earlier failed efforts to mutate himself into human form.

The graphic details of the Mayfair dolls and jars go further than any grotesquerie in Dickens, but the projection of psychological aberration onto the setting and landscape is clearly Dickensian, an acknowledgment Rice clearly makes in Michael's love of Dickens, the name of his construction company, *Great Expectations,* and references to Pip, Steerforth, and even Miss Havisham (*Hour,* 25, 26). Her spirit is most directly evoked in the obsessive Carlotta and the decay of the Mayfair house: "Spiders wove their tiny intricate webs over the iron lace roses. In places the iron had so rusted that it fell away to powder at the touch. And here and there near the railings, the wood of the porches was rotted right through" (*Hour,* 5). In Deirdre's lifetime, Aaron notes how "passersby invariably crossed the street when they approached it" and how "[s]omething evil lived in this house" (*Hour,* 551).

The Witching Hour illustrates Rice's habit of developing a variety of convincing settings in both past and present, such as the seventeenth-century French village and the eighteenth-century Haitian plantations; it also reveals her continued preference for San Francisco and New Orleans. In this novel, however, New Orleans becomes the place where the historical past and tradition are more visible in the stately old homes and lush landscapes in contrast to the more modern, transient, and affluent San Francisco. Michael and Rowan leave San Francisco and return to New Orleans to find their roots; both feel a sense of belonging in New Orleans and realize the lack of real substance in their lives on the West Coast. As a projection of the family, the Mayfair house dominates the setting in a way that no single place has in Rice's novels heretofore. It also provides an atmosphere resonant in symbolic overtones that differs greatly from the two-dimensional, stagey locations of *The Mummy.* Michael's restoration of the house to recapture its former elegance, warmth, and freshness makes it finally unsuitable as a residence for Rowan.

While Rice makes use of Dickensian houses and Hawthornian gardens to show the unnatural results when scientific curiosity and selfishness go too far in manipulating human nature, the influence of other literary figures can be seen as well. One is Mary Shelley, through *Frankenstein.* Early in the novel Rowan recalls watching *Frankenstein* on the late show and longing "to be the mad scientist." This reference to

Mary Shelley's novel prepares the reader for Rowan's future and under-scores universal concerns about the limits of scientific research that are even more pertinent in the 1990s than the 1820s. After publishing *The Witching Hour,* Rice indicated to Susan Ferraro that she hoped to work on something in the Frankenstein tradition. Both *The Mummy* and *The Witching Hour* could be viewed as variations on this myth, since the elixir brings the corpse of Cleopatra back to life, and Lasher attempts to trans-plant his own spirit into human heads before he finally succeeds in inhabiting the body of Rowan's unborn child. In *The Tale of the Body Thief,* Rice creates yet another fictional experiment to probe connections between spirit and matter and to ask questions such as what intangible spirit animates the body? Can a heart and other organs be transplanted to sustain life? Is it possible for the spirit of one person to invade or revive someone else's body?

The beauty of the human spirit that should not be exploited and the ability to hold onto the illusion of controlling or evading its own heredi-ty or life's destiny are themes that her allusion to Tennessee Williams's *Orpheus Descending* suggests, a reference that also foreshadows Michael's inability to prevent the loss of Rowan. Against all odds the valiant Michael tells the less optimistic Aaron that Lasher will not win Rowan over because he believes in her strength.

Totally confused by Lasher as to what is real and what is not, Petrie observes a butterfly in a passage that echoes Mephistopheles' cynical view of human nature in Goethe's *Faust:* "Slowly, awkwardly, a monarch butterfly climbed the screen in front of him. Gorgeous wings. But grad-ually he focused upon the body of the thing, small and glossy and black. It ceased to be a butterfly and became an insect—loathsome!" (*Hour,* 15). Mephistopheles tells the devils seizing hold of Faust,

> Watch this body! How does it seem?
> See if you see a phosphorescent gleam.
> That is the little soul, Psyche with wings—
> Pull out her wings and it's a noisesome worm." ("Interment," *Faust*)

While the butterfly could certainly be a metaphor for the struggling Deirdre, it also reflects more generally the mixed capacity for both good and evil in all humans, who also stumble awkwardly. Under Lasher's influence in this interior passage, Petrie "focuses" only on the ugly, whereas Michael later sustains his belief in the beautiful side of human nature.

Michael's faith confirms the secular morality of Rice's *Chronicles*. Less negative toward traditional religion here, perhaps because she revisits her own Catholic upbringing in New Orleans through Michael—whose family is Irish Catholic—Rice provides affectionate portraits of Father Mattingly and Sister Bridget Masrie, who mean well but are simply ineffective in dealing with Lasher. The nuns cope with the young Mayfair witches simply by sending them home from school. Father Mattingly admits his own sense of helplessness, particularly when he recalls his poor judgment in listening to Deirdre's plea for help during her confession and then asking her permission to speak with her dreaded Aunt Carlotta. Many years later he ironically misinterprets a scene where he sees a young man comforting Deirdre and leaning down to kiss her. He is sad but pleased, while the reader knows that this "man" is Lasher.

Obviously more effective in helping people with the occult is the Talamascan organization, which Aaron says the Catholic church neither likes nor understands. As Aaron explains, "It puts us with the devil, just as it did the witches, and the sorcerers, and the Knights Templar, but we have nothing to do with the devil" (*Hour,* 238). With a secular organization that parallels Catholic hierarchy, the Talamascans are more stringent, according to Aaron, because they lack dogma and ritual: "Our definition of right and wrong is more subtle, and we become angry with those who don't comply" (*Hour,* 251). Petyr van Abel tells Charlotte that the main difference between the church and the Talamasca is that the church sees anything occult as demonic rather than simply as unknown (*Hour,* 340). The Talamascans do not believe in Satan, but they do believe in evil, which they define as "what is destructive to mankind" (*Hour,* 288). Petyr's view looks forward to Aaron's moral argument with Rowan over the potential disaster for the human race if Lasher is allowed to mutate into human form.

Michael's traditionalism builds on the security of his Catholic childhood, but when he revisits his old church and thinks he should pray to the Virgin Mary, "he had no belief in the images in the altar" (*Hour,* 689). Instead, his mind shifts to Rowan, who is now the source of meaning in his life. Wishing he still had religious faith, he realizes that he still believes in the "goodness of the visions"; in other words, he is convinced that he is choosing to help Rowan fight off some threat. Though not religious, Michael is still astonished when Rowan throws a statue of the Virgin Mary across Deirdre's room, where it crashes into pieces: "He wanted to say something, some magic words or prayers to undo it" (*Hour,* 716).

Subconsciously, in this scene that prefigures the ugly birth of Lasher, Rowan is striking out at Carlotta, who put the "dreadful religious artifacts" in Deirdre's room: "a statue of the Virgin with the naked red heart on her breast, lurid, and disgusting to look at. A crucifix lay beside it, with a twisting, writhing body of Christ in natural colors even to the dark blood flowing from the nails in his hands" (*Hour,* 12). Rowan's gesture echoes the ironic use of religious symbolism in *The Queen of the Damned,* where the perversity of Akasha's schemes to be the new God is reflected in her giving her special blood to Lestat as Christ. Here Lasher parallels his unnatural mutation into human life on Christmas Eve with the birth of Christ and refers to Rowan as his mother.

The Witching Hour is Rice's most technically complex novel thus far, blending factual narrative with the suggestion of the allegorical in the psychological positioning of Michael versus Lasher in their battle over Rowan's body and soul. Moving from the vampires to mortal witches and the human Michael, Rice explores through another angle the universal themes of contacts between the living and the dead, relationships between the spiritual and the physical, and the possibilities of achieving immortality. Unlike *The Mummy, The Witching Hour* is grounded in credible scientific explanations and features a neurological surgeon as a protagonist, so that these themes appeal convincingly to a contemporary audience concerned about the implications of various forms of scientific research—genetic and fetal research, for instance. As reawakened mortals, Ramses and Cleopatra pose no serious threats in *The Mummy;* the implications of Lasher's grotesque victory are another matter. In *The Witching Hour* Rice deftly sustains the terror of the supernatural, with Michael's perspective raising the issue of whether one's life is determined by destiny or free will. As a culmination of Rice's Gothicism, the novel arouses the reader's deepest fears of helplessness in losing the self and being taken over by another.

Passages in *The Witching Hour* point to future directions for her Gothic fiction, just as mentions of mummies and witches did in *The Queen of the Damned.* Rowan asks Lasher what stopped him from "'taking over the entire organism'" when he managed to mutate the heads in the jars. Lasher replies that he is unable to change living tissue, though he can enter human bodies when they are sleeping or in a weakened state. This emphasis on the human form looks toward *The Tale of the Body Thief*. At the same time, the cultivation of an historical past and place, the focus upon the human rather than supernatural perspective, and the sensuality of her characters continue to reflect Rice's interests in non-Gothic elements that she wrote about before the publication of either *The Mummy* or *The Witching Hour,* the two historical novels written during the 1970s and the erotica in the 1980s.

Chapter Eight
The Historical Novels

Stung by some of the negative critical responses to the *Interview with the Vampire,* Anne Rice decided in the late 1970s to try her hand at a different genre, the historical novel (Ferraro, 76). Unlike those who lamented her choice of vampire subject matter yet praised her originality in treating it, reviewers of her two historical works, *The Feast of All Saints* (1979) and *Cry to Heaven* (1982), noted her unconventional choice of topic. Pat Goodfellow, for instance, said *The Feast* offers "a fascinating glimpse into a little known and intriguing segment of American history."[1] Critics also applauded the vitality of her characters: Barbara Bannon wrote that the "people and the city come alive wonderfully" in *The Feast.*[2] Beth Ann Mills, writing about *Cry to Heaven,* saw its characters as Rice's most successful creations: "deeply felt, richly imagined," compelling "attention and sympathy."[3] Reviewers perhaps accustomed to the single-focused *Interview,* however, criticized the plot of *The Feast of All Saints* failing to maintain the reader's interest[4] and the book in general for tending toward repetition. Rhoda Koenig called attention to the problems of audience in *The Feast,* which she saw as falling "somewhere between serious historical fiction and enjoyable trash."[5]

The historical novel runs the inherent risk of criticism for blending fact and fiction. As George Dekker argues, to call a novel "a 'historical romance' is . . . to direct attention to its extraordinarily rich, mixed, and even contradictory or oxymoronic character."[6] Dekker later defines the tension in this genre that is pulled "towards the contrary poles of romance and realism, myth and history" (306). Technically beginning with Sir Walter Scott's *Waverley* novels (1814–18), the historical novel fictionalizes and exploits actual characters and events. The effective historical novel gives the impression of recreating the actual past yet also engages the reader in a fictional experience. There is always the difficulty of maintaining a fidelity to the facts while not allowing these facts to stifle creativity. The past may end up as a theatrical backdrop that does not seriously pervade the characters or provide causation (as sometimes happens in Scott), or the vitality and complexity of the characters may be sacrificed in a slavish attention to historical accuracy (hence the commonsensical approach of not using historical personages as protagonists).

Scott set the standard in *Ivanhoe,* his story of warring Saxons and Normans in medieval England. He sought to portray, as C. Hugh Holman and William Harmon point out, "an age when two cultures are in conflict; into this cultural conflict are introduced fictional personages who participate in actual events and move among actual personages."[7] Elizabeth Gaskell's *Mary Barton,* Dickens's *A Tale of Two Cities,* and Pasternak's *Dr. Zhivago* are examples of this tradition, whereby large numbers of characters fit into and exemplify the impact of historical events. Yet, as Holman and Harmon state, in one variation of the Scott tradition a historical novel may also focus on fewer characters who loom larger than the cultural conflicts that motivate them, as in Hawthorne's *The Scarlet Letter* (230).

Rice's two books represent each of these well-established traditions. In *The Feast of All Saints* she follows Scott's example of a culture in conflict, specifically the racial tensions and social caste system in Louisiana during the 1840s. In *Cry to Heaven* she creates the historical novel of character, whereby the lives of the Italian castrati are represented by Marco Antonio Treschi and his opera mentor Guido Maffeo early in the eighteenth century. Painted on a large epic canvas, *The Feast* depicts characters from different generations and families illustrating all sides of the racial conflict—the whites, the *gens de couleur,* the freed slaves, and the slaves—whose lives are intricately connected and affected by their position in the caste system. In contrast, *Cry to Heaven* relies on a single, concentrated plot of revenge to aggrandize the impact of castration. In both novels the characters mature from innocence to experience as disastrous events force them to terms with themselves and the societies in which they live.

Though these factors set up a cause-and-effect plot structure in both works, in *The Feast* the causes are demonstrated through many events that affect large numbers of characters, whereas in *Cry to Heaven* the action is more psychological, revolving around Tonio's coming to terms with his forced castration, which occurs toward the beginning of the novel. While in *The Feast* the Dickensian, authorial point of view oversees all of the characters and provides many different perspectives on certain events and conditions, in *Cry to Heaven* the reader sees the world primarily through Tonio and secondarily through Guido within the omniscient voice. Making use of her native New Orleans not only connects *The Feast* to her Gothics but also provides an atmosphere rich in symbolism that Rice uses to intensify the external conflicts, foreshadow events, and establish connections in a complicated plot. In *Cry to Heaven,* she relies more on specific symbols to express the internal, psychological torment of Tonio. Though not a Gothic novel, *The Feast* nonetheless anticipates the mythic scope of *The Queen of the Damned* and the historical saga of *The Witching Hour,* while the concentrated effect and psychological focus of *Cry to Heaven* look back to the *Interview.* In both novels, the source of evil resides in the social structure, sustaining a suspense and anxiety more characteristic of the Gothic than the historical novel.

The Feast of All Saints

In *The Feast of All Saints* this evil emanates from racial prejudice. Rice focuses on the *gens de couleur,* who are below the whites in social class and above the freed and unfreed slaves. The Ste. Maries, a family of color, especially the adolescent Marcel and Marie, experience the impact of the caste system. Marcel and Marie suffer and then recover from losses: Marcel is deprived of his lifelong goal of going to Paris and educating himself; the lovely Marie is raped by five white men. The paradoxical relationship between destruction and self-renewal in their lives is evident in the quotation from John Donne that Rice uses at the beginning of the book:

> Batter my heart, three-person'd God; for, you
> As yet but knocke, breathe, shine, and seeke to mend;
> That I may rise, and stand, o'erthrow mee', and bend
> Your force, to breake, blowe, burn and make me new.

Marcel finally manages to achieve independence at the end of the novel, but during much of the action he remains naively dependent on his white father, Philippe Ferronaire, who handsomely provides for himself, his mother, and his sister, Marie. Having been raised to expect unlimited financial support, a spoiled Marcel at 14 dreams of going to Paris for an education. School in New Orleans bores him, and he often gets into trouble. Just as he is expelled, he fortunately manages to enroll in a new school opened by Christophe Mercier, a *gens de couleur* who has just returned from Paris, where he earned some fame as a writer. Marcel reveals his immaturity in his irresponsible, self-centered treatment of Anna Bella, who needs his understanding and advice, and his carefree, passionate love affair with Juliet. More important than these influences on his character development is Christophe, his teacher and friend. "Under Christophe's light," difficult subjects like history and the classics become clear, as Marcel learns "how to learn" (*Feast,* 360). Turning into an outstanding scholar, Marcel works hard to prepare himself for the exams that will ensure his entry into a French school, where he dreams that he may learn to become a teacher.

All of his dreams end, however, when a little more than a year later the financially troubled Philippe informs him that he will not support Marcel in Paris, that Marcel must become an apprentice as an undertaker with the Lermontants. Devastated, Marcel undertakes an "endless pilgrimage" on foot from New Orleans to the Ferronaire plantation (ironically called *Bontemps*) in the Parish of St. Jacques, where he confronts his father. Along the way a white man, a guard-at-the-white-gate figure, insists on inspecting Marcel's papers to be certain that he is not a runaway slave. The injustice and humiliation Marcel is soon to experience are foreshadowed here, as the well-educated Marcel realizes that the white man, who is considered his social superior in the caste system, is illiterate, unable to read the papers he has the right to demand. To reach his destination Marcel must cross the Mississippi River; the crossing marks his embarkation on his own rite of passage to adulthood and his entrance to the world of whites—where he learns he does not belong. On arriving at the plantation his white father Philippe beats him and turns him out. Marcel is taken back home to New Orleans by the gentle old Felix, Philippe's slave, who fends off a few blows himself in trying to intervene in the fight between father and son.

Ashamed of what he has done, especially the misery he has caused his mother and sister, a despairing Marcel offers himself to Christophe as a lover. Despite his real love for Marcel, Christophe declines his offer, which he sees as perpetuating Marcel's dependency on others: "I don't think you can really love anyone, Marcel, until you have that self-reliance, until the need is diminished" (*Feast,* 482). Christophe rightly believes that Marcel, who has never been truly loved by his father, has been looking for paternal love, first in his old black friend Jean Jacques, and now in him. Unable now to remain in his own home, Marcel goes his Tante Josette's plantation in the countryside, where he remains for five months and recovers.

Marcel's second trip on the river helps him regain the self-respect destroyed by his father. Before he departs for his aunt's plantation, *Sans Souci,* he thinks about the meaning of its name ("without care") and senses he is going through an important passage: "he had the strangest feeling that the acute happiness of his last few years would not come back to him for a long while, something new and perhaps far more exciting was taking its place. He had always wanted it to end, that limbo of childhood, and now it had all but come to a close" (*Feast,* 441).

Once aboard the slave steamer (ironically named *Arcadia Belle,* or "beautiful paradise"), he identifies with the degradation of the "miserable shackled human beings" being loaded onto the ship. Once at his Aunt Josie's, he learns about his own race under her wise tutelage. From the history books she makes available to him of his own people, the *gens de couleur,* in Haiti, he concludes that they "had a power and a history like nothing he had ever known in his native Louisiana in his own time. They had borne arms for their rights, and even today on that island in the Caribbean they lived along with the blacks in the Republic of Haiti fully enfranchised men" (*Feast,* 459). Experiencing a totally new regard for his race, Marcel is still uncertain about his own identity and place. Realizing that his shortcomings as a writer make his dreams of a Parisian route to teaching unrealistic, he also feels that a life in the idyllic countryside away from the racial realities of the city is too remote, so he decides to return to New Orleans.

Recognizing that "ever since he could remember, one illusion after another had been shattered," Marcel strives for the knowledge that will enable him to reconstruct his aspirations. In a passage that also occurs in different ways in *The Vampire Chronicles* and *The Witching Hour,* when protagonists come to terms with the existential nature of reality and realize that they must determine their own moral choices, Marcel considers that "[e]verything existed, perhaps, by the act of faith, and we were always in the midst of creating our world, complete with the trappings of tradition that was nothing more than an invention like all the rest." Further, it occurs to him "that the world of the white Southerner with all its doors shut in the colored man's face might also be fragile, also dependent on the same enormous act of collective faith" (*Feast,* 529). The false pride in his family's alliance with the white Philippe Ferronaire now turns into a real pride in his own race as he decides to work among the *gens de couleur* in New Orleans as a daguerrotypist. He finally reconciles himself not to "the world he would some day escape, but the world to which he'd been born" (*Feast,* 569). His ability now to recognize the true worth of the more African-looking Anna Bella, whom he had seen as a burden earlier in the novel, also marks his change. Marcel is an effective historical character, whose "deeds, values, and psychological problems have a representative historical significance" (Dekker, 305–6). His growth and self-respect as an individual are intertwined with his awareness of racial conflict and understanding of history.

While *The Feast of All Saints* is primarily Marcel's story, it is also that of his sister, Marie. Like Marcel, Marie experiences violence at the hands of whites that forces her to realize truths about herself and thereby become independent. A key figure in Marie's life is her mother, Celeste, with whom she has more complicated relationship than Marcel does with his father. Ever since Marie can remember, her mother has never been loving toward her. All of Celeste's attention has been directed to her white lover and benefactor, Philippe, and to her son, Marcel. Unknown to Marie, according to the value system held sacred by her mother and her aunts, Marie will be expected to lead the life of a kept mistress. She is both beautiful and white in appearance, and this, her mother and aunts feel sure, will attract the wealthy patronage of white male lovers.

But Marie is set against replicating her mother's life: "Never, never would she be forced into the arms of a man she could not marry . . . And never, never would any child of hers know the shame she'd known [of] a white father who could never give her his legal name" (*Feast,* 179–80). Despite the disapproval of her mother and aunts, Marie persists in her determination to marry Richard Lermontant, another person of color with whom she has fallen in love. She responds to an invitation from Richard's mother, Madame Suzette, that her own mother had neglected to show her. Just as Marcel gains respect for the *gens de couleur* in getting to know his Tante Josette, Marie comes to a new understanding of womanhood from Madame Suzette. Marie realizes that until this meeting, she has never known "a woman could have substance, simplicity, and vigor which all her life she had associated entirely with men. And this it seemed amid the usual feminine trappings which for her had spelt vanity in the past, unendurable hours with the needle, making lace to grace the backs of chairs" (*Feast,* 395).

When the Lermontants make a formal declaration to Marie's father, it appears that Philippe will consent to their marriage. Now in financial difficulty, he sees in the marriage a way to rid himself of the cost of supporting Marcel: he will agree to it if the Lermontants agree to take on Marcel as an apprentice to their undertaking business. When Marcel refuses the offer and breaks with his father, it appears that Marie will be free to marry Richard, but the death of Philippe changes everything. He has left the Ste. Maries no permanent estate or income, so Celeste and the aunts insist that Marie find her white fortune to support them as well as her brother in his desire to go to Paris. Refusing permission and insulting Richard's family, they prey on Marie's guilt and tell her she thinks only of herself and not of Marcel. Her mother explains that she hated Marie as a child because she was jealous of her beauty and of her whiteness, which led people to assume that she was Marie's black nurse instead of her mother. Celeste sees nothing wrong now in prostituting her daughter to support Marcel.

A despondent Marie is left at the mercy of Lisette, a spiteful black slave who belongs to Philippe and works in the Ste. Marie household. Lisette rightfully feels betrayed, since Philippe had promised to set her free; now that he is gone, she will belong to Celeste, who uses her badly. Lisette has further reason for revenge because she is Philippe's natural child, born of Zazu, another of his slaves. Another member of the younger generation who rebels against the system, she does not have her mother's patience and loyalty. Resenting her Cinderella-like service to her half-brother and half-sister, the sullen and dangerous Lisette has been spending her time at Lola Dede's, a voodooienne who manages a brothel of black female slaves for white men. Lisette, now an orphan, no longer has reason to restrain herself; any hope of earning her freedom is entirely gone. Already quite drunk, she has trouble sympathizing with Marie's troubles of not knowing where to go and wishing Marcel were back so that she would not be forced to take a white man. Lisette thinks to herself, "Oh, you poor baby! Such a dreadful fate!" and then hatches a plan "splendid in its evil" that ruins Marie and exacts her revenge (*Feast,* 497).

As with Marcel, the external cause of Marie's suffering is not only tied up with racism but with Marie's own internal development. Lisette takes Marie to Lola's brothel, where Marie is drugged and then violently raped by five white men. Marie staggers home to her mother, who shows no sympathy but appears to blame Marie for the loss of their future security as she roars over and over, "Ruined, ruined." Marie then manages to get to the less than reputable house of Dolly Rose, where she finds a very different reception. During her recovery Marie finds the affection and protection from Dolly that she has never known from her own mother. Just as she was surprised to find real substance in Madame Suzette, Marie comes to appreciate the kindness and wisdom of Dolly, whom she had viewed through the eyes of society as an outcast. Dolly's life, another story of racial exploitation and hard-won strength of character, has never been the same since the death of her daughter, Lisa, the child she had as a result of her alliance with the white Vincent Dazencourt, Philippe's brother-in-law. Dolly has had many random affairs with white men, whom she meets during the evening dances at her home.

Marie recovers physically, but her psychological healing comes slowly. She goes to Dolly's not only because she thinks that the life of a prostitute is what remains for her but also because she actually believes that she was to blame for what happened to her. Much earlier in the novel she had become aware of real sexual pleasure in Richard's embraces and in her own erotic dreams. When Dolly tries to explain to her that in spite of her being raped she is "free to live" as she chooses, Marie finally confesses the source of her guilt to Dolly, who replies with no "guile or solicitude": "Now I understand, *ma chere,* now we have a place to begin" (*Feast,* 522). From Dolly Marie learns to accept her sensuality; she learns "purely and so honestly the secrets of a woman's body, the passions to which all women were subject, be they sheltered or experienced, innocent or skilled." Dolly, then, leads her "farther and farther away from the voices of the past which had only deceived, distorted, betrayed" (*Feast,* 537). By the time an anguished Richard finally gets to see her, he notes that "[s]ome new fire radiated from within. It was as if the young girl he'd known had been an unstamped coin, and here was the woman" (*Feast,* 538).

Assuming that the grieving Richard has come to find a more respectable place for her rather than to accept her as his wife, Marie pretends to defend her choice to remain with Dolly. What Marie has underestimated, however, is the quiet strength of Richard's character, which gives him the courage to risk the reputation the Lermontant family has struggled to establish over the years by bringing Marie home as his wife. Richard's potential for noble action has been carefully developed throughout the novel. Never having experienced the luxuries of his best friend, Marcel, Richard has accepted the responsibility of work in his father's undertaking business and of commitment to the community. He lacks Marcel's intensity, sometimes feeling relieved "to live devoid of those peaks and valleys himself." Yet Richard stands up to his father, Rudolphe, when he vents his anger unjustly on his sister, Giselle. His strong, sensible mother recognizes the worth of Richard's character in a passage that foreshadows his bravery with Marie: "Your father is a gentleman and a man of honor because he has worked to become a gentleman and a man of honor. But you were born to it, Richard, it's bred into you without a flaw. You are of a different ilk." She advises Richard not to let his father intimidate him: "You do not value yourself for the wiser, surer person that you already are . . . remember in the future, that when you stood up to your father, your father backed down without a word." (*Feast,* 316). Once he decides to marry Marie, he approaches his father in the resolute tone of a man with the clarity and "simplicity of one who has made up his mind" (*Feast,* 544).

In marrying Richard, Marie achieves both social independence and psychological maturity, as she manages to overcome her mother's parasitic dependence on whites. The status of the Lermontant family and their assistance to people of their own race, Marcel's decision to remain in New Orleans, and finally Christophe's return from Paris to educate children of color exemplify the strength and determination of these characters to overcome racial prejudice and hatred. Indeed, the action of the novel carries out Rice's intention to pay tribute to the people of color in New Orleans. According to her biographer, she chose the novel's title to commemorate them as the "forgotten saints" celebrated on "The Feast of All Saints" (Ramsland, 183).

To demonstrate the pervasiveness of racial discrimination, Rice traces not only the maturation of Marcel and Marie but the parallel and contrasting patterns of the lives of the families and individuals representing different social classes. Within the large groups of whites, *gens de couleur,* and freed and unfreed black slaves, many comparisons are invited among members of generations, types of love relationships, and parents and children. While Grandpere Lermontant and Richard's parents applauded his bravery in challenging the status quo, Celeste and the Ste. Marie aunts "simply could not understand what had happened" (*Feast,* 529). The loving, respectful relationship between Rudolphe and Madame Suzette Lermontant is contrasted not only with the destructive alliance of Celeste Ste. Marie and Philippe Ferronaire but also with the loveless and hostile marriage of Philippe and his white wife, Aglae.

An interesting perspective on the diverse attitudes within the white side of the racial conflict is offered through the character of Vincent Dazincourt. At first Vincent's behavior does not particularly recommend him, though he is clearly a more sensitive and humane man than his brother-in-law, Philippe, in handling slaves and running *Bontemps.* Yet he is not unwilling to involve himself in white-black alliances, first with Dolly Rose, with whom he fathers the poor Lisa, and then with Anna Bella. Unlike his brother, however, Vincent comes to realize the destructive nature of these relationships and shows the same capacity for self-sacrifice as Richard—in his case, by giving up the woman he deeply loves.

Vincent entered into the alliance with Anna Bella assuming that his emotions would not be at risk. Because of his ignorance and his upbringing, "He believed all Negroes were fools" (*Feast,* 335). Yet he unexpectedly falls in love with her, a woman of substance who "was a lady to the tips of her fingers, having imbibed the principles of gentility for the very best and most profound of reasons: that gentility makes life graceful and good" (*Feast,* 336).

At first treating Anna Bella and their child badly, in the fashion of Philippe, Vincent has a change of heart. In the same nobility of spirit that prompts him to defend Marie's honor and hunt down her white rapists, he makes permanent legal provisions for Anna Bella and their child. Though Vincent demonstrates the "sins of the fathers" theme in southern historical fiction, whereby the characters are "foredoomed to defeat" because the "governing class of the old South is shown to be incapable of remedying (when it is even capable of recognizing) the social evils to which it owes its wealth and leisure" (Dekker, 295), he does show how the awareness and personal sacrifice of whites can point toward the possibility of change.

The worthy Anna Bella illustrates the interconnectedness of the characters and their impact on one another. The daughter of a freed slave who rises in status because she attracts a white man's love, Anna Bella was earlier looked down on by an immature, prejudiced Richard because of her African features and neglected by Marcel, who saw a relationship with her as an obstacle to his dreams of going to Paris. By the end of the novel, with Vincent now out of her life, Marcel's appreciation of Anna Bella shows the growth of his character. Even Christophe benefits from Anna Bella's generosity, as she nurses his friend and lover Michael through a bout with yellow fever.

The interweaving role she plays may be seen further in the *secretaire* that Marie gives her upon her alliance with Vincent, an occasion traditionally celebrated like a wedding. Marie, having received the gift from her white father, Philippe, does not realize he had stolen it from his own wife, whose grandmother had left it to her. Seeing the little treasure now housed at Anna Bella's and knowing that his sister misses it, Vincent realizes that Philippe stole it from his white family to give to Marie. This awareness increases his disrespect for his brother-in-law, and he also recognizes his own part in the system that revolts him: "He did not want the Ste. Marie family to touch his Anna Bella, and he would have liked to believe that she was not of their world. But she *was* of their world! He had only to think of that little *secretaire,* Aglae's *secretaire,* which sat so proudly on Anna Bella's bedside table to realize that of course it was Anna Bella's world, too. . . . *He* did not wish to be connected with that world" (*Feast,* 338).

The *secretaire* is just one example of Rice's keen attention to detail in establishing the impact of racial attitudes that permeate the novel. Through other conflicts within the main plots, she further establishes the complexities of the historical situation and the intricacies of the social hierarchies. The respectable Rudolphe Lermontant gets Christophe Mercier out of Dolly Rose's house when the white Captain Hamilton is expected, since Hamilton would have the right to kill Christophe in finding him there. Furious with Christophe for putting him in this position, Rudolphe tells him, "I have never never . . . cowered before any white man in my life! And never have I had to! And never, never will I endure that again!" (*Feast,* 229). At the request of Anna Bella, Vincent goes to calm down Captain Hamilton by reminding him that "a man of color cannot defend himself against a white man at all." He explains further that "in some circles it is judged an act of cowardice to quarrel with a man who cannot defend himself" (*Feast,* 233).

Not surprisingly, Rudolphe defends his daughter Giselle's honor later when a white man named Bridgeman from Virginia insults her on the street. Unable to attack a white man physically, Rudolphe verbally insults him, but since this action, too, is "a crime in itself," Bridgeman takes Rudolphe to court. When the testimony of witnesses and Rudolphe's own status in the community vindicate him, the out-of-towner is flabbergasted: In Virginia, Bridgeman says, "they would have strung that 'negra' from the nearest tree branch and lit a fire beneath him to send him on his way. What was this place, New Orleans, what with the abolitionists in the north and 'negras' attacking white men on the street?" (*Feast,* 317). While Rudolphe's experience shows his strength, it also brings home to Marcel the reality that they are "people of color living in a white man's world" (*Feast,* 320).

Christophe, too, experiences these social realities when he tries to bring the slave Bubbles into the classroom with the other students of color. As the parents withdraw their students from the school, Christophe realizes he must take Bubbles out or give up the idea of educating his own race. Rudolphe tells Christophe that he has taught many of his own black apprentices to read and write, but in private: "Teach that boy in private and everyone will respect you for it. Give him a fine education if you like, but do not sit him down in a classroom with our boys" (*Feast,* 247). He explains that they are living in a caste system, where people of color have won their "precarious place in this corrupt quagmire by asserting over and over that it is composed of men who are better than and different from the slaves! We get respect in one way, Christophe, and that is by insisting ourselves on what we are. Men of property, men of breeding, men of education, and men of family. But if we drink with slaves, marry slaves, sit down in our parlors with slaves . . . then men will treat us as if we were no better!" (*Feast,* 248).

Indeed, the lot of the slaves who hover in the background, while Rice focuses on the *gens de couleur,* is far worse, as illustrated by Lisette and Bubbles and by the glimpses she gives of slaves on the auction block, slaves loaded onto ships, and slave atrocities on the plantations, such as the beating of a pregnant slave at *Bontemps* by the overseer. Continuing Marcel's education on his race, the wise Tante Josette compares the slaves' history on Saint-Domingue plantations with those in the American South. She explains why she believes that the slaves here will not revolt as they did there: "Slaves have been bred for generation upon generation, domesticated and not by blatant atrocity, but by some system far more subtle and efficient, something akin to the cotton gin and the refining mill in its precision and its relentlessness. No, it would not happen here, because we've beaten them, cowed them, and ground them utterly *and completely into the dust*" (*Feast,* 460).

Including the experiences of both whites and slaves in her portrayal of people of color, Rice avoids the one-sidedness that can be a problem in historical fiction. Elizabeth Gaskell in *Mary Barton* (1848), for instance, concentrated on the workers but broadened her scope in *North and South* (1855) to include the factory owners. The omniscient voice moves smoothly from one group to another, as in the Ste. Maries' and the Ferronaires' reactions to Philippe's death, to provide these perspectives in what is technically Rice's most conservative novel. With a few flash-backs, such as Marcel's recalling his relationship with Jean Jacques, the stories of Marcel and Marie move chronologically with interior mono-logues used often to intensify dramatic scenes, as when Marcel makes his journey to the Ferronaire plantation and Marie regains consciousness after being raped.

As in Rice's Gothics, Catholicism provides a rich source of imagery (especially the Virgin Mary associations with Marie) but little spiritual comfort for these characters in their painful journeys toward indepen-

dence. When Marie seeks refuge in the church shortly before falling into
the clutches of Lisette, she feels "bewildered that the serenity which had
always visited her under this roof had not visited her when she needed it
most" (*Feast*, 494). Anna Bella remains convinced that God hears her
prayers, but the Catholic church seems "ornate and alien at times of real
trouble, it was a luxury like the lace she'd learned to make, the French
language she had acquired" (*Feast*, 299).

The church is merely part of the larger New Orleans scene that not
only functions as a historical setting pertinent to the racial theme, as
described earlier, but also sets the mood for particular scenes. In addition
to the great gulf between the city, with its narrow and claustrophobic
streets, and the wide open countrysides of *Bontemps* and *Sans Souci*, the
wetness and darkness of New Orleans add to the bleakness of the surroundings. In July the "rain had inundated the cemeteries so that one
burial for the parish had to be made in a veritable pool of muddy water;
and the bodies of the yellow fever victims were beginning to pile up at
the gates, giving off a stench sufficient to sicken the oldest citizen who
had seen it summer after summer" (*Feast*, 129). Before Christophe
returns from Paris, the rain beats "through the rotted shutters" of his
mother's home, where the wallpaper hangs "in yellowed strips from the
damp ceilings." Marie is led to Madame Lola's during a thunder storm,
but the menacing darkness that Richard has seen surrounding her gives
way to an "uncommon radiance" on their wedding day.

Along with the suggestive plantation names, other elements of
setting also take on broader significance, as when Marcel reminds
Christophe what he told the students about a Kerman rug: "You told us
the key to understanding this world was to realize it was made of a thousand varying cultures, many so alien to the others, that no one code of
brotherhood or standard of art would ever be accepted by all men"
(*Feast*, 246). Ramsland believes that Rice uses the rug as a central
metaphor for the richness and diversity of cultures in the South and to
convey her intentions in writing the book (186).

The novel is based on alliances between white men and women of
color, and descriptions of sensual awareness and sexual activity are prevalent. They are, however, more conservative than elsewhere in Rice's fiction. The origins of the attraction of white men for women of color are
traced to the upbringing of white children tended by black women.
Vincent recalls his own childhood, "And though he would never truly
have given in to the desire to force himself upon one of his slave women,
he had known that desire in some place a little less obscure to him than

his dreams" (*Feast,* 296). It is significant that when Vincent and Anna Bella end their alliance, she consummates her love for Marcel, experiencing the freedom of loving a man of her own race: "For her it had been a surrender of the body and the heart. She had devoured him utterly, his honey-brown skin, his clumsy passion, his feline grace, and it had cast into dim light forever those many nights with Michie Vince when, so eager to please, she had never once thought of herself" (*Feast,* 564). Like other women of color—Celeste, Juliet, Dolly, and finally even Marie—Anna Bella expresses her passionate nature openly. As in the Gothics, Rice uses sexual liberation to signify the importance of a greater tolerance, social responsibility, and freedom of personal choice.

Only the teacher, Christophe Mercier, being gay, is discreet about his sexuality because of his larger goals in the community. As the cosmopolitan outsider who leaves Paris and returns to the racial tensions of New Orleans to educate his own people and to console Marcel, Christophe is the epitome of a character who rises above an inhumane social morality to assume the personal responsibility his freedom allows. In addition to his teaching, Christophe edits *L'Album litteraire,* published entirely by men of color. However hopeless it may appear in the savage world, Marcel defends this journal to his Tante Josette and respects Christophe's commitment to his race. As mentioned in chapter 1, there is likely significance in the name Christophe, which, being a form of Christopher, the name of Rice's son, signifies a "new beginning," as Katherine Ramsland has put it (203). Christophe, as well as Marcel and Marie, like the battered persona in Donne's sonnet, are "made anew" by their suffering and self-awareness.

Cry to Heaven

Donne's plea to be made new is also appropriate to *Cry to Heaven,* where the same theme of regeneration through destructive violence is conveyed by the personal transcendence of Tonio Treschi, but in a very different social and historical context. Set in early eighteenth-century Italy, the novel takes its title from the pleas of the castrated male singers who sang in the churches and opera houses: "Children mutilated to make a choir of seraphim, their song a cry to heaven that heaven did not hear" (*Cry,* 47). As in Rice's other novels, the protagonist, whether a vampire like Lestat or a mortal like Michael Curry, must fully internalize his sense of limitation and moral insignificance, exaggerated by painful circumstances or inescapable conditions, to reconstruct a new code of morality.

Instead of portraying many groups of characters whose lives are shaped by historical events and attitudes, here Rice returns to the concentrated focus of the *Interview,* where a single character dominates the action.

In the first of the seven parts, it appears as if Guido Maffeo could be that protagonist, as the book begins with his castration in 1715. Moving back and forth between the concurrent stories of Guido's adolescence in Naples and Tonio's childhood in Venice, this section takes Guido through his loss of voice, his attempted suicide, and his painful accommodation to a life of giving voice lessons rather than preparing for his own singing career. Tonio's childhood is not perfect, but he has his father's respect and his mother's adoration, despite her alcoholic mood swings. At the end of part 1, the death of Tonio's aristocratic father, Andrea, prepares for the return of his cast-out brother, Carlo, in part 2. Andrea's will has an "ironclad provision" that the estate "could never be divided or sold. And it could be inherited only by the sons of Marc Antonio Treschi. So do what Carlo might, the future of the family belonged to Tonio. Only if Tonio was to die without issue, or prove incapable of fathering children, could Carlo's heirs be recognized" (*Cry,* 113). From Carlo himself Tonio learns the scandalous reasons for his father's disowning Carlo: Carlo had disobeyed his father by impregnating Marianna, whom his father would not allow him to marry. Banishing Carlo, Andrea married Marianna himself and raised Tonio as his son. In fact, Andrea is Tonio's grandfather, which makes Carlo Tonio's father and brother.

Carlo, determined to assume the Treschi fortune and rank in Venetian society, tries to get Tonio to say that he cannot marry or bear children. Tonio refuses to go against the wishes of Andrea: "I was born Andrea's son under this roof and under the law. And I can do nothing to change that, though you spread your abominations from one end of the Veneto to the other" (*Cry,* 127). Carlo, who has been reading *The Tempest* and hearing about Tonio's wonderful voice, hatches a plan that matches those of Elizabethan villains in its treachery: part 2 ends with Carlo ordering the brutal castration of the 15-year-old Tonio and Guido's taking him to the Naples conservatorio.

Looking for prospective pupil-singers in villages and cities but feeling disappointed at finding so few with real talent, Guido has been in Venice, where he is very much struck by the beauty of Tonio's voice. Carlo's men exploit his presence to make it appear as if Tonio has chosen this course of action for himself. They give Guido a packet of forged papers for Tonio and threaten to implicate him as a guilty party in the castration if he does not take Tonio away immediately. Horror-stricken by the "monstrous violence," Guido also understands the "appalling injustice" done to Tonio as the Treschi heir when he inspects the bloody mutilation and discovers that Tonio already shows signs of manhood. Meanwhile, news spreads through Venice that Tonio has had himself castrated to preserve his voice.

Unlike the brutal split between Marcel and his father and Marie's rape in *The Feast of All Saints,* Tonio's castration comes early in the novel; the rest of the action emphasizes Tonio's psychological reaction to this one event. With Guido and Tonio brought together in part 2, parts 3 through 7 relate to how Tonio's progress as a singer is mingled with his desire for revenge against Carlo and his gradual acceptance of what he has become. Fearing for his own life and influenced, too, by a desire to preserve the legacy of the powerful Treschi family, Tonio decides to bide his time at the conservatorio. But he refuses to sing, which he sees as capitulation, or to wear the red sash, the badge of the eunuch singers. Before the Maestro di Cappella expels him, Tonio learns that the despondent Guido has tried to drown himself. Deeply feeling his own pain, Tonio also makes a suicidal journey up the erupting Mt. Vesuvius. This ascent, however, proves to be a turning point for Tonio, as he realizes that he does not yet wish to die and that he must change the direction of his life by accepting what he is. Aware that as a eunuch he is outcast from the family and the church, he resolves to observe the rules of the conservatorio, where he will reside until Carlo produces heirs to perpetuate the Treschi lineage.

Including several homosexual love affairs and a deeply passionate relationship with Guido, part 4 traces Tonio's growth as a singer for three years under Guido's supervision and his departure with Guido for Rome and his operatic debut. Tonio realizes that the lesson of Vesuvius is that he must accept that he is not a man but a eunuch. While this awareness enabled him to return to the conservatorio and begin to sing, he still cannot perform publicly because he is unwilling to admit what he is to others. This breakthrough is finally made by his performing with the Contessa Lamberti for her guests, but he still resists his new identity by refusing to sing female roles.

Meanwhile, his cousin Giacomo's visit reminds him of the mother he loves and his unfulfilled revenge. Now that Carlo and Marianna have two children, he has no reason for delay, except for his growing love of his singing. He becomes an adept fencer to defend himself against Carlo and to exact his revenge. Handling himself adroitly in addressing an insult from a young Tuscan aristocrat, Tonio's Freudian wielding of the epee counters his feminine appearance. As he and Guido prepare to depart for Rome, the Maestro di Cappella urges Tonio to pay assassins to do away with Carlo instead of risking his own life and talent.

Despite forebodings and reminders of Tonio's family, such as the news of his mother's going back to her drinking, part 5 moves toward the climactic December debut of Tonio in the performance of Guido's new opera. While he practices endlessly with Guido, he has a passionate love affair with their host, Cardinal Calvino. After the Cardinal conquers his weakness and ends their relationship, Tonio satisfies his now-awakened desire for other men by seeking out lovers at random in the streets of Rome. He is also attracted to a painter and widow, the Signora Christina Grimaldi.

Finally the evening of the debut arrives. Still sensitive to singing female roles, Tonio nonetheless dons the female costume that transforms him and goes out onto the stage. He has been warned by Paulo that the *abbati* loyal to the famous Bettichino, with whom Tonio is performing, will cause a commotion to keep him from singing. Fortunately, Bettichino saves the day by quieting the audience and insisting that Tonio be given a chance to be heard. After the opera, Bettichino acknowledges Tonio as a worthy rival. As news of Tonio's great success spreads throughout Italy, events further develop both his destructive determination for revenge and his positive development as a singer.

Part 6 continues this dual direction. As Tonio's love for the liberated Christina grows along with his fame as a great opera star, he receives news of his mother's death and fends off an attack by Venetian cutthroats hired by Carlo to kill him. Intent on revenge, Tonio goes to make what may be his final confession to Cardinal Calvino before leaving for Venice. The Cardinal, hoping to save Tonio's life, advises him not to kill Carlo but to get power over him, satisfy himself that Carlo has indeed suffered for what he has done, and let him go if he agrees to give up his attacks on Tonio. After assuring Guido that he will meet him in Florence to sing a new opera on Easter, a date he was unwilling to commit himself to before, Tonio leaves for Venice to confront Carlo.

In part 7 the Gothic menace of Carlo hanging over Tonio's life culminates in a confrontation between the two. In a suspenseful scene on the piazza, the drunken Carlo bemoans the death of Marianna, whose dying thoughts were only of Tonio. As news comes that his paid assassins may have failed to kill Tonio, Carlo is enticed by a mysterious woman in black, who the reader suspects is Tonio. Carlo does not realize her identity until later, however, when Tonio has lured Carlo into the room of an abandoned old house and strapped him to a chair. It appears as if Tonio is willing to follow the Cardinal's advice. Though he is unable to get Carlo to admit his own pride and accept responsibility for what he has done to Tonio, he does exact Carlo's vow never to try to kill him. The minute Tonio gives Carlo the knife to cut the straps that bind him, however, Carlo lunges forward to stab Tonio, who is forced to kill him after all. His mission accomplished, Tonio leaves the freezing Venice and undertakes an arduous journey south to be with Guido and Christina in the warmer Florence, where he arrives on the Friday in Passion Week, the Feast of Seven Sorrows.

This summary of the action indicates how different *Cry to Heaven* is from *The Feast of All Saints* as a historical novel. While both works depend on the maturation of the protagonists to dramatize the historical situations, in *Cry to Heaven* the focus is entirely on Tonio and his maestro, Guido. Other castrati are part of Tonio's life at the conservatorio and in the opera, such as Domenico and Paulo, but they remain shadowy figures in comparison with the more fully developed characters in *The Feast of All Saints*. Also, Rice adds the element of forced castration at the beginning of the novel to intensify the injustice, to magnify the psychological burden Tonio must throw off, and to provide the revenge plot for suspense. Guido, for instance, has the more typical experience. Knowing "only routine hunger and cruelty among the large peasant brood to which he was born the eleventh child," he was "sold outright" by his parents and castrated when he was six. "And all of his life, Guido remembered he was given his first good meal and soft bed by those who made him a eunuch" (*Cry*, 3). While the cross Guido must bear is the tragic loss of his voice during adolescence, Tonio has been cheated out of his inheritance, expelled from his home and family, and denied his role as a husband and father: "Nor would the Church ever receive him, save for the lowest Orders, and even then only by special dispensation" (*Cry*, 183).

As Marcel and Marie had to find a way of transcending discrimination against their race, Tonio must come to terms with his sexual debility. Still a cause-and-effect plot, the structure of the action is based on two central devices that convey the psychological complexity of his character: first his positive and negative sides, which move him toward this maturity and hold him back, and second the parallel between his growing sexual maturity and his attitudes toward singing and playing female roles in the opera. The Maestro Cavalla tells Guido that Tonio "is a pair of twins in the same body, one loving music more than anything in this life, the other hungering for revenge" (*Cry,* 337). Even after Tonio has fallen deeply in love with Christina, Guido realizes that he is "being slowly torn apart. It was the battle of those twins he was witnessing: the one who craved life, and the one who could not live without the hope of revenge" (*Cry* 461).

Ramsland points out that the central metaphor for Tonio's inner conflict is Vesuvius, the dormant volcano "representing both sexual tension and the illusion of surface appearance. It becomes Tonio's symbol of restrained power . . . Carlo represents his dark side—the victim, Guido, his good side—heroic transcendence. When one side gains strength in Tonio's life, the other recedes" (Ramsland, 201). While in *The Queen of the Damned* and *The Witching Hour,* the external character arrangement suggests allegorical overtones that reflect opposing sides of moral issues, here the psychological conflict is internalized. Occasionally the repressed, violent, destructive side of Tonio erupts in his relationship with Guido and Tonio's overly defensive responses to insult.

Not to be swayed from vengeance, Tonio is, however, influenced by the power of love. As he says to the Maestro di Cavalla on leaving for Rome, "if there is one enemy of the rancor I feel against those who made me what I am, it is love for others. Love for Guido, and Apollo, and for you" (*Cry,* 328). With his great successes on the stage and his love of Christina fortifying his positive side, Tonio, in fact, has conquered the darkness by the time he meets with Carlo. He tells him: "I am done hating you, . . . Done fearing you. It seems that you are nothing to me now but some ugly storm that drove my undefended bark off course. And what was lost to me will never be retrieved, but I want no more quarrel with you, no more hatred, nor spite" (*Cry,* 524).

Within this central pattern is the parallel development of Tonio's gradual evolution as a performer and his acceptance of himself as a man castrated yet capable of deeply passionate love relationships. This connection between his life and art is invited when he first arrives at the conservatorio and refuses to sing at all: "The thought of it was too much; it was like giving in to them, and it was entering into the very nightmare role they had written for him as if this life were an opera, and they had given him this hideous part" (*Cry,* 170). As he progresses from singing for Guido in the conservatorio to singing at the Contessa's chapel and then performing at the opera, he also moves from somewhat shallow to deeply satisfying love relationships with Domenico to Guido to the Cardinal Calvino—and finally to Christina. He conquers at last his aversion to playing female parts, the final step in becoming a true castrato performer.

In keeping with the androgyny that gives Rice's vampires a liberating transcendence from sexual roles, Tonio feels a "sense of illimitable power," an "exhilarating strength" when he puts on the costume that transforms him into a woman for his performance. Shortly before his great triumph in Rome with Bettichino, he tells the costume designer, Signora Bianchi, "Make me so beautiful and so much the woman that I could fool my own father should I climb on his knee" (*Cry*, 410). Confident of his manly ability to give Christina sexual pleasure, he exploits his eunuch traits to the fullest off stage when he poses as a prostitute in black mourning to attract Carlo. This confrontation is not only delicious in meting out Jacobean justice to Carlo, but conclusive in symbolizing the maturity of Tonio, who has given over revenge and found freedom in his adversity.

Just as Marcel's and Marie's conflicts are echoed in other characters, Tonio's inner divisiveness is reflected in the fewer minor figures here. Ramsland believes that all of the characters "seem to be wearing masks. Christina, a contessa who attracts him, wants the freedom of a man; the Cardinal, a man of religious purity, exhibits brutally carnal desires; Marianna is both cruel and caring, with beauty that hides her ugliness; Carlo appears innocent of malice; Guido seems to hate Tonio when he actually longs for him; men dress as women, women as men. Even Venice, at times glorious and mysterious, has a whorish and seedy interior" (202). Going further with what she sees as a "symbolic layering" of doubles, Ramsland cites the "double imagery in the background: two recurring nightmares, two contessas, two men killed by Tonio, a duet between two castrati, and repeated attention to mirror images," among other examples.

Another variation on the dual imagery is the distinction between the two women Tonio loves, his mother, Marianna, and his beloved Christina. Both women are pressured into marrying older men, though for different reasons. Becoming Andrea's wife and hiding the truth that Tonio is Carlo's son, Marianna remains childlike herself and resorts to alcohol to cope with her secret conflicts. Upon Carlo's return she remains dependent on him, despite her anguish at losing Tonio. As Carlo explains later, "Do you know what she said to me, that I had ruined her, destroyed her, driven her to madness and drink and taken from her only comfort, our son" (*Cry*, 515). Christina, however, the "butterfly struggling from the cocoon," manages to move out from under male dependence after her husband's death and find her freedom. A skilled painter, she tells Tonio that she is not interested in remarrying: "I've been married. I was obedient. I did what I was told" (*Cry,* 449). Tonio, who has been tormented by not being able to marry Christina and give her a child, is slow to be convinced that she is truly committed to her art: "Why is it difficult for you to understand that I want to be free and to paint, to have my studio, to have my life as I please?" (*Cry,* 449). One of Rice's liberated females, she is the perfect soulmate for Tonio. As her hair spills down "a shower of corn yellow over him," she is the sunlight shining in his darkness.

The shifts between dark and light imagery, culminating in Tonio's going north to the colder climate of Venice to seek out Carlo and then arriving finally in the sunny warmth of Florence, are prevalent throughout the novel. Also countering the darkness of revenge is the brilliance of stage lights and music. Paulo's voice, for instance, fills "the room like a bright golden bell" (*Cry,* 167). Before he loves Christina, Tonio's desire for Guido radiates "out into the darkness." After the consummation of their love, the imagery suggests the coexistence of love and hate in Tonio. As they walk out into the streets of Naples, "the windows looming at every turn out of the dark were filled with lovely yellow light and then there was the blackness" (*Cry,* 249). Tonio looks over to Guido in the warm tavern and sees the flame in his eyes: "you are my love, and I am not alone, no, not alone, for this little while" (*Cry,* 250).

Toward the end of the novel, shortly before Tonio leaves to meet Carlo, Rice uses the *moccoli* in Rome, the "great closing ceremony of these last few hours before the beginning of Lent," to create suspense as well as to reinforce the symbolism of light and darkness. Climactic group scenes are a familiar device in her other novels, used to educate the main characters and intensify emotional states; examples are the performance of the vampires in the *Interview,* the rock concert in *Lestat,* the pagan orgies in *The Queen of the Damned,* and the Mardi Gras in *The Witching Hour.* Lighted candles appear everywhere; "The entire street below was a sea of dimly lit faces, each protecting its own flame while trying to extinguish another: Death to you, death to you, death to you" (*Cry,* 479). While the religious origin behind the folklore curses of death to those who hold no lighted candles (or faith in God) is apparent, so is the meaning of Tonio's love for Christina as the antidote for revenge and as the source of renewal. The merely symbolic suddenly becomes reality when Tonio must actually defend himself against Carlo's men, who attempt to stab and strangle him but are fortunately subdued by the Cardinal's guards. This scene stands out because this novel relies less upon actual violent episodes than on a pervasive atmosphere of doom and dread. Tonio feels anxious from the beginning when he is ignorant of the true Treschi family relationships; he has an "eerie feeling" connected with mystery and suspicion, with "things unspoken in this house." Guido and Christina share Tonio's dread of looming disaster when they observe him in Rome. No incident compares, however, with the real horror in the novel, the scene of Tonio's castration toward the very beginning.

Tonio's mutilation and the later confrontation between him and the villainous Carlo are carried out in the Gothic darkness, in the shabby rooms of centuries-old buildings along labyrinthine canals, which resemble the narrow streets of New Orleans in *The Feast of All Saints* in their appropriateness for crime and murder. While these streets are threatening places, they may also be filled with crowds of people engaging in religious ceremonies or going to the theater. Tonio's experiences take him into the cozy small taverns among the common people, as well as into the elegant ballrooms and salons of the grand palazzos. Rice makes careful distinctions among Venice, Naples, and Rome that are relevant to the historical subject at hand. In Naples, for instance, "Her singers, her composers, her music had fully superseded those of Venice. And they had long ago eclipsed those of Rome. Rome, however, was still the place for a castrato's debut, as far as Guido was concerned. Rome might not be producing singers and composers, but Rome was Rome" (*Cry,* 287).

Just as Vesuvius outside of Naples provides an appropriate psychological passage for Tonio similar to the Mississippi River for Marcel in *The Feast of All Saints,* Venice is the city to which Tonio returns and fulfills his father's dying wishes, though of course in a way different from what his father had intended. Andrea had told him of his ancestors, "those dim protagonists of heroic history who had first ventured into these misty marshes. The Treschi fortune had been built on Eastern trade as had so many great Venetian fortunes" (*Cry,* 59). Believing that the independence of Venice would be preserved by protecting its noble aristocratic families and referring to the present dissipation of great fortune in the corruption of "gambling, pomp, and spectacle," Andrea charged Tonio to "keep our enemies beyond the gates of the Veneto" (*Cry,* 59). Andrea had banished Carlo beyond the gate, but when Carlo returns, it is left to Tonio to assume the true responsibility of a Treschi, a role that further demonstrates his independence and maturity.

While Rice supports his transcendence through the light and warmth of Florence, she also makes use of the time of year, as Tonio arrives shortly before Easter, and the religious imagery of new birth: Florence is "as beautiful to him as the sleeping Bethlehem of Christmas paintings" (*Cry*, 529). Though the church permeates the whole musical aura of the novel, Rice is remarkably restrained in her treatment of its role in the castration of male singers, particularly in light of her criticism of Catholicism in the characters' negative experiences with the church and the ironic Christian images in her Gothic fiction. Yet the underlying truth of the church's complicity in Tonio's plight is crystal clear despite its understatement. Castrati are common. In Naples, the young Guido is proud to be one of them: "it was the soprano singer whom the world worshiped. It was for him that kings vied and audiences held their breath; it was the singer who brought to life the very essence of the opera" (*Cry*, 5). Later, Tonio realizes in Rome why "eunuchs had come into fashion and necessity. Here the Church had never relented its ban on performing women, that prohibition which had once dominated the stages of all Europe" (*Cry*, 348). As his carriage approaches the Vatican after he has just engaged in an empty sexual encounter with a man on the street, Tonio notices a sign in a small shop: "SINGERS FOR THE POPE'S CHAPEL CASTRATED HERE."

As the major cause for the boys' cries to a heaven that does not hear, the church is shown to be more ignorant than cruel in the rather sympathetic portrait of Cardinal Calvino. Tonio realizes that the Cardinal mistakenly believes that Tonio was probably an urchin saved from poverty by being castrated to sing in the holy choirs. The Cardinal also fails to appreciate the worth of aesthetic and physical pleasures. Tonio "could sense that in some way all of these pleasures—poetry, art, music, and their feverish coupling—were bound up with the Cardinal's notion of those enemies of the soul: the world and the flesh" (*Cry*, 381). Though Tonio tries to explain the sheer ecstasy and joy of singing and hearing music, the Cardinal, who manages to conquer what he sees as his depravity, cannot overcome his preconceptions of sin and redemption. Rice's savage garden is not part of this dialogue, but the narrowness of the Cardinal's perspective compared with Tonio's acceptance of physical pleasure reflects the limitations of the church he represents and the prevailing existential philosophy of Rice's fiction.

The Cardinal does not understand Tonio's lack of guilt for their sexual relationship. Unlike *The Feast of All Saints*, where these encounters are depicted in more conservative terms, descriptions of Tonio's sexual experiences with Domenico, Guido, the Cardinal, the Count di Stefano, and finally Christina preview the explicit sexual erotica that Rice would soon write. These passages answer questions concerning the capacities left to the castrati and develop the same idea in the Gothics of characters' liberation through transcendence of gender roles. Given the fact that homosexual relationships are expected of eunuchs, Tonio's freedom from social expectations comes from a heterosexual attachment to Christina. Equally comfortable playing female and male roles with his male lovers, Tonio's masculine confidence is emphasized with her, to the point of his luxuriating in discovering that she is a virgin: "He was simply and madly in love with her. She belonged to him. The sight of the blood on the sheets pushed every other rational thought out of his mind. She was his and she had been no other man's before, and he felt madness, he felt lust" (*Cry*, 447). The extent to which this confidence gives them both freedom is apparent in the scene where he invites Christina, dressed in a soldier's outfit, to get close to him backstage when he is wearing his female costume. In their inverted roles, Christina and Tonio display a rare example of humor in this serious novel, "Her little hand gathered up his skirt, it felt for the nakedness underneath, and finding the hard organ, grasped it cruelly, so that he whispered under his breath, 'Careful, my darling, let's not ruin what's left'" (*Cry*, 473).

While gender issues may account for the inclusion of a great deal of graphic sexuality, allusions to the relationship between pain and pleasure and the repetition of erotic passages point toward the sadomasochistic, entirely physical sexuality of the novels of sexual fantasies and erotica. Tonio, when still unwilling to sing female parts, believes that he will always "be divided. Always there would be pain. Pain and pleasure, intermingling and working him this way and that, and shaping him, but one never really vanquishing the other; there would never be peace" (*Cry*, 275). He refers primarily to his psychological conflict caused by castration: the joy of singing and the burden of revenge. The pain-pleasure principle is described elsewhere, however, as deriving exclusively from the nature of homosexual encounters, as when he is penetrated by a young Roman: "For one moment the pain was almost too great. And yet the pleasure blazed with it, until they were one harrowing flame" (*Cry*, 386). In the erotic novels, Rice follows up on the notion of sexual experience as the catalyst for personal liberation and leaves behind the confrontation with historical realities.

Chapter Nine

The Erotic Fiction

In an interview with Ron Bluestein on the publication of her erotic novels, Anne Rice said: "I write about how people can somehow survive, no matter how weird they are; how they can love each other and make it no matter how many strikes they have against them. Whether they're castrati or vampires or free people of color or sadomasochists, they can somehow find a moment of high romance and love."[1] The process of going from innocence to experience and thereby achieving an awareness that enables survival does indeed unite her protagonists, vampires and mortals alike: Louis, Marcel and Marie Ste. Marie, and Tonio Treschi, who come before the erotic books, and Lestat, Michael Curry, and Rowan Mayfair, who come after, are all "made anew" by the battering of experience that exposes them to existential realities, frees them from false moralities, and teaches them to trust their own moral philosophies.

It could be argued that survival through personal liberation continues to be the focus in the *Beauty* series of erotica and the two sexual fantasies *Exit to Eden* and *Belinda,* since the characters' experiences lead toward new levels of self-awareness. The actual writing of the books clearly provided a kind of liberation for Anne Rice, who, after writing them under pseudonyms, now owns up to being their author and defends them. As she explained to Dorothy Allison, "I see nothing wrong with writing sexually titillating scenes that have no redeeming social value."[2] Further, she felt that it was important for her to say that "desire is appropriate, that sex is good." Where the books fail, however, is in their focus on just one aspect of the human experience sexuality. The effect of these books is exactly opposite to that of the Gothics and historical novels. Whereas the clever adaptations of the Gothic tradition and the careful blending of historical moments with individuals serve to humanize the characters there, a relentless attention to the physical appetites of human nature creates a reductive effect that dehumanizes character. The larger liberation that occurs through the erotic elsewhere in Rice's fiction does not take place here, where it dictates the parameters of human life.

The *Beauty* series, written under the "cloak" of A. N. Roquelaure, takes the fairy tale of "Sleeping Beauty" as the springboard of its fantasy plot. It begins with the Prince's awakening of Beauty, literally and sexually, in *The Claiming of Sleeping Beauty,* published in 1983. Assuring her parents that Beauty will be returned later "greatly enhanced in wisdom and beauty," the Prince hauls her away nude to his kingdom, where as a slave her body is at the disposal of the royals, whom she must obey. Beauty is humiliated over and over again through a variety of sex acts, physical probings and inspections, donning of genital ornaments and restraints, paddlings, and instances of base servitude. Once initiated, she fits into the role of the female character delineated in the most popular erotic fantasies as described by Susan Brownmiller: "an innocent, untutored female is raped and 'subjected to unnatural practices' that turn her into a . . . dependent sexual slave who can never get enough" of the phallus.[3] Feeling embarrassed by her painfully obvious sexual readiness, moaning and longing to be satisfied, Beauty finally disobeys the Prince and is sent off to the infamous village for further chastisement, which transpires in the second novel in the series, *Beauty's Punishment* (1984).

The middle-class slave owners are just as designing in their methods of debasement as the royalty, and the same rules apply: "Not even in the village could a slave's flesh be broken; never could a slave be burned or truly harmed. No, her punishments would all *enhance.*"[4] After being sold on the auction block alongside her beloved Tristan to an innkeeper, Mistress Jennifer Lockley, Beauty goes through the humiliations she experienced at the royal palace. Beauty spends most of her time pleasing her mistress and one of her best patrons at the inn, the Captain. Not caring a whit about his conversation, she takes pleasure in being "his nude and shuddering slave," as in the episode when she is passed about from one of his soldiers to another, spread out on a broad barrel, and mounted by two men at a time.

Tristan interrupts her story from time to time to give first-person accounts of his public punishments, wallopings, whippings, sexual abuses, and harnessings as a human pony. Tristan comes to realize that he really "*wanted* the total degradation of the village" (*Punishment,* 125); he learns what his master tells him, that the slave finds great adventure in the "naked pleasure" of "yielding to the most extreme punishments" (*Punishment,* 178). Tristan is ecstatic later while being slapped and whipped on the public turntable. He describes his soul as "broke open" when he understands that his role is "to be dissolved in the will of others" (*Punishment,* 207–8). Tristan's and Beauty's lives as slaves in the village end abruptly when a raiding group of the Sultan's warriors captures them and places them in cages aboard a ship.

In the third and last novel of the series, *Beauty's Release* (1985), Beauty, Tristan, and a few other slaves arrive at the palace of the Sultan, where her sexual adventures continue and are interwoven with those of a fellow slave, Prince Laurent. Beauty assumes the role of trainer over a woman named Inanna. To her horror, Beauty discovers that Inanna, like all of the Sultan's women, has been genitally mutilated so that she will experience no sexual pleasure. Beauty finds a way to satisfy Inanna in spite of her mutilation, and she hopes that Inanna will pass on this pleasure to the other women. Nicolas and other villagers come to rescue Beauty, Laurent, and Tristan and return them to the village. In a sudden transition, Beauty is returned to her home, where she assumes her role as princess. After the death of his father, the king, Laurent returns to his home as well; he assumes control of his kingdom and subdues warring factions. Asked to choose a wife and produce an heir for the throne, he travels to Beauty and, much to her delight, carries her away to be his bride.

As this summary reveals, the series demonstrates the episodic action and lack of character causation typical of erotic novels. The emphasis on the physical at the exclusion of other human traits results in a simplistic treatment of character and more than a little repetition. Beverly LaBelle's observation on pornography as "one of the most boringly repetitious types of media" unfortunately fits the *Beauty* novels, which rely on a series of punishments "with minor variations added for spice and stimulation."[5] Unlike the innovative adventures of the vampires and witches, Rice's sensualists go through the same motions with nearly the same responses over and over again. These books are disappointing aesthetically because they lack the originality and stylistic richness that mark her Gothic and historical fiction. Rice defends the erotica, however, with arguments involving the controversial issues relating to pornographic literature.

In editing a collection of essays by women against pornography, Laura Lederer defines three major approaches to the pornographic. First is the traditional attack by conservatives, who view it as immoral; second is the support by liberals, who argue that it is one aspect of an "ever-expanding human sexuality"; third is the newest assault by feminists, who define it as violence against women and reject it as harmful on that basis.[6] Rice herself comes in on the liberal side, as she wants to explore sexuality as a means of liberation. As she stated in a 1992 interview with *Playboy,* she simply doesn't "believe women are victims who have to be

protected from everything" (Diehl, n.p.). She addresses the feminist
argument that pornography incites violence against women through the
context she creates for her characters. According to her biographer, "She
envisioned writing a book that she felt both men and women would
enjoy: elegant sadomasochism, where the desire to be dominated could
be entertained in a safe environment, where punishment enhanced
rather than restricted sexual freedom. Women could still be victims, but
only if that was what they wanted, and men could be victims, too"
(Ramsland, 213). Rice not only sets up rules whereby no one can be
injured, but has men and women serving as both trainers and slaves,
abusers and victims. Feminists who insist that pornography is demean-
ing to women make it clear that they are not objecting to the depictions
of sex acts on moral grounds. They disagree, however, as to whether or
not erotica for women's pleasure remains a degrading or liberating experience for women readers. As a result, Rice's intentions in these novels
raise complicated issues: does the limitation of sadomasochistic violence
make it acceptable or harmless, and is the inherent principle of pleasure
through pain, even though softened and applied to both sexes, an idea to
be promulgated given the incidence of rape and violent abuse in the
1990s?

The answers to these questions have to do with the efforts to define
the impact of violence on those who view pornography. Walter
Kendrick, who has traced society's futile efforts to control pornography
in *The Secret Museum: Pornography in Modern Literature* (1987), offers perhaps the most provocative observation of all. Explaining "Why
Yesterday's Smut Is Today's Erotica," he notes the recent introduction of
what used to be regarded as pornography into mainstream fiction. He
cites Anne Rice as an example of how a writer could shed a pseudonym
not only because of her established reputation but also because "the label
'pornography' was slipping off the written word and sticking to picture
magazines and videotapes."[7] According to Kendrick, "The boom in
above-the-counter sex fiction may reflect changing public attitudes
toward gender; it may mark a victory in women's long war against
oppression. Most of all, though, it means that 'verbal' porn, in the cen-
sors' eyes at least, is harmless." In other words, this "ambivalent liberation of the written word" depends on wide agreement that in a
subliterate culture, the written word in "pictureless books" is "impotent"
(Kendrick 1992, 36). Rice echoes Kendrick's points in her view that people do not "read pornography and go out and commit crimes; the vast

majority of crimes are committed by people who aren't reading any-thing" (Diehl, 56).

To what extent erotic material is harmful is taken up indirectly by the characters Lisa Kelly and Elliott Slater in *Exit to Eden* (1985). Elliott argues that "if there were a million safe places in which people could act out their fantasies, no matter how primitive or repulsive, then who knows what the world would be? Real violence might become for every-body a vulgarity, an obscenity."[8] Elliott reiterates a common defense of pornography as having a cathartic effect that indulges and assuages the viewer's sexual and violent urges in a safe way. Yet here again, this defense is based on controversial assumptions that those needs are inher-ent to the human personality, that they lie behind personal, social, and global atrocities, and that the experience of fictional aggression provides a "safety valve." Many critics and psychologists argue that pornography does not appease but rather can incite acts of violence against women. Since most issues surrounding pornography remain unresolved, includ-ing even the definition of what it is, the best way to assess this side of Rice's work may be not to address their controversial eroticism but to consider them as novels.

As with the *Beauty* series, *Exit to Eden* and *Belinda* do not fare well. Though the plots are less repetitive and the characters more developed, particularly in *Belinda,* both books resemble *The Mummy* in their thinness and predictability. Some reviewers refer to them as sexual fantasies, but these novels also fit the genre of erotic romances that have become par-ticularly popular with female readers since the 1970s. In the typical for-mulaic love plot, a man and woman may meet and go through various obstacles as they move from sexual attraction to a permanent commit-ment. The writing, according to Donna Vitek, a contributor to Kathryn Falk's *How to Write a Romance and Get It Published,* should emphasize their sexual tension, showing that "[t]he two cannot resist the delight that they give each other when they make love. Though it may seem that they should walk away from each other, they simply can't. This is the pinnacle of sexual buildup, a friction that becomes unbearable and must be eased." Confronting their problems and resolving them, they learn to trust each other and their intimacy "takes on a new and more wondrous significance."[9] In *Exit to Eden* and *Belinda,* Rice's focus on the erotic rather than emotional side of love, her virile males and beautiful females attracted to each other sexually at the outset, and the fortunate removal of obstacles separating them illustrate the criteria for the genre of sensual or erotic romance.

Exit to Eden, which Rice herself has called a "form of heightened pornography" (Ramsland, 228), at its start is similar to the *Beauty* series, with a shift from the slave's masochistic perspective (Beauty's) to that of the trainer. At 27, the protagonist, Lisa Kelly, is a master/trainer at The Club, an expensive and secret island resort she helped to establish for the purpose of allowing clients to engage in sadomasochistic sexual activities as slaves or as guests who exploit the slaves. Many of the sources of sexual pleasure and pain reappear here, such as spankings, probings, public punishments, and variations of sexual acts that establish control over the slaves. Instead of the mindless repetition of these activities, however, the action quickly focuses on the relationship between Lisa and the 29-year-old Elliott Slater, who has signed a two-year contract to be a slave.

Lisa and Elliott could both pass as models for the guidelines on heroines and heroes of romances as described in Falk's collection. The heroine, according to Falk, "is generally in her mid- to late twenties, with a fairly clear idea of who she is as an individual, and of her own self-worth. Thus, due to her intelligence, maturity, and gutsiness, she can certainly stand up for herself." The hero should be "handsome, passionate, self-assured, older than the heroine," a man who "will ultimately be successful if he is not so already. While he doesn't have to be a super macho, he must be a strong, sexy man, capable of tenderness, with his own needs and vulnerabilities."[10] Unable to maintain her dominant role as trainer with Elliott because she is so attracted to him, Lisa violates her own rules at The Club and takes him away with her to New Orleans and other places, where they greedily engage in sexual activity outside the strictures of The Club, get to know one another, and fall in love.

At the "pinnacle" of their relationship, her fellow Club directors pursue them in New Orleans, since they have broken all the regulations. Never believing that she would fall in love, Lisa has always kept her physical needs separate and hidden from her family and "real" life. Now she must reconcile the demands of two sides of her character as trainer-enjoying-sadomasochistic-pleasures and woman-in-love, which she manages to do at the end. Elliott tells her that while The Club may not appeal to them now that they have each other, they should consider the possibility of someday wanting to return. In the meantime, their marriage, he says, will be their "own little club of two" (*Exit,* 304).

While the complications of permanent commitment in *Belinda* are much more intricate than in *Exit to Eden* because they are connected with the lives of other characters, the *Lolita*-like novel ends just as happily for the lovers, Jeremy Walker, 44, and Belinda Blanchard, 16. They, too, move from sexual attraction to marriage. Interweaving their relationship with their public lives and roles as artists, Rice counterpoints the development of their love with Jeremy's liberation and artistic growth. As they come to terms with their passion and finally acknowledge the truth of their relationship to the public, Jeremy turns into a real painter.

Clearly at a crisis point in his career, Jeremy is a well-known illustrator/writer of children's books. Belinda is the daughter of an aging actress who is trying to make a comeback in a soap opera. While Jeremy's passion for Belinda must be kept secret for obvious reasons, it finds powerful expression in his art. Determined to abandon the children's books, he pours out his emotion onto daring canvases depicting Belinda. The precocious and talented Belinda does not actually develop as an actress through the course of the novel, but her love and eventual marriage enable her career to begin, since the mysteries surrounding her identity and past relationships with her mother, Bonnie, and stepfather, Marty Moreschi, are resolved. Belinda had appeared in two films herself and shown great potential, especially in the erotic *Final Score* directed by Susan Jeremiah, a film suppressed by her mother and Marty because the pornographic content would have interfered with her mother's career.

Though Belinda initially leaves Jeremy because of these entanglements, they are reunited in the suspenseful third section of the novel, where the only hope they have of avoiding arrest and irrevocable public shame is to marry before they are apprehended. With the help of friends and the legal permission of Belinda's father, "G.G.," they escape to Reno. The happy ending is not restricted to the lovers' marriage: Jeremy's paintings are well-received by critics and sold for millions; Belinda's film is a great critical success; the soap opera, "Champagne Flight," is salvaged through Belinda's generosity; Belinda's father, the gay G.G., acquires a new beauty salon in Los Angeles.

The obstacles to togetherness are more complicated in *Belinda* than in *East to Eden,* and the intrigues of Belinda's childhood and Jeremy's fame as a writer offer interesting glimpses of the film industry, the media, and the public's response to the life of artists in relation to their art. One reviewer of *Belinda* feels, in fact, that Jeremy's painting powerful erotic canvases, hiding them, exhibiting them, and then reacting to reviews are very close to Rice's own experiences with her erotica (Allison, 225), an idea supported by the fact that Rice dedicated *Belinda* to herself.

Jeremy's old friend, an aging actor named Alex, warns him of the difficult position he is in—not only as a man engaging in a criminal activity (having sex with a minor) but as an artist. He explains the "link
between sex and death" that is "as American as apple pie. For years every
movie they ever made about gay sex—or any kind of weird sex for that
matter—always ended with suicide or somebody getting killed. . . .
America makes you pay that way when you break the rules."[11] The more
confident Jeremy replies, "When everything is said and done, we'll see
who was right about sex and scandal and money and death!" Once
Belinda returns and they marry, Jeremy and Alex return to this conversation. Jeremy explains that he now has a sense of freedom that he never
had before as a man and an artist: "For the first time I could do anything
I wanted. I had passed—thanks to Belinda—out of the world of dreams
into the brilliant light of life itself" (*Belinda*, 496).

Despite the more complicated circumstances, Jeremy's experience is
similar to Lisa's in *Exit to Eden*. In both cases, a passionate love enables a
reconciliation of sides of self and ends a life of lies: Lisa, who experienced
her first orgasm at the age of eight, learns to accept her sexuality and
justify her work; Jeremy feels alive for the first time in painting the
nudes of Belinda instead of fairy-tale illustrations. He also admits to having written the last two novels published under his mother's name. Even
Belinda, who has matured beyond her years because of the "ugly pattern" of her childhood as the daughter of an alcoholic actress, is able to
leave a life of lies behind and establish independence from her mother: "I
mean, I was lying to hotel clerks and doctors and reporters before I
could remember. And, of course, we had all of us always lied to Mom"
(*Belinda*, 333). Referring to her love for Jeremy as well as to his art, she
describes the name of the painting series as "Holy Communion, Jeremy.
You've given eternal life to you and me" (*Belinda*, 372).

Rice attempts to fuse the erotic and spiritual sides of the secular love
relationship with Catholic imagery and to incorporate other techniques
prevalent in the Gothics. After Jeremy has had Belinda pose with religious props and then made love to her, he says, "Holy Communion."
"She bent down with the red wine on her lips and kissed me and she
whispered: 'This is my body. This is my blood'" (*Belinda*, 119). As
Ramsland points out, Rice "blends religious images with sex to turn the
meaning of both around. The ultimate union of person with person is
made akin to the ecstatic union of a person with God. On the one hand,
it is blasphemy to a church that views sex as duty—the ultimate degra-

dation of holy concepts. On the other hand, to someone who views sex as the ultimate human life force—the full expression of the erotic—equating it with Holy Communion means exploring and expressing its depth and power" (279). Ramsland also argues that The Club in *Exit to Eden* is a religious metaphor; the operators are referred to as an "unholy Trinity," Lisa is described through religious imagery, and The Club itself is like a heaven and hell, operating according to ritual (226). For Ramsland, these associations demonstrate once again how Rice uses Catholicism "to create vivid subliminal impressions."

Not only does the imagery preview the sacramental sanctity of blood relationships for vampires, but the couples of both novels also prefer the same settings. They flee to New Orleans, a familiar place to any reader of Anne Rice. Lisa and Elliott stay in a hotel, dine at memorable restaurants, and soak up the ambiance of the city on walks. Originally from Berkeley, as is Lisa, Elliott remarks of New Orleans, "This is a seedy place, but it's a real place. California isn't real" (*Exit,* 202). For Jeremy and Belinda, too, New Orleans is a refuge from the hectic pursuits of San Francisco and Los Angeles. They take up residence in Jeremy's mother's stately, but decaying home in the Garden District. Complete with a reference to Miss Havisham from Dickens's *Great Expectations,* this setting foreshadows the Mayfair home in *The Witching Hour.* Jeremy writes: "California just slipped away into darkness. Out of California Gothic we go into Southern Gothic" (*Belinda,* 235). The power of the setting to magnify emotional states, as in the Gothics, is apparent when an enraged Jeremy discovers that Belinda has given the negatives of his photographs of her to her mother as a way of blackmailing him to keep quiet. As he smashes his fist through an old wall of the house, "A great gaping hole broke in the pattern of leaves and roses. Stench of rottenness. Of rain and rats and rottenness" (*Belinda,* 260).

In the *Beauty* books, however, the description of carnal delights takes precedence over the creative evocations of atmosphere and mood. Rice repeats paradoxical language to describe the simultaneous pleasure and pain derived from the slaves' sexual experiences in the erotica, as when Beauty feels the "excruciating pleasure" that makes her think she is "not human" (*Punishment,* 6–7).

In an effort to divide the power in sexual relationships and therefore the sadism and masochism between the sexes—in keeping with her notion of gender equality in the erotic books—Rice has the male slaves Tristan and Laurent provide first-person accounts of their treatment along with Beauty's. The narrative in *Exit to Eden* also alternates

between Lisa and Elliott at appropriate times; when Lisa goes through
her breakdown toward the end, for instance, Elliott is the interpreter.
Though Jeremy is the main first-person narrator, Belinda is given a
chance to explain her behavior right after she seems at her worst in
betraying Jeremy. An unusually mature and rapid writer, Belinda sends
him a 100-page manuscript providing an account of her life with Bonnie
and Marty, justifying her actions, and declaring her love for him.
According to Carol Thurston, part of the appeal of erotic romances for
women readers is that they tend not only to "challenge the traditional
power relationships between men and women but depict a more bal-
anced power alignment as natural and expected—in other words, as the
norm."[12]

Although Katherine Ramsland sees the erotic books as reflections of
the different sides of Anne Rice, the Roquelaure identity providing an
outlet for masochistic fantasies, the Rampling an escape from the darkness of the Gothics (241), the underlying bond between author and art
is the larger quest for freedom and truth that finds more substantial and
significant expression in the Gothics. While this theme permeates the
worlds and characters there, in the erotica it is not blended with but
rather appended to the eroticism.

As Lisa and Elliott, Jeremy and Belinda, and even Beauty finally leave
behind wanton sexual pleasure for deeper attachments, Rice fortunately
returns to the Gothic, where she includes but does not focus exclusively
on eroticism in the complexities of human and vampiric experience. Like
The Club, which Lisa describes as a "glorious imprisonment," the erotica could have become a fictional imprisonment rather than a liberation,
an expression that may or may not be morally wrong but is ultimately
dehumanizing in its one-dimensional portrayal of men and women.
Reviewers like Dorothy Allison, who saw the "erotic charge" as becoming more and more obvious in her fiction in 1986 (24), were fortunately
inaccurate in predicting the direction her fiction would take.

Chapter Ten

Conclusion

I began this study of Anne Rice's novels with the intention of deciding whether or not we should take them seriously. Indeed, except for the erotic fiction, all of Rice's novels may be taken seriously on the grounds provided by new critical theories of historicists and culturalists, who use the popularity of a work to come to terms with the nature of the times in which it was created and the values of its readers. Rice's best novels may also be analyzed on the more traditional assessments that guarantee a lasting reputation for a major writer: philosophical substance, stylistic richness, and, most pertinent to Rice, impact on the chosen genre. She puts her own stamp on any type of novel that she writes: Gothic, historical, erotic, but it is her Gothic fiction that makes the most significant contribution to a literary tradition.

Rice's work lends itself to the ongoing critical debate on the merits of popular versus classic literature, particularly challenges to the transitional literary canon posed by new critical approaches to the texts. The impact of the debate on Gothic fiction has been to establish further the theoretical groundwork for its study. Countering Ian Watt's insistence in the 1950s on realism as the standard of assessment for the novel, critics have been identifying and justifying the goals of romantic fiction for nearly 20 years now. Yet even today some reviewers dismiss the whole Gothic genre and regard works such as *Frankenstein* and *Dracula* as unworthy of detailed analysis. While it is true that the vampire has been popularized into triviality, some contemporary critics are unwilling to acknowledge the ways in which the Gothic can imaginatively reveal psychological truths.

Though all of the new theories or approaches to text (reader-response, feminist, and multicultural, among others) may not be detailed here, perhaps the most pertinent concerning the Gothic is the cultural critic's more descriptive than evaluative approach, which promotes the study of literature as a product of and a means of understanding cultural myths, beliefs, and events. This approach is especially apt given that the nightmares of Gothic fiction often reflect the real horrors of everyday life and the shared anxieties of people at a particular time. Explaining how the cultural criticism of Janice Radway, for example, differs from Marxist studies, Linda H. Peterson states: "Rather than seeing all forms of popular culture as manifestations of ideology, soon to be remanifested in the minds of victimized audiences, non-Marxist cultural critics tend to see a sometimes disheartening but always dynamic synergy between cultural forms and the culture's consumers."[1] Harriett Hawkins, in her 1990 *Classics and Trash: Traditions and Taboos in High Literature and Popular Modern Genres,* attempts to break down the traditional division between these categories by showing their integral relationship and mutual influence. Hawkins goes so far as to argue, for example, that "the forces and energies and impacts that account for the status and indeed the survival of an 'immortal' masterpiece are pretty much the same forces and energies and impacts that assure commercial success at the box office in any age."[2]

The popular success of Rice's novels since *Interview with the Vampire* in 1976 assures her worthiness as the object of cultural studies. With her most recent novel, *Lasher,* remaining on the *Times* best-seller list for many months since its publication in 1993, she has now written 14 novels: seven Gothics, two historical romances, two erotic fantasies, and three erotica. The two historical books have not sold well, despite the current popular taste for sprawling historical fiction. Like the erotics, however, they are beginning to get more attention from readers who, drawn to Rice's Gothic novels, are curious about the others.

Many critics of the Gothic acknowledge that however the artistic fabrication takes shape, at the heart of the best examples of the genre is the confrontation with self. In *Danse Macabre,* Stephen King states that in more contemporary American Gothic, the malevolence of the Gothic villains and monsters "comes from us" (246); the dreams and fantasies in the Gothic create a confusing reality, which provides Gothic ambiguity regarding what evil is without and what is within. Rice's vampires are humanized, sympathetic characters who exaggerate the struggle for survival amid fin-de-siècle decadence. Finding personal moralities to counter the impact of overwhelming sources of dehumanization, her characters appeal to readers whose own twentieth century is coming to a close. As Susan Ferraro explains, "Trapped in immortality, [Rice's vampires] suffer human regret. They are lonely, prisoners of circumstance, compulsive sinners, full of self-loathing and doubt. They are, in short, Everyman Eternal" (67). Like Everyman, the protagonists are forced to reexamine, in a painful and violent process, the institutions and so-called universal truths of human existence to find out what to live by.

Her vampires are not all alike; they are distinguished not only physically but psychologically. For instance, to be an older vampire is to be more dignified yet less human, to have found the personal philosophy to endure. Lestat is Rice's central metaphor for the indomitable spirit of rebellion against loneliness and insignificance, but perhaps none of her vampires quite compares in impact with Louis in the *Interview,* with his search for meaning, his awareness of the demands of his existence, and his human sensitivity that brings him despair. Somewhere between Louis's depression and Lestat's superhuman will is the hopeful Michael Curry, a human being who gains the strength of his own convictions after losing Rowan in *The Witching Hour.* While the androgynous sexuality and eroticism of Rice's vampires attract contemporary readers, their larger appeal is due to Rice's atypical and imaginative development of their characters. She also endows these creatures with intellectual substance, which propels them in their quest for personal meaning and takes them well beyond the merely sensational into the spiritual and philosophical.

The spirit of liberation that Rice brings to her characters also permeates her handling of other Gothic conventions. Many critics have explored the metaphorical significance of medieval ruins and castles, dungeons, remote islands, and scenes of wilderness in traditional Gothics as reflections of psychological states, such as the imprisonment or repression of self, the fear of sexuality, the oppression of women, the claustrophobia of mental illness. Rice also utilizes setting as a symbol and perpetuates the darkness of vampirism in her characters' aversion to sunlight and their need to remain hidden during the day, but the special attributes of her vampires enable them to transcend the conventional limitations of vampirism. The world of her novels is expansive. It opens up the whole genre, as stories within the narrations move from present to ancient past and back to present, and vampire travels encompass the globe. Despite the characters' preferences for San Francisco and New Orleans, the depths of arctic waste are as convincingly portrayed as the elegant interiors of mansions decorated by vampires with exquisite taste. Adapting in dress, appearance, and behavior to the customs of the twentieth century, her protagonists may appear in Edwardian velvet or black leather. They retain their experience from the past, but they learn how to live in the present.

Instead of focusing on the predatory vampire attacks typical of the genre, Rice explores a Gothic world that includes pre-Egyptian rituals of sacrifice, rock concerts, witch trials, and fetal research. David Punter's comments concerning the ways in which the fantasy landscapes in the modern Gothic convey mental disintegration and cultural decay (374) are pertinent to Rice's existential world, where the public scenes of the past and present are linked by the desperate need for sensation and violence as antidotes to despair: the grotesque performance of the Parisian vampires in the *Interview,* including the surrealistic paintings of horror in the subterranean dwelling below the theater; the rock concert frenzy that mirrors the Druidian orgies of human sacrifice in *Lestat;* the pagan rituals of Maharet and Mekare in *The Queen of the Damned* that culminate symbolically in Akasha's goal of the massacre of males; the witch trials and perverse mutilations and mutations of Lasher in *The Witching Hour.* In acting out these scenes, the vampires echo the vulnerabilities of unfulfilled, unaware human beings and assert the importance of discovering the false motives and schemes of individuals or social institutions that feed on human need and perpetrate violence. Though Rice occasionally overdevelops these scenes, her lush, extravagant description makes them entirely credible, and their symbolic atmosphere contributes to the aesthetic realities and truths put forth in Rice's existential philosophy. Her plot structures, especially in *The Queen of the Damned* and *The Witching Hour,* make allegories of philosophical debates, such as that between the ideal of nurturing respect for humanity—represented in Maharet—and destructive rationalism—embodied in Akasha.

While Rice's Gothicism does provide an atmosphere of impending violence that contributes to suspense, the primary source of anxiety in her Gothic novels arises from the psychological passage of her protagonists, whether they are vampiric or human. Since these marginal, alienated characters usually tell their own tales, the reader identifies with their losses and confrontations with violence and wonders if they will make it. In the end, questions such as whether or not Louis will be able to endure his own despair are more important than whether or not he can conquer the Parisian vampires. Will Lestat recover his rebellious spirit and bring himself up out of his self-burial in the earth? Will Michael hold onto his secular faith in human nature? The abiding source of anxiety is psychological and philosophical, punctuated by scenes of physical horror.

Given the sense of finality with which Lestat rejects the human state in *The Tale of the Body Thief* and his murder of David Talbot, which represent a reversal of the humanization that characterizes Rice's vampires, questions arise concerning what direction her writing will take. Rice has said she believes that "the philosophical meaning of being a vampire has been fully explored" and that if she continues with the *Chronicles,* the books will be more metaphysical (Ramsland, 362). Clearly, her efforts have revitalized the Gothic and, as James B. Twitchell argues, restored the vampire figure to its original Romantic stature and ambivalent appeal (193). To date her novels have demonstrated the continuing vitality of the Gothic as a means of probing serious human concerns while appealing to the imagination.

Notes and References

Chronology

1. I am indebted to Katherine Ramsland's *Prism of the Night: A Biography of Anne Rice* for the abundance of dates of Anne Rice's life and career from which I was able to choose for this chronology. Published in 1991, Ramsland's book is an essential starting place for any researcher of Anne Rice. This study relies on it for nearly all of the biographical material, particularly Rice's own comments on her work.

Chapter One

1. Susan Ferraro, "Novels You Can Sink Your Teeth Into," *New York Times Magazine,* 14 October 1990, 28; hereafter cited in the text.
2. Katherine Ramsland, *Prism of the Night: A Biography of Anne Rice* (1991; New York: Plume Books, 1992), xii; hereafter cited in the text.
3. Anne Rice, *The Vampire Lestat: Book II of the Vampire Chronicles* (New York: Alfred A. Knopf, 1985), 124; hereafter cited in the text as *Lestat.*
4. Anne Rice, *The Queen of the Damned: The Third Book of the Vampire Chronicles* (New York: Alfred A. Knopf, 1988), 8; hereafter cited in the text as *Queen.*
5. Anne Rice, *The Feast of All Saints* (New York: Ballantine Books, 1986), 412; hereafter cited in the text as *Feast.*
6. Anne Rice, *The Witching Hour* (New York: Alfred A. Knopf, 1990), 964; hereafter cited in the text as *Hour.*
7. Anne Rice, *Cry to Heaven* (New York: Alfred A. Knopf, 1982), 47; hereafter cited in text as *Cry.*
8. Joseph Grixti, *Terrors of Uncertainty: The Cultural Contexts of Horror Fiction* (New York: Routledge, 1989), 174; hereafter cited in the text.

Chapter Two

1. David Punter, *The Literature of Terror: A History of Gothic Fictions from 1765 to the Present Day* (New York: Longman, 1980), 408; hereafter cited in the text.
2. J. M. S. Tompkins, *The Popular Novel in England 1770–1800* (Lincoln: University of Nebraska Press, 1961), 129.
3. Stephen King, *Danse Macabre* (New York: Berkley Books, 1982), 43; hereafter cited in the text.
4. Janice Radway, *Reading the Romance: Women, Patriarchy, and Popular*

Literature (Chapel Hill: University of North Carolina Press, 1984); hereafter cited in the text.

5. Helen Hazen, *Endless Rapture: Rape, Romance, and The Female Imagination* (New York: Charles Scribner's Sons, 1983), 35; hereafter cited in the text.

6. Cynthia Griffin Wolff, "The Radcliffean Model: A Form for Feminine Sexuality," *Modern Language Studies* 9 (Fall 1979): 102; hereafter cited in the text.

7. Whitley Strieber, *The Hunger* (New York: Pocket Books, 1982), 304.

8. Leonard Wolf, *A Dream of Dracula: In Search of the Living Dead* (New York: Popular Library, 1977), 130.

9. Brian J. Frost, *The Monster with a Thousand Faces: Guises of the Vampire in Myth and Literature* (Bowling Green, Ohio: Bowling Green State University Popular Press, 1989), 24; hereafter cited in the text.

10. Digby Diehl, "Anne Rice Interview," *Playboy,* March 1993, 60; hereafter cited in the text.

Chapter Three

1. Edmund Fuller, review of *Interview with the Vampire, Wall Street Journal,* 17 June 1976, 14.

2. Charles W. Gold, review of *Interview with the Vampire, Booklist,* 15 June 1976, 1453.

3. Pearl K. Bell, "A Gemeinschaft of Vampires," review of *Interview with the Vampire, New Leader* 59 (7 June 1976): 15.

4. Phoebe Lou-Adams, review of *Interview with the Vampire, Atlantic Monthly,* June 1976, 105.

5. Leo Braudy, review of *Interview with the Vampire, New York Times Book Review,* 2 May 1976, 7.

6. Edith Milton, "*Interview with the Vampire* by Anne Rice," *New Republic,* 8 May 1976, 30.

7. Anne Rice, *Interview with the Vampire* (New York: Alfred A. Knopf, 1976), 79; hereafter cited in the text as *Interview.*

8. James B. Twitchell, *The Living Dead: A Study of the Vampire in Romantic Literature* (Durham, N.C.: Duke University Press, 1981), 5; hereafter cited in the text.

9. William Patrick Day, *In the Circles of Fear and Desire: A Study of Gothic Fantasy* (Chicago: University of Chicago Press, 1985), 192–93; hereafter cited in the text.

10. Constance Casey, "Literary New Orleans," *Publisher's Weekly,* 9 May 1986, 154–58.

Chapter Four

1. Nina Auerbach, "No. 2 with a Silver Bullet," review of *The Vampire Lestat, New York Times Book Review,* 27 October 1985, 15.
2. Walter Kendrick, review of *The Vampire Lestat, Village Voice Literary Supplement,* November 1985, 28–29; hereafter cited in the text.
3. Sybil Steinberg, review of *The Vampire Lestat, Publisher's Weekly,* 16 August 1985, 63.
4. Michiko Kakutani, "Vampire for Our Times," review of *The Vampire Lestat, New York Times,* 19 October 1985, 15.
5. Gregory A. Waller, *The Living and the Undead: From Dracula to Romero's Dawn of the Dead* (Chicago: University of Illinois Press, 1986), 8.
6. J. E. Cirlot, *A Dictionary of Symbols,* trans. Jack Sage (New York: Philosophical Library, 1962), 328; hereafter cited in the text.
7. Anne Rice, ". . . Playing with Gender," *Vogue,* November 1983, 434, 498; hereafter cited in text as "Gender."
8. Katherine Ramsland, *The Vampire Comparison: The Official Guide to Anne Rice's "The Vampire Chronicles"* (New York: Ballantine Books, 1993), 396; hereafter cited in the text as Ramsland 1993.

Chapter Five

1. Laurence Coven, "A History of the Undead," review of *The Queen of the Damned, Los Angeles Times Book Review,* 6 November 1988, 13; hereafter cited in the text.
2. Sybil Steinberg, review of *The Queen of the Damned, Publisher's Weekly,* 12 August 1989, 440.
3. Eric Kraft, "Do Not Speak Ill of the Undead," review of *The Queen of the Damned, New York Times Book Review,* 27 November 1988, 12.
4. Michael Rogers, review of *The Queen of the Damned, Library Journal,* 1 October 1988, 101.
5. Lindsy Van Gelder, "Biting Satire: The Final Installment in Anne Rice's Vampire Trilogy," *Ms.,* November 1988, 76.
6. Walter Kendrick, review of *The Queen of the Damned, Village Voice Literary Supplement,* November 1988, 5.
7. Review of *The Queen of the Damned, Booklist,* 1 September 1988, 4.
8. Northrop Frye, "Theory of Genres," in *Anatomy of Criticism: Four Essays* (New York: Atheneum, 1969), 304.
9. Sir James George Frazer, *The Golden Bough: A Study in Magic and Religion* (New York: Macmillan Company, 1951), 514; hereafter cited in the text.
10. Eric Neumann, *The Great Mother: An Analysis of the Archetype,* trans. Ralph Manheim (New York: Pantheon Books, 1955), 39; hereafter cited in the text.

Chapter Six

1. David Gates, "A 200-Year-Old Problem Drinker," review of *The Tale of the Body Thief, Newsweek,* 26 October 1992, 62.

2. Ralph Novak, review of *The Tale of the Body Thief, People,* 2 November 1992, 33; hereafter cited in the text.

3. Roz Kaveney, "Undead Again," review of *The Tale of the Body Thief, New Statesman and Society,* 30 October 1992, 38.

4. Walter Kendrick, "Better Undead than Unread: Have Vampires Lost Their Bite?" *New York Times Book Review,* 18 October 1992, 55.

5. Michael Rogers, review of *The Tale of the Body Thief, Library Journal,* 1 September 1992, 216.

6. Review of *The Tale of the Body Thief, Publishers Weekly,* 13 September 1992, 72.

7. Anne Rice, *The Tale of the Body Thief: The Vampire Chronicles* (New York: Alfred A. Knopf, 1992), 6; hereafter cited in the text as *Thief.*

8. *Goethe's Faust Parts I and II,* trans. Louis MacNeice (New York: Oxford University Press, 1951), 298.

Chapter Seven

1. Sybil Steinberg, review of *The Mummy or Ramses the Damned, Publishers Weekly,* 5 April 1989, 70.

2. Frank J. Prial, review of *The Mummy or Ramses the Damned, New York Times Book Review,* 11 June 1989, 9, and Steinberg 1989, 70.

3. Victoria Neumark, review of *The Mummy or Ramses the Damned, Listener,* 5 October 1989, 33.

4. Rita Mae Brown, *"Witching Hour* Rice's Best," review of *The Witching Hour, Springfield Sunday Republican,* 25 November 1990, D-8.

5. Patrick McGrath, "Ghastly and Unnatural Ambitions," review of *The Witching Hour, New York Times Book Review,* 4 November 1990, 11.

6. Anne Rice, *The Mummy or Ramses the Damned* (New York: Ballantine Books, 1989), 4; hereafter cited in the text as *Mummy.*

7. A. Conan Doyle, "The Ring of Thoth," in *The Captain of the Pole-star and Other Tales* (New York: A. L. Burt, Publisher, n.d.), 262; hereafter cited in the text.

8. In *Lasher* (1993)—published too close to the print date of this volume to incorporate its study in the text—Michael finally manages to destroy Lasher by crushing his skull with a hammer. Rowan, too, who had been imprisoned by Lasher and become deathly ill as a result of miscarriages from his attempt to impregnate her and from the bizarre birth of his offspring, escapes Lasher and recovers to destroy their "daughter," Emeleth. Despite their role in defeating the evil figure whose identity goes back to pre-Christian Scottish times and includes an exemplary life as the holy St. Ashlar, Michael and Rowan are not the central focus here that they were in *The Witching Hour.*

In *Lasher* the shifts in stories and narrative perspectives typical of Rice's technique in her other Gothics concern Mayfair females threatened by Lasher and others. A disillusioned Aaron Lightner separates himself from the Talamascans, whose motives in tracking down Lasher become suspect here. Given Lasher's brutal treatment of Rowan, his egotistical plan to replace human beings with his own kind to "subdue the earth," and his ruthless rapes of Mayfair women who die from hemorrhaging in instant miscarriages, he remains an unsympathetic villain like Akasha in *The Queen of the Damned*. With Lasher no longer a threat at the end of the book, the character who offers a new place to continue the saga of Mayfair witchery is Mona Mayfair, the precocious 13-year-old who seduces Michael at the beginning of the book, who has more Mayfair blood in her than any other member of the family.

Chapter Eight

1. Pat Goodfellow, review of *The Feast of All Saints*, *Library Journal*, 15 January 1980, 226.
2. Barbara Bannon, review of *The Feast of All Saints*, *Publishers Weekly*, 26 November 1979, 41.
3. Beth Ann Mills, review of *Cry to Heaven*, *Library Journal*, August 1982, 1483.
4. Review of *The Feast of All Saints*, *Virginia Quarterly Review*, Summer 1980, 107.
5. Rhoda Koenig, "Two Novels," review of *The Feast of All Saints*, *New York Times Book Review*, 17 February 1980, 17.
6. George Dekker, *The American Historical Romance* (New York: Cambridge University Press, 1987), 26; hereafter cited in the text.
7. C. Hugh Holman and William Harmon, *A Handbook to Literature*, 6th ed. (New York: Macmillan Publishing Company, 1992), 229.

Chapter Nine

1. Ron Bluestein, "Interview with the Pornographer," *Vogue*, April 1986, 216.
2. Dorothy Allison, "Sex, Sin, and the Pursuit of Literary Excellence," *Village Voice Literary Supplement*, December 1986, 26; hereafter cited in the text.
3. Susan Brownmiller, "Excerpt on Pornography from *Against Our Will: Men, Women, and Rape*," in *Take Back the Night: Women on Pornography*, ed. Laura Lederer (New York: William Morrow and Company, 1980), 32.
4. Anne Rice as A. N. Roquelaure, *Beauty's Punishment* (New York: Plume, 1984), 8; hereafter cited in the text as *Punishment*.
5. Beverly LaBelle, "The Propaganda of Misogyny," in *Take Back the Night*, 177.
6. Laura Lederer, ed., introduction, in *Take Back the Night*, 19–20.
7. Walter Kendrick, "Increasing Our Dirty-Word Power: Why

Yesterday's Smut Is Today's Erotica," *New York Times Book Review,* 31 May 1992, 36; hereafter cited in the text.

8.   Anne Rice as Anne Rampling, *Exit to Eden* (1985; New York: Dell Publishing, 1989), 221; hereafter cited in the text as *Exit.*

9.   Donna Kimel Vitek, "Building Sexual Tension," in *How to Write a Romance and Get It Published: With Intimate Advice from the World's Most Popular Romance Writers,* ed. Kathryn Falk, rev. ed. (New York: Signet, 1990), 154.

10.   Kathryn Falk, ed., "Examples of Tip Sheets," in *How to Write a Romance,* 18–19.

11.   Anne Rice as Anne Rampling, *Belinda* (1986; New York: Jove, 1988), 435; hereafter cited in the text as *Belinda.*

12.   Carol Thurston, *The Romance Revolution: Erotic Novels for Women and the Quest for a New Sexual Identity* (Chicago: University of Chicago Press, 1987), 7–8.

Chapter Ten

1.   Linda H. Peterson, ed., "Cultural Criticism and Wuthering Heights," in *Emily Brontë: Wuthering Heights: Complete, Authoritative Text with Biographical and Historical Contexts, Critical History, and Essays from Five Contemporary Critical Perspectives* (Boston: Bedford Books, 1992), 423–24.

2.   Harriet Hawkins, *Classics and Trash: Traditions and Taboos in High Literature and Popular Modern Genres* (Buffalo: University of Toronto Press, 1990), 118.

Selected Bibliography

PRIMARY WORKS
Novels

Beauty's Punishment. New York: Plume Books, 1984.
Beauty's Release. New York: E. P. Dutton, 1985.
Belinda. 1986. New York: Jove, 1988.
The Claiming of Sleeping Beauty. New York: E. P. Dutton, 1983.
Cry to Heaven. New York: Alfred A. Knopf, 1982.
Exit to Eden. 1985. New York: Dell Publishing, 1989.
The Feast of All Saints. New York: Simon & Schuster, 1979.
Interview with the Vampire. New York: Alfred A. Knopf, 1976.
Lasher. New York: Alfred A. Knopf, 1993.
The Mummy or Ramses the Damned. New York: Ballantine Books, 1989.
The Queen of the Damned. New York: Alfred A. Knopf, 1988.
The Tale of the Body Thief. New York: Alfred A. Knopf, 1992.
The Vampire Lestat. New York: Alfred A. Knopf, 1985.
The Witching Hour. New York: Alfred A. Knopf, 1990.

Other

"The Master of Rampling Gate." *Redbook,* February 1984, 50–57.
". . . Playing with Gender." *Vogue,* November 1983, 434, 498.

SECONDARY WORKS
Books, Articles and Reviews about Anne Rice

Auerbach, Nina. "No. 2 With a Silver Bullet." Review of *The Vampire Lestat. New York Times Book Review,* 27 October 1985, 15.
Bannon, Barbara. Review of *The Feast of All Saints. Publishers Weekly,* 26 November 1979, 41.
Bell, Pearl K. "A Gemeinschaft of Vampires." Review of *Interview with the Vampire. New Leader,* 7 June 1976, 15.
Bluestein, Ron. "Interview with the Pornographer." *Vogue,* April 1986, 212, 214, 216.
Braudy, Leo. Review of *Interview with the Vampire. New York Times Book Review,* 2 May 1976, 7.
Brown, Rita Mae. "Witching Hour Rice's Best." Review of *The Witching Hour. Springfield Sunday Republican,* 25 November 1990, D-8.

Casey, Constance. "Literary New Orleans." *Publishers Weekly,* 9 May 1986, 154–58.

Coven, Laurence. "A History of the Undead." Review of*The Queen of the Damned. Los Angeles Times Book Review,* 6 November 1988, 13.

Diehl, Digby. "Anne Rice Interview." *Playboy,* March 1993, 53–54, 56, 58–64.

Ferraro, Susan. "Novels You Can Sink Your Teeth Into." *New York Times Book Review,* 14 October 1990, 27–30, 67, 74, 76–77.

Fuller, Edmund. Review of *Interview with the Vampire. Wall Street Journal,* 17 June 1976, 14.

Gates, David. "A 200-Year-Old Problem Drinker." Review of *The Tale of the Body Thief. Newsweek,* 26 October 1992, 62.

Gold, Charles W. Review of *Interview with the Vampire. Booklist,*15 June 1976, 1453.

Goodfellow, Pat. Review of *The Feast of All Saints. Library Journal,* 15 January 1980, 226.

Kakutani, Michael. "Vampire of Our Times." Review of *The Vampire Lestat. New York Times,* 19 October 1985, 15.

Kaveney, Roz. "Undead Again." Review of *The Tale of the Body Thief. New Statesman & Society,* 30 October 1992, 38.

Kendrick, Walter. "Better Undead Than Unread: Have Vampires Lost Their Bite?" Review of *The Tale of the Body Thief. New York Times Book Review,* 18 October 1992, 55.

_____. "Increasing Our Dirty-Word Power: Why Yesterday's Smut Is Today's Erotica." *New York Times Book Review,* 31 May 1992, 3, 36.

_____. Review of *The Queen of the Damned. Village Voice Literary Supplement,* November 1988, 5.

_____. Review of *The Vampire Lestat. Village Voice Literary Supplement,* November 1985, 26–29.

Koenig, Rhoda. "Two Novels." Review of *The Feast of All Saints. New York Times Book Review,* 17 February 1980, 17.

Kraft, Eric. "Do Not Speak Ill of the Undead." Review of *The Queen of the Damned. New York Times Book Review,* 27 November 1988, 12.

Lou-Adams, Phoebe. Review of *Interview with the Vampire. Atlantic Monthly,* June 1976, 105.

McGrath, Patrick. "Ghastly and Unnatural Ambitions." Review of *The Witching Hour. New York Times Book Review,* 4 November 1990, 16.

Mills, Beth Ann. Review of *Cry to Heaven. Library Journal,* 4 August 1982, 1483.

Milton, Edith. Review of *Interview with the Vampire. New Republic,* 8 May 1976, 30.

Neumark, Victoria. Review of *The Mummy or Ramses the Damned. Listener,* 5 October 1989, 33.

Novak, Ralph. Review of *The Tale of the Body Thief. People,* 2 November 1992, 33.

Prial, Frank J. Review of *The Feast of All Saints. Virginia Quarterly Review* 56 (Summer 1980): 107.

_____. Review of *The Mummy or Ramses the Damned. New York Times Book Review,* 11 June 1989, 9.

_____. Review of *The Queen of the Damned. Booklist,* 1 September 1988, 4.

_____. Review of *The Tale of the Body Thief. Publishers Weekly,* 13 September 1992, 72.

Ramsland, Katherine. *Prism of the Night: A Biography of Anne Rice.* 1991. New York: Plume Books, 1992.

_____. *The Vampire Companion: The Official Guide to Anne Rice's "The Vampire Chronicles."* New York: Ballantine Books, 1993.

Rogers, Michael. Review of *The Queen of the Damned. Library Journal,* 1 October 1988, 101.

_____. Review of *The Tale of the Body Thief. Library Journal,* 1 September 1992, 216.

Steinberg, Sybil. Review of *The Mummy or Ramses the Damned. Publishers Weekly,* 5 April 1989, 70.

_____. Review of *The Queen of the Damned. Publishers Weekly,*12 August 1989, 440.

_____. Review of *The Vampire Lestat. Publishers Weekly,* 16 August 1985, 63.

Van Gelder, Lindsy. "Biting Satire: The Final Installment of Anne Rice's Vampire Trilogy." Review of *The Queen of the Damned. Ms.,* November 1988, 76.

Books, Articles, and Reviews about Gothic Fiction and Related Issues

Brownmiller, Susan. "Excerpt on Pornography from *Against Our Will: Men, Women, and Rape.*" In *Take Back the Night: Women on Pornography,* edited by Laura Lederer, 30–34. New York: William Morrow and Company, 1980.

Cirlot, J. E. *A Dictionary of Symbols.* Translated by Jack Sage. New York: Philosophical Library, 1962.

Day, William Patrick. *In the Circles of Fear and Desire: A Study of Gothic Fantasy.* Chicago: University of Chicago Press, 1985.

Dekker, George. *The American Historical Romance.* New York: Cambridge University Press, 1987.

Falk, Kathryn. "Examples of Tip Sheets." In *How to Write a Romance and Get It Published: With Intimate Advice from the World's Most Popular Romance Writers,* edited by Kathryn Falk, 15–23. Rev. ed. New York: Signet Books, 1990.

Frazer, Sir James George. *The Golden Bough: A Study in Magic and Religion.* New York: Macmillan Company, 1951.

Frost, Brian J. *The Monster With a Thousand Faces: Guises of the Vampire in Myth and Literature.* Bowling Green, Ohio: Bowling Green State University Popular Press, 1989.

Frye, Northrop. "Theories of Genres." In *Anatomy of Criticism: Four Essays,* 243–337. New York: Atheneum, 1969.

Grixti, Joseph. *Terrors of Uncertainty: The Cultural Contexts of Horror Fiction.* New York: Routledge, 1989.

Hawkins, Harriet. *Classics and Trash: Traditions and Taboos in High Literature and Popular Modern Genres.* Buffalo: University of Toronto Press, 1990.

Hazen, Helen. *Endless Rapture: Rape, Romance, and the Female Imagination.* New York: Charles Scribner's Sons, 1983.

Holman, C. Hugh and William Harmon. *A Handbook to Literature.* 6th ed. New York: Macmillan Publishing Co., 1992.

King, Stephen. *Danse Macabre.* New York: Berkley Books, 1982.

LaBelle, Beverly. "The Propaganda of Misogyny." In *Take Back the Night: Women on Pornography,* edited by Laura Lederer, 174–78. New York: William Morrow and Company, 1980.

Lederer, Laura. "Introduction." In *Take Back the Night,* edited by Laura Lederer, 15–20. New York: William Morrow and Company, 1980.

Neumann, Eric. *The Great Mother: An Analysis of the Archetype.* Translated by Ralph Manheim. New York: Pantheon Books, 1955.

Peterson, Linda H. "Cultural Criticism and *Wuthering Heights.*" In *Emily Bronte: Wuthering Heights: Complete Authoritative Text with Biographical and Historical Contexts, Critical History, and Essays from Five Contemporary Critical Perspectives,* edited by Linda H. Peterson, 415–25. Boston: Bedford Books of St. Martin's Press, 1992.

Punter, David. *The Literature of Terror: A History of Gothic Fictions from 1765 to the Present Day.* New York: Longman, 1980.

Radway, Janice. *Reading the Romance: Women, Matriarchy, and Popular Literature.* Chapel Hill: University of North Carolina Press, 1984.

Thurston, Carol. *The Romance Revolution: Erotic Novels for Women and the Quest for a New Sexual Identity.* Chicago: University of Chicago Press, 1987.

Tompkins, J. M. S. *The Popular Novel in England, 1770–1800.* Lincoln, Neb.: University of Nebraska Press, 1961.

Twitchell, James B. *The Living Dead: A Study of the Vampire in Romantic Literature.* Durham, N.C.: Duke University Press, 1981.

Vitek, Donna Kimel. "Building Sexual Tension." In *How to Write a Romance and Get It Published: With Intimate Advice from the World's Most Popular Romance Writers,* edited by Kathryn Falk, 146–54. Rev. ed. New York: Signet Books, 1990.

Waller, Gregory A. *The Living and the Undead: From Stoker's Dracula to Romero's Dawn of the Dead.* Chicago: University of Illinois Press, 1986.

Wolf, Leonard. *A Dream of Dracula: In Search of the Living Dead.* New York: Popular Library, 1977.

Wolff, Cynthia Griffin. "The Radcliffean Model: A Form for Feminine Sexuality." *Modern Language Studies* 9 (Fall 1979): 98–113.

Other

Doyle, A. Conan. "The Ring of Thoth." In *The Captain of the Pole-star and Other Tales*. New York: A. L. Burt, Publisher, n.d.

Goethe's Faust Parts I and II. Translated by Louis MacNiece. New York: Oxford University Press, 1951.

Scott, Sir Walter. "Introduction." In *Ivanhoe*. 1830. New York: Collier Books, 1982. 13–22.

Strieber, Whitley. *The Hunger*. New York: Pocket Books, 1982.

Index

The Author

Bette B. Roberts is a professor of English at Westfield State College in Massachusetts, where she has been chair of the English Department for five years. She teaches courses in composition, British literature, and the novel. She is the author of *The Gothic Romance: Its Appeal to Female Writers and Readers in Late-Eighteenth-Century England* and of many essays on Gothic fiction. She lives with her husband in Belchertown, Massachusetts.

The Editor

Frank Day is a professor of English at Clemson University. He is the author of *Sir William Empson: An Annotated Bibliography* and *Arthur Koestler: A Guide to Research*. He was a Fulbright Lecturer in American literature in Romania (1980–81) and in Bangladesh (1986–87).